"Are you going to be okay?" Cade asked

"I always am," Jessie said over the phone. "I'll be doing stunts in no time."

Cade could say what he felt—that she was better off not working in such a dangerous field. But what he did know was the passion she brought to her work. *Passion*. Bad choice of words. He pictured himself kissing her, holding her, doing a lot more with her.

"Damn," he muttered.

"What?"

"Just realized I forgot to turn off the slow cooker," he lied.

"I've never met a man who rescues damsels in distress by day and cooks and cleans at night. You might very well be perfect."

"I'm a single dad. If I don't do it, nobody does. And as for rescuing you, that was more a matter of being in the right place at the right time."

After they hung up, Cade sighed. Jessie made him remember he was a man who hadn't been with a woman in a long time. Which made him realize inviting the Bouchard twins into his life might well have been his worst idea to date.

Dear Reader,

We are nearing the end of the Spotlight on Sentinel Pass series. It seemed appropriate that the final two books would begin to draw us away from the Black Hills. Ironic, given the title of this book, right? But in romance, all is never what it seems at first glance.

Jessie Bouchard, a successful stuntwoman, has sacrificed a great deal for her career. She's chosen an "extreme" lifestyle of physical challenges and relentless travel as a way to avoid those sticky, unpleasant emotional tangles she witnessed in her mother's life.

Prodigal son Cade Garrity returns to his Black Hills roots knowing exactly what he wants: to build a safe, nurturing home for his daughter. Would Cade be open to finding a mate? Absolutely. But his late wife chose her career over her family. He won't go down that road again—even for someone like Jessie, who tempts him to make a short-term exception to his rules.

In researching Jessie's backstory, I learned a great deal about the sports called Parkour and Free running. These athletes are fearless, dedicated and exciting to watch. I knew I'd found my heroine when I saw stuntwoman Luci Romberg's Incredible Egg commercial on TV. Thanks, Luci, for friending me on Facebook. It's a joy to follow your interesting career.

Next month, Jessie's twin sister, Remy, will close out this series. I hope you've enjoyed all nine Spotlight on Sentinel Pass books. If you've missed any, Harlequin has released them all as ebooks. As a new devotee of electronic books, I highly recommend you give downloading these titles a try. What a great way to store a library!

Debra Salonen

Return to the Black Hills

Debra Salonen

TORONTO NEW YORK LONDON
AMSTERDAM PARIS SYDNEY HAMBURG
STOCKHOLM ATHENS TOKYO MILAN MADRID
PRAGUE WARSAW BUDAPEST AUCKLAND

Recycling programs
for this product may
not exist in your area.

ISBN-13: 978-0-373-71698-2

RETURN TO THE BLACK HILLS

Copyright © 2011 by Debra K. Salonen

www.eHarlequin.com

Printed in U.S.A.

ABOUT THE AUTHOR

In her heart of hearts, Debra Salonen knows she could have been a stuntwoman—if only the job didn't involve running and jumping. She likes to think she's mastered the art of sitting still for long periods—a physical challenge that in Debra's opinion is highly underrated. She's also a fairly good walker—thanks to her dog, Sydney, who somehow manages to guilt Debra out of her chair every day.

Books by Debra Salonen

Michael, Jamie, Madelaine and Parker Daisy—
thanks for breathing new life
into "The Compound."
We're glad you're here. Jan would be, too.

CHAPTER ONE

"A LITTLE TO THE LEFT. *Puuuush*. Harder. Keep it coming. That's it. Almost. Yes," Jessie Bouchard cried in triumph. "You're in."

She stepped back and looked skyward at the massive man-made climbing tower that she and her team would be scaling a few hours from now. "What do you think?" she asked her sister Remy, who was standing a few feet away.

"It's definitely phallic."

Jessie ignored the humor in her twin's voice. "I meant does it look plumb? Not the tower itself—the computer on the truck handles that—I mean the lightning rod thingie we added."

Remy moved closer. "It looks straight. And dangerous. You aren't really going to climb this thing, then jump off the top holding one of those little, bitty ropes, are you?"

"That's the plan," Jessie answered, watching Zane and Eerik—the oldest and youngest members, respectively, of Team Shockwave—crisscrossing each other's paths in an attempt to beat the other to the top.

"Hey, guys, cool it. Shane won't pay us if you break his new toy."

And the money was important. Jessie needed every penny to fund her three-month training hiatus this summer. By the end of August, she planned to be in Japan with her name at the top of the leaderboard of *Kamikaze*—the adrenaline-rush game show she'd lost so spectacularly last year. Her reputation was on the line, along with her career and self-esteem.

"Well, the plan looks downright dumb to me," Remy groused. "But since when have you ever listened to anyone else?"

Jessie turned to look at her. "Nobody is twisting your arm to watch the show, you know. If you hadn't suddenly popped in to check up on me, you never would have known about this."

"I was worried. You stopped answering your phone. And emails. The Bullies figured you were still pouting about Mom's funeral, but I told them something else was going on. Something serious and life-altering. I felt it."

Some people would have taken that kind of woo-woo prophesy from the lips of Remy Bouchard seriously. Not Jessie. She knew all of her twin's secrets. Well, most of them, anyway. And she knew Remy wasn't the semipsychic Dream Girl the citizens of Baylorville, Louisiana, thought she was.

"I told you. I lost my cell phone and sublet my apartment for the summer, so I turned off the landline. And my laptop died. I borrowed a friend's to update my Facebook page, which is how you knew where to find me, right?" Family was great and all, but, seriously, the way they looked over her shoulder could be claustrophobic. "The point is I'm not hiding or pouting or taking crazy risks. Just the opposite, in fact." She pointed at the tower. "This thing is completely safe. A thousand little kids will be climbing it this summer."

Remy's perfectly outlined deep pink lips—her sister knew makeup the way Jessie knew car engines—formed a moue. "What about the lightning rod?"

Jessie gestured to the six-foot pole from which two lines—one red, one black—were partially visible. "That was Zane's idea. He thought our routine lacked pizzazz. He and I are going to jump backward and rappel back and forth, like Tarzan and a really hot Jane," she said, pounding her chest.

Remy crossed her arms. The pinched look on her face was so much like their mother's Jessie felt a shiver pass down her spine. Mom had been gone for nearly ten months, but Jessie thought about her every day. The way she died. The way Jessie let everybody down. Again.

She looked at her watch. "I'm supposed to meet a guy over at the community center in a few minutes. Are you sticking around or what?"

Remy gave her a "well, duh" look. "Of course I'm sticking around. Think I came all this way to ask why you weren't answering your phone? I figured since you're here for the summer, this would be a great chance for us to spend some time together."

Some time? How much? Before Jessie could ask her to elaborate on her plans to stay in the Black Hills, Eerik shot toward them on a skateboard. At nineteen, the guy was part fearless maniac, part laid-back surfer dude. "No killing yourself before the show, Eerik. We need you to play a menacing bad guy."

"No prob, Jess. Just staying loose."

"I hope he remembers his stocking cap," Jessie said, watching him show off. "A blond ponytail isn't very threatening, is it?"

She glanced over her shoulder when Remy didn't answer right away and found her sister's gaze following the fit, sexy, young Brad Pitt–looking kid. Not that Jessie blamed her. Eerik was hot, but Jessie didn't date coworkers. She'd learned that lesson the hard way. Plus, romance was so far off her radar at the moment it was a non-issue. Men were one luxury she couldn't afford.

"Watch where you're going, a-hole," Jessie heard someone shout. She turned in time to see Zane stiff-arm Eerik, sending the younger man stumbling.

Eerik rebounded with the grace and nimbleness of a highly trained Parkour athlete, executing a backflip to land on his feet. The average person would have been on their butt on the ground. He spun around, fists raised. Before Jessie could voice her protest, Marsh, the third member of their team, dashed between the two men. "Take it down a notch, guys. We have a show in forty minutes."

Zane, who at the moment looked very much like the Special Forces commando he claimed to have been, flipped them both off and stormed away. Marsh looked at her, hands out in a what-the-heck motion.

Jessie had no idea what was going on with Zane. He'd been more short-tempered than usual the past few days. A veteran stuntman and co-captain of Team

Shockwave, their eight-member competitive Parkour/
Freerunning team, Zane brought strength and cunning
to the mix. But his team name was Inzanity, which,
lately, seemed a little too apropos.

"Come on," she said, changing direction. "I need
some water before my meeting. There's a cooler in
Yota."

Her impossible-to-miss, 1971 turquoise Toyota Land
Cruiser was parked midway between the post office,
where the show would originate, and the tower. In Parkour, athletes incorporated existing landmarks, like light
poles, walls, parking meters, even cars in their routines.
Yota was used to playing the foil for Jessie and her
troupe.

She opened the rear doors and reached for her cooler.
She smiled when she saw Remy lovingly pat the car's
dusty fender. They'd bought the car together shortly
after graduating from high school. Jessie had replaced
the engine twice, but she had no plans to trade it in
on a newer model. She loved the boxy old thing like a
member of the family.

The vehicle lacked an authentic tailgate and Jessie
had removed the rear seats years earlier to allow for
more cargo space, but Remy didn't let that stop her from
making herself comfortable. She turned and hopped
backward to sit on the threshold, adjusting the fall of
her gauzy purple-and-blue cotton skirt. As usual, she
looked pretty and feminine.

Jessie stripped off her sweaty black T-shirt and
grabbed the green, sleeveless blouse she'd worn the
night before. Not too wrinkled, she decided, buttoning it

partway. Her bright orange tank with the built-in work-out bra didn't clash too badly, she decided, checking out her reflection in the passenger-side mirror.

Remy tilted her head to scrutinize Jessie's outfit but didn't comment. Instead, she asked, "Who did you say you were meeting?"

"Cade Garrity. His sister, Kat, is friends with Libby Lindstrom. Cooper Lindstrom's wife," Jessie added meaningfully. She knew her sister wasn't a big fan of television, but she didn't live under a rock, either. *Sentinel Passtime* was a legitimate TV hit and a stunt double's dream. Jessie loved this annual trip to the Black Hills of South Dakota to film on location. Since they already had the permit to film scenes in this part of town, Shane, the director, had decided to give the stunt demonstration as a thank-you to the locals for so gener-ously sharing space with Hollywood types.

"I asked Libby if she knew of any rentals in the area. Kat said her brother had a place—a ranch somewhere north of here. It sounds perfect. So I emailed him last week."

Remy frowned. "If you wanted to do your train-ing someplace other than L.A., you could have come home."

Jessie heard something not-quite-Remy in her sister's voice. Grievance? Complaint? Remy was the one person Jessie could always count on to be in her corner. She never complained about Jessie's choices or lifestyle. Obviously that had changed.

"Okay. Out with it. What's going on?"

"I lost my job."

"At Shadybrook? No way. You're the best thing those old people ever saw."

"Budget cuts. They lost their funding for my program and didn't want to raise their rates."

Jessie gave her a one-arm hug. "I'm sorry."

"It's okay. I needed a change. Plus, I figured I'd find you to deliver this in person." Remy settled her oversize carpetbag of a purse on her lap and pulled out an envelope, which she handed to Jessie.

"What is it?"

"Open it and see."

She let the envelope rest in the palm of her hand a moment. Thin. Cheap, ordinary paper. Nothing special—except for her name written in her mother's hand. *Jessie.*

Her throat tightened, making it hard to swallow. "Where'd you find this?"

"In her desk in the kitchen. You know Mama. One desk wasn't enough, ten were too many."

The old joke helped ease the tension. Jessie had had a turbulent relationship with her mother for most of her life, and one point of contention was Marlene Bouchard's penchant for buying estate-sale furniture she didn't need, couldn't afford and didn't have space for in her Louisiana shotgun-style home.

Jessie ripped open the envelope and quickly scanned the one-page missive. Without conscious thought, she gently rubbed the tender spot on the side of her forehead. The stitches were gone but the pain lingered. "You got one, too, I assume?"

"We all did."

Jessie reached for her duffel bag. She found the plastic vial of prescription pain pills the doctor had given her. She didn't like to take them before a job, but one wouldn't hurt, she figured. She choked it down with a swig of water.

"So, what changes? She'd already told everybody how she wanted her will handled. Now we have it in writing. Big deal. I still don't want anything—including my half of the house. You know that. You didn't have to come all this way to hear me say so in person."

Remy blew out a huff of exasperation. "That's exactly why I had to come. To talk some sense into you. Just because you don't want your share of Mama's estate doesn't mean you might not have kids someday who would treasure a small piece of their grandmother's past. I refuse to let you give away your inheritance simply because you feel guilty."

Jessie heaved the duffel deep into the car and turned her back on her sister. "I don't want to talk about this. Not now."

"No problem. Like I said, I think I'll stick around for a while. We can be roomies. Like when we lived in Nashville."

"What about the house? Aren't you afraid the Bullies will make off with all those so-called treasures you think I deserve?" The Bullies was the pet name the twins had for their three older sisters.

Remy gave her head a shake, making her white-blond hair shimmer in the intense noon sunlight. "They've already taken everything they want. I told them when

I left I might not come back right away, depending on your plans. Luckily, since Mama's house is paid for, I can help you out with rent and it won't feel as if I'm paying double. How big is this place?"

This sort of spur-of-the-moment planning was more her than Remy. "I don't know all the details. That's what I'm here to find out. This Cade guy said he was willing to trade part of the rent for a few hours of child care during the week."

"Child care? You?"

Jessie spun on one heel. "See? You're as bad as the Bullies. You all assume certain truths about me that aren't based on any actual facts."

Remy put up her hands defensively. "I'm sorry. I didn't realize you actually liked kids. You have to admit you've never had much to do with our nieces and nephews."

"That would have meant spending time with their parents. I've learned that I can get along with my older sisters just fine if I keep a few states between us. Which is another reason I want no part of Mom's house."

"But—"

"Not now, Rem. I gotta go. This ranch sounds perfect. Out of the way. Practically off the grid." A bonus given the mess she'd left in L.A. "So, stay here. I'll feel him out about renting to two tenants. If he doesn't have a problem with the idea, I'll mention that you're in town and thinking about staying. Okay?"

"I could kick in more rent."

Jessie thought about Cade Garrity's initial reply to her query: brief—almost terse—as if he were doing something he wasn't totally happy about. "I don't think he's doing this for the money. His main focus seemed to be his daughter. She's twelve. He said he wanted someone to pick her up at the bus stop and supervise her after-school time until he got home."

"A teen. Good luck with that," Remy said, with a slight smirk.

"Hey, for your information, last year I coached two Girlz On Fire gymnastics teams. A couple of the girls came very close to placing at the district level. Not bad for our first try." First, and probably the last, Jessie thought.

She pushed the memory away. What was happening with Girlz on Fire was out of her hands at the moment. Maybe someday, after the dust had settled, she might be able to resurrect the pieces of the dream, but that was going to take a lot more money than she currently had. Another reason to win *Kamikaze's* million-dollar prize.

She looked at her watch. "Damn. I have to run. I only have a few minutes to talk to him before the show starts. Stay put. I'll be right back."

She jogged across the street even though there was no cross traffic at the moment. In fact, the street was completely empty thanks to the bright yellow Do Not Cross tape that Marsh and Eerik had put up early that morning before they started filming.

Spectators were starting to collect along the sidewalks and storefronts. She probably should have scheduled this meeting for later, but she had to admit she'd wanted to show off a bit for Cade Garrity. If the guy was going to be her landlord, he deserved to know what kind of person she was—and her work pretty much defined her.

When she reached the plaza adjacent to the community center, she glanced over her shoulder. Remy was still by Yota, but she wasn't alone. Eerik—skateboard in hand—had stopped to talk to her.

Jessie wasn't surprised. Remy was, without a doubt, one of the most beautiful women Jessie had ever known. The irony was they were identical twins. They just didn't look—or act—anything alike.

With a shake of her head, she hurried across the open plaza, which had been packed with tourists and paparazzi earlier that morning during filming. At the moment, the area was empty save a tall man in jeans, a white shirt and cowboy boots. No hat. A few feet away, a young teen she assumed was his daughter, lounged against the town's mascot—a pony-size concrete dinosaur named Seymour. The girl was dressed similarly, except she *was* wearing a cowboy hat and a bright pink T-shirt sporting a Lady Antebellum logo.

"Hi," Jessie called out. At the curb, impulsively, she did a round-off, ending in a backward flip to land a foot in front of the pair.

"Wow," the girl exclaimed, pushing off to step closer to her father.

Twelve going on twenty, Jessie thought. *Been there and then some.*

"That was very cool," the girl said. "Can you teach me how to do that? Dad says you're a stuntwoman.

I plan to ride bulls someday, but maybe I could be a stuntwoman, too."

Jessie wiped her hands on her pants. "I'm Jessie Bouchard," she said, shaking Cade's hand first. "Sorry about showing off. It's what I do."

"Show off?" His tone wasn't insulting or rude, but Jessie could tell her stunt had left him underwhelmed.

"I meant the flip. I do stunts for a living, but my passion is Parkour. It's also called Freerunning. Ever hear of it?"

"As opposed to paying to run?"

She couldn't decide if the question was meant to be serious or snide.

"Oh, Daddy, stop. I promise not to bug her about teaching me how to jump off buildings. Really. I mean it."

Jessie looked between them, trying to follow the debate, which obviously had been going on for a while.

"Fine. Okay. I believe you." To Jessie, he said, "Sorry. We were rude. I'm Cade Garrity. This is my daughter, Shiloh. We aren't in complete agreement about renting to you. I like the fact that you don't smoke, don't have pets and only need the house for three months. Which, hopefully, is about how long my dad will be at his spiritual retreat. My reservations have to do with your job."

"My job?"

"You jump off buildings for a living, correct?"

"When the script calls for it," she said, slowly. She was beginning to not like this man—even though he was handsome enough to be on some Western-wear billboard. "And when all the proper safety precautions are in place and the stunt's been cleared by all the right people. I wasn't planning to jump off any of the buildings on your ranch, if that's what you're asking."

He had the grace to blush a small degree, but his daughter saved him from having to apologize. "See, Daddy. I told you she was normal. She just has an extreme job. Like Mom used to." She looked at Jessie and explained, "My mother was a barrel racer. Her saddle slipped and she got trampled by her horse when I was a baby. I never knew her."

The stark, emotionless announcement left Jessie speechless. She looked at the man across from her in a different light. No wonder he wasn't crazy about her career. He probably assumed it held the same kind of risk as the one that killed his wife. Before she could formulate any sort of reply, a voice said, "Hi. Sorry to interrupt. I'm Remy Bouchard, Jessie's sister. Has she asked you, yet?"

There are two of them? Cade looked from the athlete to the Southern belle. *Sisters?*

"Hey. You two look alike. Are you twins?" Shiloh asked, her tone suddenly very girlish and young.

Cade still couldn't believe she'd dumped a lapful of personal information on a perfect stranger. They were going to have a long talk about personal boundaries and privacy. Especially since Shiloh was the reason he was here today. His perfect little girl seemingly overnight had turned into a rebellious hellion with a snippy attitude and secrets that could easily get her in a lot of trouble. Cade had felt panicky and out of his depth. Instinct told him he needed help. Family.

Unfortunately, returning to the Black Hills meant trusting his father. *And we all know how well that turned out.*

As usual.

"Ask me what?"

He directed his question not toward the vivacious blonde but to the woman he'd been emailing for the past week. Jessie Bouchard, aka Jess DeLeon. He'd checked out her website. Very hip, jazzy and impersonal. Nowhere did it say anything about a twin sister.

He saw her give her sister a scalding look. "Remy has unexpectedly come by some free time and she thought it would be a good reason to drop in on me. If you're not comfortable renting to two people, that's perfectly understandable."

The idea of renting his father's house for the summer had seemed logical. He needed another set of eyes on Shiloh for those times when he was in the field. He'd read the horror stories about online predators. That alone made his blood run cold, but discovering his daughter would go behind his back to do exactly the sort of thing her mother had…well, that nearly killed him.

"The house has two bedrooms. The problem is it's my dad's place. He's on some spiritual quest and I don't have a real clear timeline on when he plans to return."

"Well, we're flexible, aren't we, Jess? Worst-case

scenario, you have to come home with me to finish your training."

Cade's gaze hadn't left Jessie. He could tell by the small flicker in her cheek muscle that going home wasn't something she was in any hurry to do. He could sympathize with that easy enough. He'd resisted his father's overtures to come home and claim his inheritance for years.

Now, here he was. Different reason, but still.

"I need someone to pick up Shiloh from the bus stop five afternoons a week."

She nodded. "You said that in your email. Three-to-four hours after school. Saturday mornings. Maybe a few evenings if you have meetings. None of that is a problem. I'm an early riser. I'll probably be a few miles into my run by the time you get out of bed," she boasted.

He doubted that, but he couldn't fault her work ethic.

"I'm not an early riser, but I am a bit of a night owl," Remy said. "So, if you got called out on a farm emergency, I would happily hang out with Shiloh until you got home."

He stifled a sigh. There were nights like that when you were in charge of a ranch. His father had promised to be that go-to person for his son and granddaughter.

She might have said more but a sudden ringing sound made Remy clutch her giant bag. "That's me." She stepped away to take the call.

"It's Bing," she told her sister. "I told her I'd call

her as soon as we spoke. She saw your rollover. We all did."

Rollover? He didn't like the sound of that.

Jessie didn't comment, but her gaze followed her sister as she returned to the brightly painted box on wheels across the street.

"Is that your car?"

She nodded. "Yes. That's Yota."

"Your car has a name?" Shiloh asked. "Cool. We should name your truck, Dad. How 'bout…Demon?"

"How 'bout we don't?"

Jessie's unpainted lips moved suspiciously, as if working to suppress a grin.

"So," he said, a bit more severely than necessary, "you're planning to stay in the area until mid-August?"

"Yes. I've been invited to try out for a game show in Japan. I participated in it last year and didn't do as well as I would have liked. There were extenuating circumstances but that doesn't mean a lot in the end. I lost. I don't intend to lose this year. That's where the training comes in."

"What kind of training?"

"A lot of running to build up my endurance. Balance work. Wind sprints. Weights, if I can find them. I figure there must a gym in the area, right? If not, I can make do. I'm adaptable."

"The nearest one is probably twenty miles away. Do you need any special equipment besides weights?"

"No. Not really. I always carry a couple of mats with me." She did a half-squat, drawing his attention to her legs and derriere. Her legs were shapely, the muscles well-defined by skintight black pants. "Jumps are a big part of Parkour. I try to lower the impact on my knees whenever possible."

His gaze traveled up to her face, but not quite as quickly as it probably should have. She was everything an athlete should be: trim, compact, coiled energy in repose. Just like Faith.

She spoke, drawing him back to the present. "Hey, listen, if you don't want to do this, I understand. I would have told you about my sister, but, honestly, I had no idea she was thinking about staying. Apparently, she lost her job, and, well, our mother passed away last fall. I think Remy's been feeling a bit lost lately."

"There's a lot of that going around," he said, recalling the argument he'd had with his dad a week earlier.

"I didn't see this coming when I asked you to move back, son," his father had said. "People die. You don't know when and you sure as hell don't know in advance how that death is going to make you feel."

Dealing with loss was one thing Cade did understand.

Despite his misgivings about Jessie's career, Cade was tempted to accept her and her sister as tenants, if only to cross one problem off his list. There were still a dozen more he needed to handle.

"Let's be clear. Shiloh rides the bus, but if she misses it for some reason or needs to come home early, I'd expect you to go after her. Is that a problem?"

"No. Have a cell phone. And, contrary to what some people believe, I *can* drive a car without rolling it."

Her dry humor made him smile. He looked in her eyes and saw a genuine person. His gut said he could trust her not to do something stupid. Of course, his gut had been wrong in the past. Dead wrong.

"Hey, Dad, look at me."

He looked around, shocked to discover his daughter wasn't standing a few feet away from him.

"This is so cool," she hollered, adding a little squeal of delight as she continued her climb up the tower that had been erected in the middle of the street. Yellow caution tape fluttered in the light breeze. Tape she'd obviously ignored.

"Shit," he swore, and took off running.

Even fueled by pure adrenaline, he was quickly passed by Jessie, who somehow levered herself from the ground to a spot parallel with Shiloh before Cade even reached the bottom of the tower.

"Hey, Shiloh. You need to stop. Right now."

Shiloh reached for another knob an arm's length above her head. "Why? This is fun."

Don't tell her it's dangerous. That'll only make her keep going. He'd learned that the hard way six months earlier.

"It's also extremely uncool to climb without the right gear. The friction tape on these holds is killer on bare feet. You might not notice that going up—adrenaline does that, but believe me, you will when you start down. It's going to sting like hell."

Shiloh froze. "Really?"

Jessie moved horizontally several pegs. She could

have been standing on solid ground, she seemed so at ease. "Really. Plus, you might not know this, but it's against the law for a child under the age of eighteen to climb one of these without protective gear. Your dad can get in trouble for this."

Shiloh looked down. "Nuh-uh."

"Oh, yeah. Big fine. They call it child endangerment. He could go to jail."

"Jail?" Shiloh looked over her shoulder and momentarily lost her balance. One foot slipped out from under her, but, luckily, Jessie was there to stabilize her.

"Grab the purple knob with your left hand and hold on tight until the dizziness passes," she ordered, her tone calm and reassuring.

His neck ached from looking up but he wouldn't start breathing normally again until Shiloh was on the ground. Jessie continued to talk in a low, reassuring voice, adding authority to her speech by using phrases such as *personal liability, safety first* and *taking risks not the same as brave.*

Hadn't he said the exact same thing to Shiloh's mother? Not that it did a bit of good. Faith claimed her career was the key to her self-identity.

"What about being a wife and mother? Doesn't that count?" he'd asked.

She'd refused to answer. But as they said, actions spoke louder than words. Saddling a horse, riding into an arena, slipping beneath that horse at a full gallop... actions that spelled the end of her being a wife and mother.

He let out the breath he'd been holding the minute he

saw Jessie and Shiloh start to descend. They probably weren't more than ten to twelve feet above him. But it was enough to make every muscle in his body tense in nervous anticipation.

"Oh, my," a voice said beside him.

He knew it was Remy even though he didn't dare take his gaze off Shiloh.

He crushed Shiloh to his chest a few moments later, safe and sound. "You are grounded," he said, his voice gruff with emotion. "For life."

She wiggled free of his clasp. "Oh, Daddy, I wasn't very far up. I wouldn't have broken anything if I fell. Would I, Jessie?"

Jessie, who was still perched above them like a lizard on a branch, suddenly launched up and out to land beside them. She picked up the boots Shiloh had kicked off. "It only takes seven pounds per square inch—that's seven PSI—to break your collarbone. If you had landed wrong, you *would* have broken something, Shiloh. And if you ever do anything that stupid again, *I* will break something for you."

Her tone was part teacher, part drill sergeant and part mother. And, at that moment, Cade wanted to kiss her. She was exactly what had been missing from his life for so damn long that he felt like a blind person who suddenly acquired sight.

Shiloh's look of smug triumph disappeared and she flung herself back into his arms, sobbing.

He patted her back with soft words of comfort, but his gaze never left Jessie. She looked first at the boots in her hand, then at her sister. He couldn't read whatever silent communication passed between them, but when she looked at him, he was ready. He knew what he wanted to say.

"So, when can you two move in?"

CHAPTER TWO

"HOW 'BOUT THIS AFTERNOON? After the exhibition?"

Jessie couldn't say she was surprised by the offer—he probably felt her owed her something for rescuing his kid, but she knew better than to pass up a golden opportunity. And even though she'd scolded the girl, Jessie couldn't blame Shiloh for giving the tower a try. Jessie would have been the first one on it when she was that age—safety harness or no safety harness.

"Sounds good. Shiloh is going to go into the community center and use the computers to print you a map. Aren't you, Shiloh?"

Shiloh heaved a sigh and took her boots. "Sure. I can do that." She smashed her feet into the boots then stomped across the street and straight into the building.

"Thank you," he said, his voice so low Jessie had to lean in to catch what he was saying. "I didn't think she'd do something that stupid in public."

"Sure. No problem."

The show would be starting in a few minutes and she hadn't had time to go through her usual warm-up routine. She looked at her sister. "Rem, would you do me a favor and stick around for the map? I need to meet the guys to make sure we're all on the same page. Have you seen J.T.?"

"Who's that?"

"Our camera guy."

"The one you used to date?"

Jessie winced. She didn't want to be reminded of that mistake. She never would have gone out with J.T. in the first place if not for Dar—J.T.'s mom *and* Jessie's mentor. In hindsight, Jessie should have recognized the blatant manipulation for what it was—a last-ditch attempt to solidify Jessie's loyalty against the coming firestorm.

"We went out a couple of times." Until his possessiveness got him in trouble. "Anyway, you know what he looks like. Have you seen him this morning?"

Remy shook her head.

"Damn," she muttered under her breath. "I really need someone to film this." She paused. "Wait a minute. I have a camera you could use if he doesn't show up."

Remy put one hand to her heart dramatically. "Me?"

"Wait here. Don't move. I'll be right back."

She raced to her car. The camera was right where she left it on the floor of the backseat. She returned inside a minute. "Here," she said, handing Remy the compact black bag. "It should have a full battery, but just in case, don't turn it on until the action starts."

Remy looked doubtful. "Are you sure about this? I'm a rank amateur at best. What if I screw up?"

"Just do the best you can. I have to go."

"Good luck," Cade said.

Jessie paused. "Thanks. I'll try to give you a good show."

Then, she took off at a slow jog, mentally running down her pre-performance checklist. "Everybody ready?" she asked, joining the group assembled at the picnic table behind the Sentinel Pass Post Office. A quick head count told her someone was missing. "Where's Zane?"

"We don't know," Eerik answered. "He left on his bike before I finished passing out the Team Shockwave fliers and hasn't come back."

Winding mountain roads, a Harley and a speed demon. What could possibly happen?

She fished out her cell phone. No messages. "Crap," she muttered. "If he found some bar and forgot about the show, I'm going to throttle him." She replaced the phone in her knapsack and pulled out the gray-blue shirt she'd borrowed from wardrobe that morning. She quickly changed shirts. "What about J.T.? Anybody seen him?"

"Yeah, he's around here someplace. Probably too ashamed to show his face."

Jessie looked at Marsh—by far the most stable, easy-going member of the Shockwave team. "Why?"

"He said he got drunk last night and forgot to charge his battery. He used the spare for the shoot this morning. Sorry, Jess, I know you were counting on the footage."

The producers of *Kamikaze* had asked her to submit a new audition tape. Apparently, they'd seen the YouTube video of her rollover and wanted proof that she was healthy enough to participate. With any luck, Remy would get sufficient footage to send with her formal application.

"So, no Zane means one of you gets to be my hero. Drag J.T. into position and make this happen. No excuses," she said, quickly buttoning the ugly shirt. She swept her hair into a loose ponytail and pulled on a regulation U.S. Postal Service employee cap.

She did a couple of deep stretches while she ran over the story line in her mind: ordinary postal worker trudging back to work gets accosted by three—no, two—hoodlums. Movie-star hero-type comes to her rescue. After a brief skirmish, good guy realizes he can't fight them all and urges the woman to run for it.

The Freerunning that followed would pack its usual visual punch, employing existing structures, as well as a couple of well-placed obstacles—her car, for one. The tower at the end of the street was the ultimate challenge. Jessie and her hero would make it to the top; the bad guys would fail spectacularly.

"Cue the music," Jessie hollered. "Stay safe, everybody."

There came a point in any stunt where backing out was not an option. And for Jessie, forward momentum was her personal mantra. Keep moving. Keep doing. Keep going. *And maybe, just maybe, the demons won't catch up.*

Then she picked up her fake mailbag and marched to the yellow tape. "And go," she called out.

Once she rounded the corner, she let instinct take over.

Fear—the thing every smart stunt person knows to expect and respect—made her senses sharpen. She and the others weren't *actors* per se with marks to hit and set lines to say. This was mostly ad lib, although the five of them had worked together often enough to know each other's strengths and weaknesses.

Marsh and Eerik would play the bullies, she gathered, when the two entered Main Street near the corner coffee shop. *Please let that mean Zane is back,* she prayed.

The crowd parted to let them through. Low-riding pants, sloppy sweatshirts, hats worn off to the side, they looked like gang members out for trouble.

Jessie walked fast to reach the first mark they'd sketched out the day before. She ignored them completely, although she never completely lost sight of them in her peripheral vision.

"Yo, postal beyotch," Marsh called. "Whatcha got in your bag?"

He did an impressive little hop, twirl and backflip to land directly in her path. The crowd let out a small cry of surprise. Eerik ran straight at the brick wall of the building to her right and continued up the side then dropped backward to land on his feet, eliciting applause.

Not to be outdone, Marsh grabbed the old-fashioned metal pole that supported the building's overhang with both hands and swung around so his body was perpendicular to the pole, creating a pencil-straight line blocking her path.

The cheers pleased her. The guys were on their game and things were only going to get better, she hoped.

Marsh swung around and let go of the pole to reach for her bag. "Gimme that. I bet there's money in there."

Her character wasn't the weep-and-cry kind of girl. She'd put up a fight even if the odds were against her.

"Messing with the mail is a federal offense," she said, speaking loudly so her voice would carry to the onlookers.

"Oh, yeah? Who cares about Uncle Sam? We want what's in that bag, ho," Eerik snarled.

The script had called for Zane to rush to her rescue the moment Marsh picked her up and twirl her overhead like a sack of potatoes.

Marsh reached for her, but before he had them both in position, she heard a voice cry, "Leave her alone."

The wrong voice. *What the hell?* Jessie spun around to see J.T. approach. J.T.? She nearly groaned out loud. "What are you doing here?" she asked—the right line but with a different meaning than originally intended.

"I'm here to help. Because, no matter what you do or say, I love you. And I know you love me. And need me."

Jessie was honestly and completely speechless. Either his acting had improved or he really meant what he was saying. Yes, Dar had told her as recently as a week ago that J.T. was still mooning over Jessie, but even Dar admitted the two were completely incompatible. J.T.

was a control freak. A micromanager. Jessie was as independent as they came.

She looked over her shoulder toward where she hoped Remy was filming. Her sister wasn't there. She didn't know what to do—yell "Cut" or try to fake it.

"I…" She looked at her two colleagues, pleadingly.

Marsh made the call. He grabbed the front of J.T.'s shirt and gave him a shake. "Ain't that sweet. Her hero decided to show up. Let's show him what we do to heroes."

The script called for a fight scene—an artfully choreographed kind of battle where no true contact was made. Jessie doubted J.T. knew how to avoid walking into a punch. She decided to jump ahead in the program.

"Leave him alone, you bums," Jessie shouted. "Did I forget to mention I have a black belt in karate?"

She assumed a fighting stance. Eerik understood to keep a visibly squirming J.T. restrained while Jessie did her thing. Her skirmish with Marsh was like a dance— feign, dip, twirl, kick, duck, roll, rebound.

The crowd cheered for her and booed every time Marsh knocked her down. On cue, Eerik released J.T., faking a loud "umph" as if J.T. had elbowed him in the gut.

J.T. stumbled in his haste to reach Jessie, but when he did, he grabbed her arm and pointed toward Yota—the only car parked on the street. Its boxy shape and overall height was perfect for launching yourself into the air for a couple of backflips or twists.

"Run," J.T. cried, pulling her arm the same moment

she pitched her mailbag through the open door of the post office. Although she could appreciate his enthusiasm and lack of experience or training, the force of his tugging wrenched her off balance. She would have fallen flat on her face if he hadn't been there to catch her. Once she regained her balance, she had to stifle the urge to send him to the ground in pain with a swift kick to the groin.

The script called for her anonymous hero to lead them on a circuitous route up and over Yota, vaulting across strategically placed planter boxes and making use of light poles in an attempt to lose the bad guys. Unfortunately, it quickly became apparent that the only way J.T. could keep up with her was by not doing any of the stunts. That was fine with Jessie. This was supposed to look serious, not comedic.

"Wait here," she cried, pushing him into the doorway of the abandoned building they'd been given permission to use. A narrow alley between two brick exteriors provided the right gap for her to spider-walk from ground level to the roof. With hands and feet pressed firmly against the opposing walls, she hopped upward a foot or so at a time.

The crowd cheered, but the effort was so taxing, Jessie barely heard a thing over the sound of her breathing and the blood rushing through her veins. When she reached the top, she dug the fingers of her left hand into the lip of the roof to swing her body over.

"Oh," the crowd cried as she dangled by one arm.

With a graceful arc, she lofted up and over the edge. Breathing hard from the effort, she bent over to watch her team follow. The script called for only one of the mock bad guys to make it, although both were perfectly capable of doing exactly what she did.

She turned and danced across the edge of the roof, balancing like a gymnast above the street.

"Be careful."

"Watch out."

"Oh, no," people cried from their vantage point across the street.

The wall she was running across was actually two feet wide, which is why she'd picked this building. That and the fact it had an exterior fire escape within view of the street. Made of wood nearly a hundred years ago, the rickety-looking structure was surprisingly sound. Jessie eschewed the steps, choosing to dive for the open railing then swing from level to level like a monkey in a rain forest until she reached the bottom landing.

With only a few feet to get up to speed, she pumped her legs hard: step, step, go. She launched her body into the air, flying up and out toward the street. When she was certain she'd cleared the sidewalk, she executed a neat tuck and roll to come up on her feet in front of the climbing tower.

J.T. was waiting for her.

"You can't do this trick," she whispered, her breathing strained from the exertion.

"Neither can you," he said. "Not alone."

She looked over her shoulder. As scripted, only one bad guy was still on her trail. Marsh. Unfortunately, the script also had called for Zane—not J.T.—to lead the way up the tower. Partly because he was supposed to be her hero; partly because the two dismount lines that had been added to the tower were slightly outside Jessie's reach. A design flaw she blamed on Zane's ego. In practice that morning, Jessie had needed his help to reach her line.

But Zane would not be waiting for her at the top. Was that J.T.'s plan? Had he convinced their friend to let Jessie face failure so she'd be forced to see that she needed him?

She looked him straight in the eyes. "Watch me."

As planned, she ripped off her ugly blue shirt and kicked it to one side. The crowd cheered. Jessie knew her bright orange tank enhanced her image of a strong, fit, woman athlete. Now, she had to live up to her image.

Instead of reaching for the blue route—the one she'd picked during the practice run—she chose Zane's path. Black. "Scary enough to make the spectators piss their pants," he'd crowed.

In the back of her mind, she hoped Remy was positioned close enough to get the best perspective. She'd watched the others practice and had been impressed. The person climbing resembled a superhero...or a very large bug.

Although her fingers were starting to cramp from a couple of the holds and her triceps burned, she ignored the discomfort and visualized hauling herself onto the very top where her dismount rope was waiting.

She heard a muffled commotion below and assumed Marsh and J.T. were faking some kind of skirmish. The pounding in her head made everything surreal.

For her, climbing produced a sense of moving in slow motion, even though she was pressing hard not to lose her momentum. Finally, after what felt like minutes but was probably only seconds, she took a deep breath and power-lifted herself up as high as possible to grasp one of the corner uprights and swing herself onto the top.

The obelisk was designed to be raised and lowered by a hydraulic pistonlike contraption. When deflated, the unit could be hauled by a semitruck from venue to venue. It wasn't meant to be straddled like a bony horse. The molded fiberglass—or whatever the thing was made of—was bumpy and irregular on the very top. And surprisingly slick.

She locked her feet under one of the steel braces as she tried to figure out how best to reach the rope— just inches outside her reach. She started by scooting closer to the corner. Hand-over-hand, she carefully inched forward then pulled her knees up to the topmost handholds.

Since the other side had an indentation in the same spot, she had to trust her balance as she pulled herself up. *Almost. Almost. I can do this.*

"Yes," she cried softly, her fingers closing around the rope.

Her heart rate began to normalize once she had the safety line in hand. She pulled her opposite leg over the top to balance on the lip of the tower a moment. After a few seconds, the noise from the crowd sank in. The applause drowned out the shouts coming from her colleagues, who were now grouped around J.T. at the base of the edifice.

Jessie waved with one hand and gave a quick bow that nearly unseated her. Silently scolding herself for showing off, she shook out the rope. As planned, it stopped six feet short of the ground. The script had called for her and Zane to make back-and-forth passes, swinging close to each other until they finally united, literally, at the end of their ropes. From that point, they'd do a tumbling dismount and take their bows to thunderous applause. They hoped.

Reaching up slightly so she could turn around and rappel backward down the climbing tower, she felt the rope slide a tiny bit. She dug her toes in and looked down, trying to make sense of the odd sensation.

Vertigo?

She checked all four guylines, worried for a moment that the twenty-five-foot edifice was going to topple over.

The tension on the outriggers appeared rock solid, but when she looked at the rope, it struck her that this was not the same one she'd use in practice. Smoother. A slightly different weight. And the surface appeared slicker.

"What the hell?"

More disgusted than panicked, she wrapped the rope around her fist then pushed off. She hung there a moment, recalling how she and Zane had joked about which of them had the better Tarzan yell. In truth, they'd both sucked.

As she bounced back toward the tower, she relaxed her knees and tried to place her feet for the best advantage of angle. Unfortunately, her shoe lost its grip at the worst possible moment, knocking her off balance. She overcorrected and the rope slipped through her fingers a good five or six inches, as if greased. Had it not been for the safety loop she'd instinctively used, she might have kept going, like a runaway train without the least bit of friction to slow her down.

What is going on? she thought, desperately locking her legs around the part of the rope dangling below her.

So much for grace and showmanship.

She needed to get down in one piece, and at this point, that was not a sure thing.

Another thought followed.

Someone did this on purpose.

CHAPTER THREE

CADE HAD TO ADMIT THAT watching Jessie Bouchard climb that ridiculous tower, freehand, without any of the safety harnesses novice climbers would be required to wear, was heartbreakingly exciting. She was power, grace and determination combined in one sexy package.

He could feel Shiloh's fingers digging into his arm the closer Jessie got to the top. His heart rate had kicked up a notch or two and his mouth was so dry he couldn't have spit if he'd wanted to.

"It's really tall, isn't it, Dad?"

"Uh-huh."

"How far up it was I?"

He looked at her. "Too far. Now you know why I was scared."

"What are those men fighting about?" she asked, pointing to the three men at the base of the tower. Cade couldn't hear their words over the cheering of the crowd, but they appeared to be having a real argument, not a staged one.

"Oh, God," a voice said from behind him. "She's in trouble. For real. I can feel it."

Cade turned to see Remy a few steps away, a digital

camcorder in her hand. He looked from her to the tower. It took him less than a second to realize she was right. Instead of the graceful descent Jessie had been making a moment earlier, she was now floundering, her descent rope wrapped around one calf, her fingers grasping and regrasping the rope as if it were greased. She made a desperate grab for one of the knobby, molded plastic handholds and her fingers slipped from it like butter.

"Oh, shit," he swore. "Shiloh, stay here. I mean it.

"Hey," he said, approaching the trio of stuntmen. "Your friend is in trouble. What are you going to do about it?"

The guy who had been running beside Jessie earlier— the one who looked least like a stuntman—groaned fatalistically. He looked upward, his face showing a full gamut of emotions Cade didn't completely under-stand. Fear, for certain. But something else, too. Regret? "Didn't I tell you something was going to happen? Why wouldn't she listen to me? She thinks she's freakin' in-vincible, but she isn't. Tell her I'm sorry. I gotta go."

He turned and took off running. The blond surfer dude started after him, but the other man stopped him. "Let him go, Eerik. Jessie needs us." He looked to Cade for direction. Obviously, these guys either followed a script or waited for a director to tell them what to do.

Cade looked at Jessie. She'd grabbed the second rope and appeared to be stable for the moment. From the corner of his eye, he spotted the rustic wood building that housed the Sentinel Pass Volunteer Fire Depart-ment. There had to be someone on duty, he thought.

"Go get some help. A ladder. A fire truck. Something. And call 9-1-1 while you're at it."

"No way," the younger guy protested. "We can get her down safely. All we have to do is lower the tower."

The dark-haired one looked at Cade for confirmation.

Cade threw up his hands. "So, where's the operator? There must be a key, right?"

The young one let out a low groan coupled with a colorful string of cusswords. "I forgot. He told me he'd seen this kind of thing a hundred times and was going into Rapid with friends. He won't be back here until three."

"Let's try the fire department. Come on." The dark-haired guy took off like a sprinter.

As he surveyed the situation, Cade heard murmurs of doubt and concern coming from the audience. Were they finally starting to understand this wasn't part of the show?

Then another sound came to him. A cry of pain— muted, but unmistakable. He stepped directly below where Jessie was hanging. The rope that had at one time been her salvation was now knotted around her ankle. She'd managed to grab on to a bright purple knob a couple of feet to her right, but he could see her fingers desperately working to maintain her grip. A second later, she lost hold and swung, pendulum-like, in the opposite direction, the back of her head connecting with at least two of the climbing knobs.

His stomach turned over. No wonder she'd been so

adamant about Shiloh climbing with protective gear. This was even more dangerous than he'd imagined.

"Jessie," he called out. "Your friends went for help. What can I do?"

The minute she stopped thrashing, her body dropped like a plumb bob on the end of a string. Her ankle, the part visible above her shoe, had turned an ugly shade of purple. He could see on her face how much pain she was in. "A knife. Somebody get me a knife."

His hand automatically went to the small leather holster at his waist. "Could you catch it, if I tossed you one?"

With what he knew had to be a Herculean effort, she wrapped her right leg around the rope and arched her back to look down. "I'll try."

Cade heard others approaching. He looked around, hoping it was Jessie's friends and half a dozen firefighters. No such luck.

"I can climb up and give her the knife, Daddy," Shiloh said, sitting down to take off her boots.

"No," Jessie cried. "The rope has some kind of oil or lubricant on it. That's why I slipped. Everything I've touched is slick. You can't come up here, Shiloh. Nobody can. It's not safe." To Cade, she reached out both hands. "Throw me your knife. I'll catch it. Throw it now. Hurry."

"Stand back, Shy. I need room to move." His heart was racing and he prayed his sweaty hands didn't screw this up. "Here it comes."

He braced to dive for it when she missed, but somehow Jessie managed to catch his much-too-small pocketknife, midair while dangling upside down.

"She did it," Shiloh yelled. "Oh, my gosh, she did it."

"Now what?" Remy asked. "Jessie, you do know that if you cut the line, you're going to fall, right?"

Jessie didn't answer. She was already pulling herself upright. She used the other rope for leverage, but whether due to her slippery hands or something on the rope itself, each handhold required her to loop it around her fist. Cade had no idea where she found the strength and grit, given her obvious pain.

Finally, she reached an angle that would allow her to cut into the line.

Remy, he noticed, was still filming. He didn't know whether that was a good thing—there would be an investigation, he figured—or slightly sadistic. He looked toward the fire station, relieved to see the massive door opening, and the red light above the door flashing.

He waited, expecting to see a truck to pull out. Instead, two men—the stuntmen—raced out, carrying a large yellow extension ladder. Where the hell was Mac McGannon? They'd talked at his sister's wedding. Cade knew his old friend was one of the town's first responders.

"Nobody was there," the surfer said.

His pal positioned the ladder and quickly dashed upward. The rough surface made it bounce.

"Ouch. Stop." Jessie looked up from her intent sawing. "Marsh. Don't. You're making me swing again. I need to stay still until I get this cut."

"Sorry. What can I do?"

She glanced down. "I don't suppose you have a bounce pad on you."

He shook his head. Needlessly.

"If we can find a blanket," Cade called out, "we could catch you."

"Oh," Remy cried, suddenly. "I know where one is. In Yota. I'll be right back. Here," she said, shoving the camera into Shiloh's hands. "Keep rolling. She's going to want to see this."

Cade quickly organized the three volunteers who rushed forward, along with the two stuntmen—after they moved the ladder out of the way. They made a circle below Jessie and all looked up expectantly. He gave her credit for sheer focus and strength of will. This was no simple task and the swaying movement had to be extremely painful.

"Here it is," Remy called, racing toward them.

The blanket wasn't huge—twin-size, at best. The baby-blue fleece with a stylized panda design seemed more appropriate as a child's blankie, but it would have to do.

"Everybody grab a hunk and hold on tight."

"I'm almost through," she called. "Are you ready below?"

Cade widened his stance and braced his shoulders. "As ready as we're ever going to be."

Keeping his focus completely on her, he held his breath. In an effort to land on her back, she used her free foot to push off at the very last second before the rope gave. The timing was critical. She did everything right, but, regardless, the impact knocked Cade and two of the other volunteers off their feet. His knees hit the pavement hard, but he barely felt the sensation because he was concentrating intently on keeping her from crashing to the ground.

She rolled his way. His arms scooped her up as if he were catching a grounder in the biggest game of the year. He pulled her close and then leaned sideways, colliding with another man. The surfer. The three of them landed in a heap on the street with Jessie on top.

Breathing hard, adrenaline pumping through his veins, he held on tight. Half-afraid to let go. In the chaotic seconds before reality fully sank in, a stupid thought passed through his mind. *She's softer than she looks.* An even stupider thought followed. *I like the way she feels in my arms.*

"CAN I GO, NOW?" JESSIE asked. "What's it been—four hours?"

Cade, who had been sitting beside her on the park bench practically the whole time, checked his watch.

"One. One and a half, max."

His tone was a bit too cheerful for her taste.

"Yeah, well, nothing is happening, so why can't I leave?"

She leaned down to adjust the cooling pack the EMTs had given her. The ambulance with its red flashing lights was still parked across the street; the two EMTs were filling out forms and talking to the sheriff's deputy.

"The sheriff said he wanted to talk to you again.

Besides, I think everyone is hoping you'll change your mind and go with the paramedics."

"Hospitals are for sissies," she muttered, risking a peek at her swollen ankle. Purple and red. Not a pretty sight, but she was certain it wasn't broken. Wrenched and possibly sprained, but nothing permanent. Thank God. It could have been worse. Much worse.

"I thanked you, right? For catching me and throwing the knife so accurately? You kept your cool under pressure. That's not typical. I do appreciate it."

He gave her a look she'd seen several times in their short acquaintance. Patient. She'd classified it as a dad look. "You thanked me. And you're welcome."

"Are you sure I'm not keeping you from something?"

He shook his head. He had great hair, she'd noticed. Sun-streaked wheat—not the bleached-blond color of Eerik's. "Shiloh texted me a few minutes ago. She's playing video games with her cousins."

The only time Cade left her side was to make arrangements to send his daughter with her aunt and cousins. Kat, a familiar face around the *Sentinel Passtime* set, had stopped by to extend her sympathy and concern for what happened.

"This sucks, Jessie. I hope your ankle is okay. I called Libby right after it happened. She said Shane and Jenna are somewhere over the Rockies. But I know they'll want to hear all about the accident when you're feeling up to a call." To her brother, she'd added, "Let me know if there's anything Jack and I can do to help."

The accident. That was what everybody was calling

it, but Jessie wasn't so sure. In fact, she was almost positive the ropes had been tampered with. She couldn't prove that, of course, but she planned to keep asking questions until she got some answers.

"Shouldn't the C.S.I. people be here by now?"

Cade's laugh seemed to originate deep inside his chest. He immediately apologized. "Sorry. I forgot. You're from L.A. I wouldn't hold my breath waiting for a bunch of lab guys to show up."

She'd guessed as much the moment she heard the semi driver start the truck and engage the hoist to collapse the tower.

"You're afraid someone is going to blame you for what happened, right?"

She didn't like it that he could read her so easily. "Wouldn't be the first time," she muttered.

Operator error. That had been the final verdict on her rollover despite her claim that she'd done everything exactly according to plan.

"Well, if it's any consolation, I think Mac is bagging the ropes." He gestured toward the now-lowered tower.

"Mac," she repeated. "Libby's brother, right?"

The burly guy in a black Sentinel Pass Volunteer Fire T-shirt had been the first "official" responder to appear. He'd come unglued when he found Cade lowering Jessie to a park bench beside the community center. "Holy shit, Cade," he'd cried. "You don't move an accident victim. You could have made her injuries worse. If she had a broken rib, carrying her could have punctured a lung."

"My ribs are just peachy, thank you," Jessie had insisted. "It's my foot that hurts, and Cade didn't do anything to make it worse. In fact, if it weren't for him, those paramedics might be dealing with a self-inflicted amputation. That's how bad it feels to hang upside down by one foot."

"Mac was right about one thing. You really should get your leg X-rayed."

She made a negating motion with her hand, as if brushing away a pesky fly. "I thought he was a miner, not a doctor."

She knew she was being a pain in the ass, but she hated being told what to do almost as much as she hated sitting around doing nothing. And the longer she sat here, the less likely the police would find out who tampered with her ropes.

"Is she being a grouch?"

Remy. Jessie had almost forgotten her sister was still there. She'd brought Jessie a bottle of water, then disappeared. "Where's the video camera?" Jessie asked. "I want to see the tape."

Remy made a face. "I gave it to the deputy. He said he'd return it in a day or two."

Jessie jumped to her feet without thinking. The pain was instantaneous and she hopped on her good foot, cussing under her breath. "What? No. You should have asked me first. You know perfectly well they aren't going to take this seriously. Cops always think people who do Parkour get what's coming to them. If we're dumb enough to vault off a building, we shouldn't complain when something winds up broken, right?"

Her rant apparently fell on deaf ears, because Remy looked at Cade and said, "Obvious deflection. She hates hospitals. Perfectly understandable, of course, given all the time she spent—"

"Damn it, Rem, shut up," Jessie snapped. She could use her toe for balance only if she avoided putting any weight on the limb. That was not good. She knew that, but a person who failed to make it to the hospital in time to save her mother's life had no business hauling her sorry butt into one for a bruised ankle.

Cade stretched out an arm to pick up the ice pack that had fallen to the ground. She glanced down but the movement made her dizzy. She had no choice but to steady herself using his broad, substantial shoulder. His head lifted and a second later, he was standing with one arm around her back.

"This is foolish. If your foot is hurt worse than you think, you could be causing permanent damage."

"But if it's not hurt that bad, then I will have wasted my money for nothing."

Remy and Cade exchanged a look. "Don't you have insurance?" he asked.

"Of course I do. But I carry a superhigh deductible."

"Because of your line of work," Cade said.

Because of my so-called preexisting condition. But she was happy to let him believe what he wanted. "The average stunt person probably gets injured on the job less often than the average bus driver or mail carrier, but stuff happens. I was involved in another incident a few weeks ago and had to spend the night in the hospital for observation. They might cancel my policy because of this." She was pretty sure her union wouldn't let that happen, but it seemed like a valid excuse.

"What happened the last time?" Cade asked.

She looked at Remy. He didn't know? Her rollover had gotten a million or so hits on the internet. The video might not have made his radar, but she was willing to bet Shiloh had seen it.

"She rolled a car," Remy answered. "The video was a big YouTube sensation. If you saw it, you would have sworn nobody could have walked away alive."

Jessie involuntarily touched the tender spot near her temple. "It wasn't that bad. A couple of stitches and nurses waking me up every hour or so to flash a light in my eyes."

Lack of sleep hadn't been the worst part, of course. No, the smells and the noises brought back memories she'd worked most of her life to forget. Phantom pains had made lying on her back impossible. But the very worst was the desolating sense of loneliness and fear that made her want to curl up in a ball and disappear.

"Jessie? Are you okay? You're shaking."

"Okay, this is silly. You need to get checked out," Cade said firmly. "No more arguments." Without giving her a chance to respond, he called to the men across the street, "Hey, guys, your patient is ready for you now."

She leaned into him. It was hard not to, and besides, his strength offered a tiny respite. She could allow herself that. For the moment. Nobody could be strong all the time. She'd learned that the hard way.

The clatter of the gurney wheels bouncing over the

pavement made her turn her face against Cade's shirt. Fabric softener and sweat. A very male smell that made her wish for something she couldn't quite name.

"Where are your keys, Jessie?"

Jessie looked up, blinking to get her bearings. "They're in the mailbag. That's the only prop we borrowed, but somebody has to take that back to the studio. Where are Marsh and Eerik?"

"They left. The blond—Eerik, right?—said they had to check out of their motel and get to the airport."

"Are you kidding? They left without saying goodbye?" She gave a snort of exasperation. "Did they even talk to the cops? I mean, come on, they're witnesses."

"To an unfortunate accident," a deep male voice said. "Isn't that what you told me when I first talked to you, ma'am?"

Jessie swallowed hard and looked at the deputy. Miller, the little nameplate above his breast pocket said. "I'm not sure what I said. I was pretty shook up and in a lot of pain."

He looked at Cade, then the two paramedics. "But you refused care."

That might have been a mistake, she realized. She'd called her fall an accident and downplayed the severity because nobody in her field enjoyed filling out the paperwork that followed a stunt person around after a stunt went sour.

But now that she'd had time to think about what happened, she could honestly say she'd done nothing to cause this. She could also say with some conviction that somebody else did.

Before she could answer the man, Cade asked, "Have you looked at the video, Hank?"

It irked her that *Hank* seemed to put aside his skepticism the moment Cade opened his mouth. She knew all about the good-ol'-boy network. Hadn't she been fighting for a place in it her entire career?

Hank held up the camera her sister had given him. "We were just looking at it. Seems to me, you're damn lucky to be alive. If I hadn't seen the look on Cade's face when all this was happening, I mighta thought it was kind of a publicity stunt."

"What? No. I would never do something that stupid or dangerous on purpose. And the dismount pole was never my idea. Ask Zane. Zane Whorley. He was supposed to be on the ropes with me, but he didn't show up, so I had to do it alone."

"Where is he now?"

"I don't know. Marsh said he took off on his bike. I tried his phone..." She wondered if that excuse sounded as lame as she thought.

"Listen. People—especially insurance investigators—love to blame the stunt artist when something goes wrong. But I should have been perfectly safe doing that dismount alone. Zane and I practiced on those ropes less than an hour earlier. Everything was fine. But when I got to the top and grabbed my rope, I knew instantly that something wasn't right."

She held out her hands for them to inspect. Small, functional hands, calloused from years of gymnastics. Hers were not girly hands. Outlining the heels of both hands and along the edges of her fingers was a white ring. "Somebody put something on the rope. It felt like I was holding on to an icicle."

The cop frowned. He rubbed one spot with his finger then sniffed and tasted the sample. "Salty. Like sweat. But you're alleging someone tampered with your rope."

She hesitated. Did she really want to open this can of worms? *Must you always make such a fuss,* a voice in the back of her mind questioned. Her mother's voice. "Yes."

"Any idea who? Or why?"

"No."

"And you didn't see anyone hanging around the tower?"

She shook her head.

"Unfortunately, she was talking to *me* immediately before the show started," Cade told the man. "Jessie and Remy are going to rent my dad's place for the summer."

"Where's Buck?"

"That, my friend, is anybody's guess." Her future landlord—she'd almost forgotten about that part of this strange saga—sounded resigned and a little bit pissed off. "You know Buck. Got a mind of his own, and, now that I'm here to run the ranch, he decided to take off for a few months."

When he shrugged his shoulders, Jessie felt the motion all the way through her body.

The cop nodded as though he understood completely. He looked at Jessie. "So, if I have this timeline right, you set up the climbing tower, took a practice run, then walked away and left it completely unguarded prior to your performance."

A bad feeling started low in her belly. He made her team out to be a bunch of flakes. Why had she hoped the authorities in the Black Hills would be any different from the ones she'd met at Parkour events around the world? "We put yellow caution tape around the base to keep people away."

Cade nodded. "That's true. Unfortunately that wasn't enough to stop Shiloh." At the cop's confused expression, Cade explained, "My daughter was halfway to the top before I noticed. Luckily, Jessie was here to talk her down safely."

"And there was no sign of sabotage at that time," Hank observed.

"Going up was not the problem."

Hank looked toward the parked semi where the deflated tower rested like a garishly colored sarcophagus. "Could someone have tossed a slushy or a soda or something that landed on top of the rope?"

Jessie looked at Cade. "The area where the ropes were coiled was narrow. Under a foot wide. That would require amazing accuracy."

"Or really bad luck on your part."

Cade reached around her with his free hand and ran two fingers across her hot orange tank, an inch or so above her left breast. There wasn't anything sexy or suggestive about his touch but a shiver passed through her lower abdomen. A definite I-am-woman kind of shiver.

"I don't know, Hank. This doesn't look like soda to me." To the paramedics, he made a come-here motion with his chin. "I think her foot should be elevated. It's swelling."

Jessie shifted her gaze downward and gulped, loudly. He was right. She glanced at Remy and sighed, giving her a look only her twin would understand.

Before she knew it, she was on her back on the gurney with a blood-pressure cuff attached to her left arm and a fresh cold pack on her ankle. The pain she'd managed to block returned with a vengeance, but she made herself pay attention to the deputy, who seemed to be giving her declaration of foul play some credibility.

"So, this Zane guy? Where's he staying?"

"No idea. He wasn't at our motel. But you can't miss his bike. It's got a skull for a headlight."

The man scribbled something in his little notepad. "And what about the other guy? Cade said there was a third stuntman who took off after you fell."

"His name is J. T. Feathering." Jessie felt a pang of guilt for even hinting Dar's son might have had something to do with the sabotage. "Both of their numbers are on my phone. Remy, could you grab my backpack for me? I think I have an address book in it somewhere."

She watched her sister walk away, then added, "J.T. and I used to date but we broke up after a couple of months."

"You broke it off?"

She nodded. "We weren't that close. But his mom kept pushing us together."

"His mother?"

"Darlene Feathering. My ex-business partner. J.T.'s a decent cameraman. He works a lot of the same jobs I do. But he's not into the physical side of things. If he did climb the tower to put something on the ropes, it was payback for Dar."

"For what?"

She looked at Remy, who was returning with the backpack. Jessie hadn't told anyone in her family about the financial meltdown she'd returned to after their mother's funeral. "Dar embezzled from Girlz on Fire—the nonprofit corporation she and I started three years ago. We provided a safe harbor for at-risk young women. Dar was the hands-on manager. I was in charge of fund-raising. I collected pledges tied to Team Shockwave's performance."

"What's Team Shockwave?"

"Our eight-member Parkour team. Zane and I are co-captains. We…um…didn't do so hot at our last event," Jessie said softly. "I was eliminated earlier than I should have been."

She stared at the sky to avoid seeing the look on her sister's face. Remy was smart enough to put two and two together. "When I got home, Dar accused me of throwing the game. She said I'd sabotaged Girlz. Claimed she was going to have to file for bankruptcy." She closed her eyes, wishing she could forget the ugly confrontation that came so close on the heels of her mother's funeral. "Something about that didn't feel right to me, so I hired an independent auditor."

"How much money are we talking about?"

"Half a million dollars, give or take."

The cop whistled.

"Dar claims it's all a mistake. I'm not worried. She'll land on her feet. She always does. When I left L.A., I heard she was negotiating a plea bargain. She has a lot of support in Hollywood. She was one of the first female stuntwomen in the biz. When she was injured on the job, the outpouring of donations was pretty substantial. She says that generosity is what made her want to give back. I doubt very much if she'll go to jail."

And, honestly, Jessie had never wanted that. Dar had been like a second mother to her. Being a burn victim, too, Dar had seemed to understand Jessie in a way her family never had. But apparently that empathy and camaraderie and love came at a price.

"Ahem. We need to get going, sir," one of the paramedics said. "Could you finish this interview at the hospital? We're taking her to Sturgis General."

The two men started pushing her toward the ambulance. Cade rushed ahead to stop traffic. There wasn't much, thankfully. But watching him brought her gaze in line with her car—parked on the space directly below a prominent No Parking sign.

"Yota," she cried, lifting up on her elbows. "What about—"

"I told you," Remy interrupted, "I'll drive it."

That was hardly reassuring. Remy had a terrible sense of direction. "Are you sure you won't get lost? And what about the keys?"

Remy, who was walking beside her, held up a familiar key fob. "Somebody put the mail sack on the driver's seat. I'll be right behind the ambulance. Don't worry."

Don't worry? That was like telling her not to run. Jessie always worried. It was her job. Especially where members of her family were concerned.

Not that she was able to take care of the people she loved and keep them from dying. Her mother had proven that. But she never stopped worrying about them.

"One second, guys." Cade joined them. He leaned over so Jessie could see his eyes. *Someone should name a color of contact lenses after those eyes.* A silly thing to think, she realized about the same time he said, "I'll follow Remy to make sure she gets to the hospital safely. And I'll hang around until we hear what the verdict is on your ankle. Even if you decide not to stick around the Hills to train, you and your sister are welcome to stay at the ranch for as long as you need."

Not stick around…? What did he think was going to happen? Surgery? Amputation? Before she could say a word, the two men in uniform unlocked the wheels on the gurney with a loud clang and shoved the whole unit into the back of the ambulance, then closed the doors.

The blood-pressure cuff on her arm filled up, pinching her skin. "A little high," the man sitting beside her said. "How's the pain? Give me a number. If ten is the worst pain you could possibly imagine and one is no pain at all, what's yours?"

"Four," she lied. The steady throbbing in her foot and ankle was probably closer to an eight, but she could handle it without drugs. She'd survived weeks upon weeks of ten and worse. This was manageable.

Besides, she needed her mind to stay sharp if she was going to figure out who sabotaged her stunt…and why.

CHAPTER FOUR

CADE REGRETTED HIS IMPULSIVE decision to play white
knight even before the odd-looking caravan left Sentinel
Pass. Mac had stopped him in the parking lot to find
out where the paramedics were taking Jessie.

"Sturgis? Why Sturgis?"

"I guess it's closest. I don't know. Maybe Jessie told
them she was planning to move into Buck's place."

Mac had blinked in surprise. "You're renting your
dad's house to Jessie Bouchard?"

"Yeah. Why?"

Mac put up his hands defensively. "No reason. She's
cool. Coop and Shane were talking about some spec-
tacular rollover that put her in the hospital a few weeks
ago. Most people seem to think it was her fault. I heard
she lost her mother a while back. Maybe she's lost her
edge."

"She looked pretty damn sharp when she kept my
daughter from falling off that climbing tower and possibly breaking her neck."

"Shiloh did that?" Mac made a face. "Damn. Kids
never think, do they? Speaking of kids, I gotta run.
Good catch today, buddy."

Cade didn't know why he felt the need to defend

Jessie's reputation. He was certainly no fan of reck-less behavior and risky jobs. Hell, he'd lost his wife to exactly that sort of self-centered, all-eyes-on-me job. He'd never understood Faith's decision to put her career over the good of her family. That choice had cost her everything. But it had cost him, too.

And their daughter.

Speaking of Shiloh...once he had Jessie's funky blue box of a car in sight, he used his Bluetooth to call his sister. "Hey, Kat, how's Shiloh?"

"Great. The kids are out back with Jack, assembling our new barbecue. I'm thinking it's about time to order pizza."

Her happy laugh made him smile. She was the good part about moving back. Buck...not so much. "Will you buy enough for Shiloh? I'm on my way to the hospital. I would have swung by and picked her up but Jessie seems to think her sister could get lost following an ambulance."

"She told you that?"

Her pretty, mostly very unexpressive face had still communicated loud and clear. Cade had learned at a very young age to read the nuances behind the words. Probably a skill most children of alcoholics learned. "I read her silence."

"Oh." Kat seemed momentarily lost for words. Not surprising, Cade thought, she'd grown up with Buck for a father, too. But she was nearly ten years younger than Cade. With a different mother. Helen. The woman who recently passed away and whose death sent his father into an emotional tailspin.

"How's her foot?"

Ugly. "Don't know. I'll call you as soon as I hear something, okay?"

"Sure. Don't worry about Shiloh. She and the boys are having a blast. Just like you hoped when you moved back here."

Nothing was exactly as he'd hoped it would be when he returned to the Black Hills, but Kat and her sons were a start. Maybe Shiloh would act her age again if she spent more time with her cousins. And Kat was bound to be a good female influence on her, too.

"Thanks. I appreciate it."

"No problem. Tell Jessie I hope her leg is okay."

"I'll keep you posted." He pushed the disconnect button and let out a deep sigh.

Cade turned on the radio and settled into driving. Today was his first day off in two weeks and he was spending it chasing after a complete stranger who may or may not wind up living across the yard from him. Was he crazy? Probably. But that's what happened when you had a father like Buck Garrity.

"OHMMMMM."

Buck Garrity let the strange word resonate through his throat and chest the way his instructor had taught him. He'd heard someone say the sound was supposed to mimic the tone of creation. He had no idea what that meant, nor did he believe it, but he'd paid an exorbitant amount of money to stay at the Mount Madonna spiritual retreat, so he planned to give this meditation stuff a shot.

What did he have to lose?

He'd made a helluva lot of mistakes in his life. He'd loved and lost two good women. Of his four children, only two were still living. His oldest son passed in the prime of his life—angry. Mad at Buck. Mad at life. A sad way to leave things.

His eldest daughter was gone, too. At least as far as Renata had been concerned. She lived on the East Coast. Married. No children. She might as well be living on the moon. She'd formally resigned from being Buck's daughter the day she left for boarding school—a choice she made completely on her own when she was fourteen.

"I'm never coming back, Daddy. Just so you know. The ranch is not my life. It wasn't Mommy's, either. She wouldn't want this for me."

She was wrong. Her mother had loved living in the Black Hills. She called it her spiritual home. It's where she wanted to die—although not so young and from a disease no one completely understood. Especially not Buck. Bulimia. A hateful word. Almost as detestable as *drunk*. That was his claim to fame.

He'd been too weak, too big a coward, to face raising three kids alone, so he'd left his poor, grieving family with a housekeeper and drove west looking for someone to ease his pain and tell him it was going to be okay again.

He met Helen. The second love of his life. A single mom with three kids of her own.

He married her too fast. He figured his word alone would make the two families mesh. His word was a joke. The children hated each other and hated him more. All except for Cade. His bighearted youngest son. Cade tried to get along. And he loved baby Kat when she was born.

But in the end, Buck managed to drive Cade away, too. Determined to make his own way, Cade turned his back on his sister, the ranch, his inheritance, but, most of all, his father. Buck bided his time, keeping the lines of communication open via Kat. Fishing, hoping for a miracle.

And six months ago, he got a nibble.

Slowly, with finesse—the way you landed a fifteen-pound trout on a five-pound line—he and Cade worked out an arrangement. Cade and Shiloh would move home. At long last, Buck was going to have a chance to get to know his granddaughter. With any luck, he'd die a happy man on the ranch he'd built, his family around him.

Perhaps even be partially forgiven.

But then Helen died. The woman he'd been divorced from longer than he'd been married to. They'd loved each and hated each other. They'd made a daughter together and then fought over her for so long Kat claimed to feel like the knot in a giant tug-o'-war.

Helen died after a long and difficult illness. Everyone knew the end was coming. Buck thought he was prepared. He wasn't. Her funeral brought all of his losses crashing down upon him. Their faces. Their pain. The multitude of mistakes he'd made. The lost opportunities when he could have said "I love you, son. I love you, dear." But he didn't. And those chances never came again.

So, he did what he always did when life got too hard to handle without a stiff drink—he ran. This time, he left the bottle in the cupboard. Two years sober. He planned to stay that way. Instead, he ran to a sanctuary that promised to help him come out of his pain a better man. Wiser.

Forgivable.

He hoped.

"Sir, we have a short break before yoga. You're welcome to use the phone if you'd like."

Buck looked at the serene face of his tutor—that's what they called the person who helped guide a novice practitioner through the early days of the retreat. "Thank you, Matthew. Not today. My family is probably getting along much better without me. I think I'll keep it that way for the time being."

He would call Cade soon. He'd talked to Kat, once, but had asked her not to mention the call to her brother. She'd told him about Cade's plan to rent Buck's house for the summer. "He needs an extra set of eyes on Shiloh," she'd explained. *To fill in for Shiloh's missing grandfather.*

Buck stood, stretching slowly. He wondered if he'd ever get used to this slow pace. Running a ranch was a 24/7 sort of job. Having a resident grandpa on staff was supposed to be part of the plan.

Plans changed.

Cade knew that better than anybody.

"How did you say this happened again?"

Jessie looked at the doctor presently handling her foot as if it were an eggplant. The purple color and general shape resembled an eggplant. Inverted, though. With the plump part toward the top.

"I tried to secure the safety line around my foot to use as a brake while I was falling off a climbing tower, but I lost my hold on the rope and flipped upside down. The rope became knotted around my foot."

"I'll say," he agreed. "I can feel the knot right here."

He pressed with his thumb and she came completely off the exam table. "Ouch. That hurt."

"I'm not surprised. It's badly bruised. I'm thinking you tore something."

"Something?" She gave him the once-over. Short. Trim. Asian. Thick black hair. Round glasses and a bow tie. He looked about twelve, but his lab coat said Dr. Tan. "Don't you know the name for it?"

"I'm not an orthopedist. You need to see one. There's no obvious break on the X-ray, but that doesn't mean one won't show up in the fine bones in a day or two." He sounded a bit more professional now. "A sprain can take even longer to heal than a break. You might need surgery."

She let her elbows splay outward so she dropped like a rock to the exam-room gurney. To her great surprise, the hospital was bright, quiet and extremely efficient. According to the first nurse who took her vitals, this was the slow season. That worked for Jessie. Even if the doctor finished med school before junior high.

"I don't have time for this."

"Well, you should have thought of that before you climbed a fake mountain. I've seen those. They don't look safe."

"It was an accident."

"Falling off a stool is an accident. Falling off something you had to climb? Not so much."

She didn't have the energy to explain or argue. "So, what do I do now?"

"Rest. Stay off the foot. Alternate hot and cold compresses to help the swelling. I'll prescribe something for the pain."

"I still have a few pills left from…" She changed her mind. Telling him she'd had concussion a couple of weeks earlier would no doubt further confirm his opinion of her inability to distinguish between safe and reckless behavior. "Okay."

"And I'll give you a referral to Dr. Means. Don't let the name fool you—he isn't."

He laughed at his dumb joke, obviously not bothered in the least that his patient didn't appear amused.

"You'll need crutches, too," he said, getting to his feet. He scribbled something across the paper on his clipboard. "No cast today. We have to get the swelling down. I have a fancy boot you can wear, but you still need to be careful. You've severely compromised the ligaments, and ligaments are like politicians—they don't like compromise."

Jessie snickered at that. "You're funny. Are you sure you're old enough to be a doctor?"

"That's what they told me at Harvard."

She made a face to let him she know she was impressed.

He paused at the door of the exam room. "It'll take a few minutes to find the right boot. Do you want me to send in your family?"

"Sure." She looked at her bare legs. She didn't know why the nurse had insisted on removing Jessie's leggings, but, regardless how grouchy Jessie felt about being in a hospital, she never talked back to a nurse. The nurses had been her only salvation in the burn unit. Every one of them had treated her like their own child.

Of course, that was their job, she thought, pushing the memory away.

"Hey," a male voice said, "what's the verdict?"

Jessie startled, realizing too late that Dr. Tan had assumed Cade was related to her. She modestly tried to yank down the thin cotton gown that presently stopped midthigh. "Where's Remy? I thought she was coming."

Cade leaned around the partly closed door. "She stepped outside to take a call. When the doctor motioned for me to come, I thought maybe there was some kind of emergency. Are you okay? Is your ankle broken?"

"Too early to tell for sure. I need to see a specialist next week." She swallowed. "Um…I guess that means I need a place to stay. Are you still okay with Remy and me moving in?"

"Sure. Why wouldn't I be?"

"They're fitting me for a soft cast. They're bulky and

awkward, so I probably won't be able to drive. That was part of the bargain."

"Right. Well, I followed your sister the whole way here, and she seems like a very safe driver, so…maybe she could handle that part of the deal."

"Safe," she repeated softly. "Yeah, definitely. Remy's all about playing it safe. Safe job—now defunct. Safe boyfriends—most of them currently married to someone else. Safe life. The only time she took a big risk was when I dragged her to Nashville when we were eighteen."

"Nashville? Are you singers?"

Jessie let her head fall back against the thin, practically flat pillow. She didn't normally talk about her past, but job interviews were different. Cade was going to be her employer. "Remy has a beautiful voice. I play guitar. We waited tables by day, worked the clubs—really, really small, out-of-the-way clubs—at night."

"No big break, huh?"

She shrugged. "We weren't that good. But being on stage gave me a leg up in front of the camera, so I have no regrets. And Remy needed to get away for a while. She had… Well, let's just say it was the right time for both of us to fly the coop. Eventually, she went back, commuted to college from home and got her degree."

"And you started doing stunts."

She snickered softly. "I wish it were that easy. I followed a boyfriend to L.A. I worked a lot of different jobs, but for recreation, I played beach volleyball on Venice Beach. A guy came up to me and said he was making a commercial, and did I want to be in it? One thing led to another and, before you knew it, I was making low-budget slasher films. Crazy as it sounds, I got my big break because of Katrina."

"The hurricane?"

"Our hometown is about an hour north of New Orleans. I went back to help, and my agent called to tell me a Hollywood director was looking for locals to appear in his next film, which, coincidentally, was about a tourist town hit by a hurricane. He fast-tracked my Screen Actors Guild card and the rest, as they say, was history."

"I'm here," Remy said, bursting through the door so fast she sideswiped Cade. "Oops, sorry. I was on the phone with Bing."

"Did she call to say 'I told you so'?"

Remy made a face. "No. She called to tell me Shasta got her braces." To Cade, she said, "Bing is our sister. The youngest of the Bullies. That's what Jessie and I call our three older sisters. Shasta is about Shiloh's age. You're lucky Shiloh has perfect teeth." She rubbed her thumb and fingers together in the universal gesture of money. *"Pri-cey."*

Jessie sat up. An air-conditioned breeze across her backside reminded her that she wasn't going anywhere without her clothes. She pointed to the far end of the counter. "The doctor said I could get dressed. Cade, would you mind…?"

"Oh. Of course. Sorry. By the way," he said, glancing at his watch, "I need to pick up Shiloh from my sister's. You have the map, right?" he asked Remy.

"Right here," she said, patting her oversize purse.

She'd always had hideous taste in purses in Jessie's opinion. "And thanks to your description, I should be able to find your ranch without getting lost."

Jessie stifled a snort. Remy had been known to get lost going to the portable potties at a rock concert. *And when did these two get all buddy-buddy,* she thought, strangely peeved by their evident camaraderie.

Not that she was surprised. Remy was beautiful, personable, friendly, easy to like. Nothing like Jessie.

Why does everything have to be so hard with you, Jessie? their mother had asked the last time they saw each other. A couple of weeks before Mom ate the fateful E coli-laced burrito.

I don't know, Mom. I guess I didn't get the easy gene. A snide comment with several connotations. And given their mother's undeniable history—bastard twins born with no father named on their birth certificates—it was an obvious slam.

I suck. No wonder everyone likes Remy best.

"Jess?"

"Huh?" She looked between the two, blinking. What had she missed?

"Cade asked if he should pick up a wheelchair."

"Kat's mom had one before she passed. I don't know if it was a rental or what, but I could ask."

"No," she cried, swinging her legs around so she could face them. "The doctor's giving me crutches. I'll be able to get along fine."

"But you said—"

"I can't tell you what's going to happen long-term, but, I promise, if you're still okay renting to us, one of us will stick around as long as you need help. If I can't drive for a while, then Remy will have to play chauffeur, but no matter what, we'll make sure Shiloh's covered. Is that okay with you, Rem?"

"I guess so. When do you have to be in Japan?"

"The tryouts start in mid-August."

Cade had one hand on the door. "Is this show the one where people get dunked into water and stuff?"

"No," she snapped. Why did everyone always ask that? "*Kamikaze* pits world-class Parkour athletes against the clock. The top team wins a humongous trophy, but the big-money prize goes to the individual who completes the courses the fastest with the fewest mistakes. Not to be cliché, but the courses are extreme."

He didn't say anything or give her any reason to assume he thought that sounded like a crazy idea, but something his daughter said came back to her. His late wife was an extreme athlete. She died when Shiloh was a baby.

"You think that's crazy, right?" Jessie asked.

"It's not something I'd do, but you're an adult. You're obviously in great condition…except for your foot. I don't have a problem with your job, but I would appreciate it if you didn't glamorize the risk when you're around Shiloh. She has a bit of her mother in her. I didn't realize that until last winter when I caught her sneaking out of the house to help a seventeen-year-old stable hand who was trying to break a mustang."

He looked discouraged, frustrated. "She was only eleven at the time. The kid and I had a long talk. He thought he knew what was he doing, and Shiloh was utterly fearless. But horses are unpredictable, and a range-bred mustang can strike faster than a rattlesnake. She knew the barn was off-limits on a school night, but she went anyway."

Risk. Obedience. Respect. Jessie got it. Too bad she'd have probably done the same when she was Shiloh's age.

But Jessie was a responsible adult, now. And her sister *never* broke the rules. So, between the two of them, his daughter should be perfectly safe. "I've worked with at-risk girls the past couple of years. We had some success redirecting behaviors. Yoga. Martial arts. Kickboxing. Things like that. Would Shiloh be interested?"

He smiled. A really nice smile that made her go soft and mushy inside. "She'd probably follow you around like a puppy if you'd take her on as a student, but—" he looked at her foot "—I think it'll be a while before you're kickboxing."

Her warm feelings disappeared, but he left before she could come up with a snappy reply.

"He's cool," Remy said. "You like him."

"Hand me my pants," Jessie snapped. It sounded a great deal more adult than what she almost said: "Nuh-uh."

She did like him, but she had no intention of acting on those feelings. She had a pretty crappy track record with men she didn't have any financial dealings with; she hated to think how badly she'd screw up things by dating her landlord.

And, *Kamikaze* or no *Kamikaze,* going back to

L.A. was not in the cards at the moment. Was it cowardly of her hide out in the Black Hills? Not cowardly, circumspect.

"Lie low for a few weeks," Zane had advised. "Let the legal system do its thing. When the truth comes, everyone will know Dar screwed you over and stole from those needy kids."

Speaking of Zane… "Do you have my phone?"

"Yeah, but the battery is dead. I turned it off a few minutes ago. Cade said something about 'roaming.'"

Great. A bum foot, a nosy sister and a useless phone. "Things just don't get any better," she muttered under her breath. "Where's that doctor with my crutches?"

CHAPTER FIVE

CADE SAT IN THE CAB OF his truck in the hospital parking lot, not bothering to start the engine. He needed a minute to sort through his thoughts. He still couldn't quite believe his carefully considered plan to rent his dad's house until Buck finally "found God" or himself or whatever the goal of this self-imposed quest turned out to be was this close to fruition.

He'd asked his sister to put some feelers out. Less than a day later, he had an email from Jessie Bouchard. On paper, she seemed like the perfect renter: didn't smoke, short-term, low maintenance—as in no dogs, cats or kids. When he checked out her website, he was sold.

The nonprofit she supported was called Girlz on Fire. She even volunteered when she wasn't jumping off buildings and rolling cars. The stated goal of the organization was to serve at-risk teenage girls. Shiloh wasn't officially a teen, but she wasn't his sweet, happy, easygoing little girl, either.

He wished he knew how that had happened. He'd been certain he and his daughter had the perfect relationship. It had been the two of them against the world since she was three. He hadn't tried to shield her from ranch life or rodeos or any of the things her mother loved—except barrel racing. He'd never lied about Faith's career or her passion for the sport that killed her, but he encouraged Shiloh to explore other hobbies: dance, karate, gymnastics, soccer.

His job didn't always mesh with his daughter's schedule, but he'd sidestepped career advancement in ways Faith never would have. And he'd been certain his diligence as a parent had paid off. He and Shiloh were on the same wavelength. Until the night he walked into that barn and saw his daughter leading an unbroken two-year-old mustang around a pen.

"She is her mother's daughter," Faith's mother had predicted before her death when Shiloh was six. "She always was a wild one." Faith, not Shiloh. Cade had made damn sure of that.

Or had he?

Shiloh was the reason Cade was sitting in this parking lot today. He'd needed to find someone to fill his father's shoes while he was away. Was Jessie Bouchard the right person?

He didn't know. Her twin seemed sweet, demure and mannerly. The perfect role model for an impressionable young teen.

But Jessie was the twin he couldn't get out of his head.

He let out a sigh and put the key in the ignition. Before he could start the engine, his phone rang.

He glanced at the screen, his eyes widening in surprise.

"Buck?"

"Damn," the voice on the other end of the line cursed. "You were starting to call me Dad again. Now, we're back to *Buck*." His father sighed. "I guess I should have expected that, given the way I left things."

Cade wouldn't argue the point. "What do you want? Has something changed?" Knowing Buck, that could mean anything.

"No. I still plan to stick with this spiritual retreat. We only have a few chances to call. I wasn't going to bother you, but I saw a hummingbird zipping around a sage and I thought of Shiloh. How's she doing?"

Like you care. Like you ever cared. "She's fine. We made your bison chili recipe this morning."

"Oh, man, that sounds good. We eat a lot of vegetables here. And tofu," Buck said, his tone a bit baffled.

Well, you're the one who had to go all the way to California to make peace with your maker, Cade almost said. He didn't. He held his tongue and let the emptiness between them fill the line.

"Where is my granddaughter? May I talk to her?"

"She's at Kat's. I'm on my way there now to pick her up. I told you before you left that I might look into renting your house. Well, I sealed the deal with one of the stuntwomen from the *Sentinel Passtime* show. Her name is Jessie Bouchard. Unfortunately, she had a little mishap this morning. Twisted her ankle pretty bad. She'll be on crutches for a while, but she still wants to rent the place."

Buck didn't reply right away. When he did, his tone was somber and reflective. "You always were a bighearted kid. You were the only one who was nice to Helen."

Cade didn't like to think about that time in his life. *Chaos* didn't come close to describing the petty war carried on between his older siblings and Helen's three brats. As the youngest of the six, Cade had done his best to disappear. Sometimes that had meant hiding behind his stepmother's skirts.

Buck sighed weightily, then added, "I did love her, son. More than I realized. That's why her death hit me so hard. I have to try to figure out how something so good and real could turn so ugly and mean."

"I hope the retreat helps, Dad." The man had put Cade's name on the deed and all the bank accounts before he left. Unfortunately, that good fortune brought along a whole hell of a lot more responsibilities. Time-consuming responsibilities. "I have to go now. Shiloh's waiting."

"I knew you weren't gonna be happy about this, son, but you gotta admit, this is a lot better than me sitting around drowning my sorrows in a bottle."

Cade had to give him that one.

"Just one thing, Cadence." Helen was the only person who ever called him that. "Is she pretty?"

"Who?"

"That stunt gal who's moving into my house. Is she easy on the eyes?"

Cade started to grin. "Yeah, Dad. They both are." He pretended to stop and think a second. "Wait. Did I forget to mention that Jessie has an identical twin named Remy and they're both gorgeous? Yep, that new pool you put in for Shiloh is going to be looking pretty nice in a few weeks. You enjoy that tofu, now. See you in August. Bye."

He was still smiling when he pulled out of the parking lot.

"Wow. THIS PLACE IS unbelievable," Jessie said, rolling down her window as they passed under a massive arch of metal and carved wood. Garrity Ranch.

The car's right front tire hit a pothole and the crutches she'd been given toppled sideways, nearly smacking her in the face. She shoved them between the seats, but the big rubber tip on one of them got wedged beneath the sole of her snow-boot-size protective brace.

"What do you think of my designer footwear?" she asked. "Doesn't it remind you of that nursery rhyme where the lady has too many kids? I remember thinking that was our life—particularly when Mom's friends came over with their broods."

"That was the best part of Mama's house, for me," Remy said. "The Bullies were always in and out with their friends. They had the coolest clothes and…oh…the perfume." She inhaled deeply as if smelling something besides the faint locker-room scent of the car.

"They were stuck-up cows—just like the Bullies."

Remy frowned but she didn't refute the charge. Instead, she said, "I'm going to blame your negatively slanted memory on that shot the nurse gave you in the butt for pain."

"Yes, you are a pain in the butt," Jessie joked. "Finally something we agree on."

She could tell by Remy's tight-lipped profile she wasn't amused.

"Speaking of pain, I don't have any. Isn't that cool?"

"It won't last," Remy said sagely.

"Nothing ever does."

Jessie closed her eyes and let her head rest against the seat. The bounce and jolt of the gravel road should have prompted her to check out the landscape of her new, albeit temporary, home, but all she really wanted to do was sleep.

Damn painkillers. When she'd been hospitalized as a child, she'd come to hate the gray numbing fog each IV brought. She should have welcomed the brief cessation of red-hot pokers tormenting her back, but, without her mother by her side, Jessie was afraid she'd drift so far into the fog she'd never be able to find her way out.

"Remy? Can I ask you something?"

"Yes."

"Was Mama in pain when she passed?"

Remy didn't answer right away. When she did, her voice sounded serious, truthful. "No. She was on morphine. All of her organs started shutting down—not only her kidneys. The end came pretty fast."

Fast was good, Jessie imagined, even though a part of her wished Mama could have hung on a bit longer.

"Are you still beating yourself up for not being there?"

"No."

"Liar."

"I don't want to talk about it."

Remy made a scoffing sound. "Then why'd you bring it up?"

"I don't know."

Yes, she did. Guilt. Jessie had done everything that was asked of her when Mama's sickness turned systemic—simply not *when* it was asked of her. The Bullies accused Jessie of dragging her feet as a way of payback.

"She did the best she could when you were in the hospital, Jessie," Bossy, the oldest of the Bullies had shrieked at her—the telephone connection with Japan as clear as if they'd been standing in the same room. "Get over it. Mama needs you now."

What Mama needed was a kidney. And if Jessie had been a donor match, the operation would have effectively killed her career—the one thing that defined her, gave her life purpose and proved to the world she was not a scarred victim who deserved pity, not love. Jessie had agonized over the dilemma from halfway around the world, and as much as she hated to admit it, there had been a part of her that remembered feeling abandoned by the woman she was now expected to save. That sense of righteousness pointed out Jessie's commitments—her moral obligation to her team and her financial obligation to Dar and Girlz on Fire—as reason enough to keep from hopping the first plane back to Louisiana.

"Maybe if I'd tried harder…" *What?* She didn't know. Her mother would still be dead.

Remy slowed the car to pass over a metal cattle guard. Yota rocked like a small boat on a rough sea. A moment later, they crested a slight rise, which afforded a vista of a cluster of buildings and trees a mile or so ahead.

"You know, Jess, I could have mailed Mama's letter and your copy of the will, but I could tell lately that you've been a little down. I was afraid you might be stewing about what happened at the funeral."

"I'm used to being the family scapegoat. Nothing new there."

Remy didn't argue the point. They'd talked about their family dynamics many times. The fire that destroyed their childhood home, the costs—from Jessie's hospital stay to the many subsequent operations, the terrible emotional toll for everyone—especially their mother. All assumed to be Jessie's fault, since everyone believed she'd lit the candle that ignited the curtains that became a fuse.

"I know, but remember what Mama always said about you? 'Jessie's shoulders are broad. She can handle anything.'"

Jessie sat up a little straighter. Mama had said that. Many times. About many situations. A surge of emotion swelled upward, nearly choking her. No tears, though. Jessie never cried. "The heat from the fire sealed my tear ducts," she told people.

"So, this is the place, huh?" Jessie asked, leaning forward to look around. "Not bad."

"Not bad? How 'bout freaking amazing?" Remy came to a stop in front of a four-stall garage. The roofline extended across a breezeway to join up with a postcard-perfect two-story log house the color of burnished gold. A forest-green metal roof and matching shutters completed the Cartwright-ranch look. Set back slightly and perpendicular to the big house was a far more modest, one-story home that was saved from looking like a tract home by its wide, wraparound veranda.

"But where are the barns?" she asked, swiveling in the seat. "Shouldn't a ranch have a bunch of barns and outbuildings and corrals and stuff?"

Jessie rolled up her window and opened her door, carefully maneuvering her new walking sticks so she could get out of the car without help. A hospital orderly with a wheelchair had insisted on helping her into Yota, but she was determined to figure this out on her own. "I don't know, but I'm sure we'll get a guided tour sooner or later."

"You made it," a familiar voice called. Cade and his daughter exited the house through the door closest to the garage. "Shiloh and I made bison chili. My dad's recipe. He won a local chili cook-off a few years ago and has been coasting on the glory ever since, but it's good. We hoped you'd get here in time for supper."

Jessie's stomach had been growling for miles. "Bison, huh? I don't think I've ever tried that."

Once she was standing and the car door was closed, she put her crutches under her arms and hobbled toward him. "Lead the way, I'm starved."

He pointed to a sidewalk linking the two houses. "Shiloh and I were discussing this. We think it will be easier for you to get up and down the front porch steps. They're wider and there's a handrail."

Jessie looked at the door he'd used.

"This goes through the laundry room. It's closer, but there are more things to trip over, including," he said meaningfully, his gaze going to his daughter, "Shiloh's pet raccoon."

"You have a raccoon?" Jessie exclaimed. "I had one when I was a kid. Her name was Bandit." She looked at Remy and grinned. "Not very original, but we were… what? Ten?"

Remy shook her head. "No. More like six or seven. Bandit was before the fire." She looked at Shiloh. "Sometimes wild things don't stick around the way you hope they will."

Shiloh's smile disappeared. She looked at her dad, who rubbed his hands together to hurry things along. "Can I carry anything for you or do you want to eat first and bring in your stuff later?"

"Food first," Jessie said. "Definitely."

Shiloh and Remy led the way, with Jessie moving slowly and carefully—the damn pain meds were making her dizzy—bringing up the rear.

Jessie found her rhythm using the crutches pretty quickly. The tricky part came from trying to walk and look around at the same time. And there was plenty to see.

"You have a pool," she said, motioning toward an inground pool that seemed to take up at least half of the lawn between the two houses.

"Yeah. My dad put it in last fall. Right before winter. Dumb time to put in a pool, if you ask me, but I guess he had his reasons. It is solar heated, though, so that's cool. Do you swim?"

She loved the water. "Water aerobics would be good low-impact exercises for my ankle. You wouldn't mind if Remy and I use it?"

"No. Feel free. I'll show you how to operate the cover, and maybe you can help me figure out the filter system. So far, nobody's used it—still too cold. But the days are starting to warm up. Shiloh's been asking to get in, haven't you, Shiloh?"

The girl nodded with enthusiasm. "But I have to get a new swimsuit. I want a two-piece, but Dad gets all weird whenever I show him any suits online."

Cade blushed slightly. A manly blush, Jessie decided. If there was such a thing. "Two-piece suits are one thing. Triangles with strings are something else."

"Hey, look," Remy exclaimed, stemming off a full-blown fashion debate. "Are those buffalo?"

She and Shiloh were standing on the porch that extended the entire length of the house. The building was angled in a way that afforded a view of distant fields. The closest pasture was dotted with large, woolly beasts.

"Wow," Jessie said, slightly breathless from climbing the steps. For someone in as good a shape as she was, the four, wide redwood stairs shouldn't have her puffing. "Those are buffalo. The same ones we're going to eat tonight?"

Cade shook his head. "No. That's Kat's herd. She knows each animal by name, I think. Dad and his friend trade butchered beef for butchered bison."

The interior of the house was impressive, with a wall of windows that offered an unobstructed view of the rolling hills and—yes—buffalo. The decor was understated and rustic in a manly way—the occasional stuffed deer head shared wall space with a watercolor landscape. "Nice," she said, meaning it.

"A huge improvement over that log cabin we stayed at with Mama. Remember that dump in the Bayou? It belonged to her banker boyfriend."

"A major slimeball," Jessie said. "He told us there were gators everywhere and we couldn't leave the house, but there was nothing for a fifteen-year-old kid to do." She looked at Cade. "Remy read a book and listened to her Walkman. I flagged down a passing airboat and partied with a bunch of river rats all weekend. I don't think Mama even knew I was gone."

"She knew," Remy said.

"The kitchen's this way," Cade said, motioning toward the left.

"When I was a kid, I thought alligators were giant snakes with teeth."

Jessie looked at the Shiloh. She was still wearing jeans and a T-shirt but she'd added a black apron with the words *Heat Happens* spelled out in chili peppers. "That's funny. I like your apron."

"I made biscuits. From a can," she added. A second later her eyes went wide and she took off running. "I forgot to set the timer. Damn. Damn. Darn. I mean… Darn." She dropped out of sight behind a high-end, eight-burner stove.

"Does your dad like to cook?" Jessie asked, pressing ahead, keeping one eye out for tripping hazards.

Cade walked around her, heading toward the counter, where four bowls were sitting on bright, Mexicali-colored woven placemats. "Yeah. Kat says he won a popular chili cook-off a few years back. This is his recipe. He was going to teach Shiloh how to make it, but didn't get around to it before he left."

Jessie picked an outside stool so she could prop her leg on the empty stool beside her. She leaned her crutches against the thick granite countertop and unfolded her napkin in her lap. "Where did you say he went?"

"West."

Cade took the vibrant yellow bowl from her spot to fill it from a giant caldron on the opposite counter. With his back to her, she studied him with an athlete's eye. He'd changed shirts, she noticed. Like the white one, this short-sleeve blue-and-gold check was tucked into the belted waistband of his denim jeans. Name brand, but the kind favored by working-class joes, NASCAR drivers and, of course, cowboys.

She heard a soft noncough and glanced sideways to the neighboring stool. Remy had caught her studying Cade.

Jessie grabbed her spoon and nudged the bowl a little closer. The aroma made her mouth start to water. "Yum," she said, savoring her first bite. "Nice heat. Well done, Papa Garrity, wherever you are."

Cade finished filling the other bowls then pulled a stool to a spot directly across from her. Remy and

Shiloh anchored the side to her right. Only three sides of the square island were meant for stools, she realized. Cade could have squeezed in with his daughter and Remy, but he chose to sit where he could see her. Did that mean something? she wondered.

"So, Jessie, my cousins and I went to your website today and watched all your videos. Man, you have been all over the world, haven't you?" Shiloh said.

Jessie reached for the basket of slightly toasty biscuits. "I've been lucky," she said, slathering on a big dollop of butter. Normally, she could eat as many calories a day as she wanted and never worry about gaining a pound because she burned off every bite. She looked at the biscuit for a few seconds before dunking it in the glistening red stew.

"What's your favorite country?"

She finished chewing before answering. "I don't know. Japan was interesting. High-tech and fast-paced. I would have liked to visit the countryside, but I wasn't there long enough."

"You travel a lot?" Cade asked.

She'd taken too big a spoonful and couldn't answer right away, so Remy stepped in. "She's always on the go. We never know where to find her. One day you call her cell phone, thinking she's in her apartment in L.A., and she answers half-asleep because it's 2:00 a.m. in Beijing."

Jessie frowned. "It's not quite that bad."

Remy snorted. "Remember when I called you in freakin' Iceland? Iceland," she repeated, looking meaningfully at Shiloh. "She was filming a vodka commercial."

"Men's deodorant, not vodka." She doubted anyone in the States had seen it. "I fell backward out of a window into the arms of some Nordic god. Literally. The guy had lightning bolts strapped to his chest. If I fell wrong, I could have been impaled."

"What's *impaled* mean?"

Remy pretended to stab herself in the chest.

Cade did not look amused.

"Can you teach me how to do those backflips and midair twists?" Shiloh asked. "Those look so cool. And, man, would the kids at school freak if I learned how to run up the side of a building. Whoa."

Jessie looked at Cade. She wasn't surprised to find him scowling. He'd rented his father's house to her so she could watch out for his daughter's health and safety, not teach her how to do stunts.

She pushed her bowl away. "This was really great, Cade. Thank you so much. Shiloh, your biscuits were delish. Extra crunchy—exactly the way I make them. But—" she drew the word out as she reached for her crutches "—I was supposed to start hot-and-cold therapy on my ankle as soon as I got settled. Would anyone mind if I checked out my new digs?"

"Of course not," Cade answered. "I'll show you the way. Shiloh, you're in charge of cleanup. Remember?"

"I know."

"I'll help," Remy said. "Unless you need my help, Jess."

"No. No, problem. You put the prescription in my duffel, right?"

"Yep. I left both our bags sitting beside Yota."

Cade detoured toward the side door. "I'll collect them and meet you at Buck's." He stopped suddenly. "Oh, that reminds me. Grandpa called today, Shiloh. He said to tell you he misses you, but he's doing well and has developed a fondness for fried tofu."

Jessie snickered softly to herself as she headed across the simply landscaped yard. She breathed deeply, taking in the smells of moist grass and some unfamiliar scents. She felt strangely at peace. She had no idea how that was possible. Given the fact her life was in chaos and somebody screwed with her ropes today.

The meds, she thought.

"Hey, Cade," she called. "Any chance you have the number for that cop...I mean...deputy from today? You know what they say about squeaky wheels."

"They're the first to fall off the car?" He grinned, obviously amused by his own joke.

He lugged the two suitcases to the door. "Speaking of car wrecks, the kids found the video of your famous rollover on YouTube today."

Her chili made a wrong turn in her stomach. "It wasn't my fault."

"Hmm."

A sound that could mean just about anything.

He reached past her to set the bags inside the door. His shoulder brushed against her breast. An innocent accident that set off a not-so-innocent response in her body. Normally, if she felt her nipples pucker when they weren't supposed to, she'd cross her arms. Impossible to do when they were straddling two bulky padded crutches.

He stepped back, his gaze dropping like radar to her chest. A second later, his chin popped up. His expression didn't change, but something between them did. She would have sworn to the fact. Not that you could tell that by his friendly, perfectly innocent "Sleep well."

She stepped into the room and closed the door firmly.

Well? Probably more like *hell*.

CHAPTER SIX

CADE WALKED SLOWLY TO THE house. He wasn't sure what just happened. Wrong. That much he knew. He'd been married, for God's sake. He'd dated a dozen or so women before he and Faith got together. He'd felt that thing that happened between a certain man and a certain woman more than once. A spark. A look. A hint that maybe the other person felt a tiny bit of possibility, too.

But not with Jessie Bouchard, damn it. He was her landlord. Her short-term, temporary landlord. When he went looking for a new someone, he sure as hell intended to pick one who planned to stick around—the Hills *and* life.

He shook his head. That wasn't fair. He knew Jessie wasn't Faith. Faith's death had been an accident. It couldn't be called a freak accident because saddles slipped more often than people wanted to admit or talk about. The horse breathes in, expanding its belly, the person tightening the cinch forgets to knee the horse or give the cinch an extra tug… Who knows what happened that night? The end result was still the same.

It was wrong of him to associate Jessie's job with Faith's. He didn't know anything about her career—other than the fact she'd wound up falling into his arms this morning. And he knew she was damn lucky not to have been hurt worse.

What more did he need to know about her chosen profession? Nothing. She was not the sort of woman he was looking for. Not that he was actively looking, of course. His life was still in flux at the moment. His relationship with Shiloh was changing. He'd returned home to try to rebuild some kind of relationship with his father…who wasn't here.

He pushed the thought away. The point was he had no intentions of getting involved with another dedicated athlete type. He wouldn't. He refused.

Then why was he pacing on the porch instead of going inside and having a normal—*boring?*—night with his daughter?

He slammed the heel of his hand against the railing of the deck. *No. Where the hell had that thought come from?*

"Oh, hi, Cade. Great place you have. Shiloh just showed me around."

"Thanks. It's—" He stopped himself from saying *my dad's.* It wasn't. Not anymore. "Shiloh and I still have a way to go before it feels like home."

Remy cocked her head. "Wasn't this always your home? I must have misunderstood."

"No. You didn't. This is where I grew up, but I haven't spent much time around here for a lot of years. Buck remarried after my mom passed, and Helen, my stepmother, did a bunch of remodeling. Added the second floor, actually," he said, looking up. "And Buck's done a lot to the place over the years. Including the new *granny* house." The word always made him smirk. Buck hadn't been much of a father; Cade didn't have high hopes that he'd make a better grandfather.

"Oh," she said, smiling. "So, you have a little of the wanderlust, too. Like Jessie."

He didn't see the parallel. Texas was a long way from Iceland. But he didn't say so. "I'd better get inside and make sure Shiloh isn't online. Punishment for climbing that tower today."

"Yeah, wow. That was scary. Jessie makes it look so easy, but you wouldn't catch me up on that thing. No way, no how."

Although the two women were both fair and there *was* a strong family resemblance, he had a hard time reconciling the fact they were twins. Identical twins.

How identical? he wondered.

When she moved to walk past him, Cade turned, too. His shoulder bumped her shoulder, and he politely steadied her with a hand on her arm.

Nothing. Not a hint of tingle.

"Have a good night," he said. "Dad has satellite in both the bedrooms, if you're interested."

"Cool," she said, blithely traipsing down the steps— obviously also unaffected by their contact. "I wouldn't even own a TV if it weren't for *Sentinel Passtime*. I love watching Jessie."

He blinked in surprise. "I thought the goal of a stunt person was to look so much like the star nobody could tell the difference?"

"It is and she does. She's the best. But Jess and I have

a special kind of bond. Twin sense. Believe me, I know her when I see her. G'night." She wiggled her fingers and strolled across the lawn.

He thought a moment. He was pretty sure he had a couple of episodes of *Sentinel Passtime* on his digital recorder. Would he be able to spot Jessie if he saw her pretending to be someone else?

He opened the door and walked inside. He'd check it out after Shiloh was in bed. He was curious. That was all.

DAWN.

Holy spitwad. Buck couldn't remember the last time he got up this early. Probably on one of his hunting or fishing trips. He'd been semiretired from ranching for several years and paid good money to have someone else wake up in the wee hours of the morning.

Stumbling along a pitch-black trail to reach the pinnacle of what passed for a mountain in these parts was not part of the brochure, he thought grumpily.

Faith Mountain, Matthew called this place. "That's not its given name," he'd said last night when he talked Buck into joining the small group planning the hike. "But those of us who come here often know it's a very spiritual epicenter."

Buck didn't think that word meant what Matthew thought it meant.

"The moments just before dawn are especially porous," he claimed. *Porous?* "If you truly want to reach someone who has passed over to the other side, this could be your best chance."

Baloney. Complete and utter hoodoo nonsense, Buck thought. But he decided to make the climb anyway. He didn't know why. To prove he could? Probably. Both of his wives had called him bullheaded. "You'd spend a hundred bucks to prove the dollar in your hands was worthless, wouldn't you?" Helen once asked.

He would. He probably had. Numerous times.

Take this retreat, for example. He was paying ten times that to prove what? That he wasn't a complete and utter screwup where relationships were concerned?

He didn't know. Maybe he'd ask Helen when he *saw* her this morning.

His thick-sole hiking boot caught on the tip of a jagged rock and he stumbled, catching his balance using the brand-new high-tech walking sticks he'd purchased at the retreat store the day before.

"Careful," Matthew said, suddenly materializing a step away from Buck.

The leader of the group—a silver-haired fellow in his sixties—motioned for everyone to fan out around him. "We've reached the pinnacle," he said in a hushed whisper, his voice so achingly poignant you'd have thought they were looking at a double rainbow.

Buck covered his snicker with a fake cough.

"Are you, okay, Buck?"

"I'm fine, Matthew. Thank you."

"Good. We use this time to meditate individually, and then rejoin everyone to chant *Ohm* before we head back down." He directed his flashlight toward a generous-size flat rock a few feet away.

Buck followed the light and sat. The rock was cold

but he ignored the distraction. He was here to focus. On the past, mostly. On memories he'd felt certain had been flushed away by a million or so bottles of Jack Daniel's. The people he'd loved. The ones he'd lost. When he looked at Matthew, his tutor, he was reminded of Charles. His firstborn.

The two were nothing alike, but Charles would have been Matthew's age now if he'd lived. Hard to believe he'd been gone thirty years or better. Funny the things that stuck out in his memory, Buck thought.

Like his firstborn's first tooth, which the baby promptly buried in the fleshy part of his father's thumb. Buck had carried the scar for years. He reached up and rubbed his thumb across his nose.

God, how he'd loved that boy.

Proud? His pals had claimed Buck had turned into the most obnoxious, boastful parent they knew. "My kid did this. My kid did that."

A heaviness settled over him.

My kid thinks I killed his mother.

And maybe I did.

Not on purpose, of course. Neglect. Pure and simple. Too busy acquiring land, juggling government contracts, investing in his breeding program, drinking with his buddies. He'd missed what his kids saw every day. His wife was disappearing. Literally.

He'd never even heard of an eating disorder before his wife was diagnosed with bulimia. He took her to the University Of Minnesota Medical School for treatment. He got her the best care he could find. But they couldn't undo the damage her self-starvation had inflicted on her body—especially her heart.

Passed away. Too young. In the prime of her life. Such a waste.

Platitudes became his new reality.

If he could overlook the fact that his wife was barfing up the elaborate meals she cooked for her family, how could he possibly be in charge of three kids all by himself? He was a failure. He only had to look in his eldest son's eyes to see proof of that. He went searching for help.

"I married Helen for your sake, Charles," he remembered telling his then seventeen-year-old son. "You and Renata and Cade. Cade, especially. You're almost grown, but Cade needs a mother. He's still a little kid."

Buck looked into the murky near light of daybreak. He could almost see him. Handsome as sin. Filled with potential—and fury.

That's a lie, Dad. For once in your life, admit the truth. You married Helen because you were a coward. A complete and utter coward.

"Dawn," a voice said.

Buck turned to stare at the red ball inching above the indistinct curve of the earth. Blurry. Not from clouds, but from tears. The kind that came from shame.

"Good morning. You're up bright and early."

Jessie looked from under the hood of her car to find Cade standing a foot or so away, a cup of coffee in his hand.

"I forgot to check the oil yesterday. I'm about ready to replace the engine again."

"Again?"

"The first was a couple of years after we got it. My mom's boyfriend at the time owned a body shop. He showed me how to drop the tranny. It's not all that hard if you have the right tools."

He didn't look convinced. "And the second?"

"I bought a crate motor and rented a stall at a garage down the street from where I live."

"You're pretty self-sufficient."

She was—and proud of it. And while there was nothing overtly judgmental in his tone, she felt defensive. "I think every woman should know about car engines. If for no other reason than to be aware if some unscrupulous mechanic is trying to screw you."

He walked closer. "I agree. Do you think you could teach Shiloh how to change the oil? I was starting to show her some of those things when she suddenly decided I was a mean and controlling father. Not someone she wanted to learn squat from."

She replaced the dipstick and closed the hood, balancing on her good foot. "Sure. I could do that. And I wouldn't worry too much. Kids butt heads with their parents. That's a given."

"Are you speaking from experience?"

"Absolutely. My mother and I were polar opposites. She never understood why I did the things I do, and, I guess you could say, I felt the same way about some of her life choices."

"Like what?"

She grabbed her crutches, glad for the support. "Do you have any more of that?" she asked, motioning toward his cup with her chin—partly because she needed a caffeine fix and partly to avoid the much-too-personal question. "I live within walking distance from four fabulous coffee houses. I haven't made my own since I moved to L.A."

"Sure. I'll meet you on Dad's veranda with the pot."

He smiled that friendly puppy-dog smile that had stayed in her mind all night. She'd even dreamed about him, for heaven's sake. A nice dream. The kind that was probably illegal in several states in the South.

Jessie had been awake for a couple of hours. She'd been too wiped out the night before to shower, so that was the first order of business. After another hot and cold compress therapy, she felt fairly optimistic that the specialist would have good news for her when she saw him.

But she wasn't taking any chances. She moved slowly, carefully skirting the collage of outdoor furniture. Instead of taking a chair at the table, she eased her butt into a chaise so she could elevate her foot.

"Hey," Cade said a couple of minutes later. "Your ankle looks a lot better." He set an insulated Thermos on the table and handed her a mug that said World's Best Grandpa. "Do you like sugar and cream? I can run back inside."

"Black is good. Thanks."

He pulled out a chair at the table and joined her, refreshing his plain green ceramic mug, too. "I don't mean to sound nosy, but you and Remy have both mentioned your mother. I understand she passed away recently, and I'm sorry to hear that. But could I ask about your father? I thought Shiloh and I had a pretty great relationship until about six months ago."

Jessie brought the mug to her nose and inhaled deeply. She loved coffee, but there was nothing like the kind her mother used to make. She took a sip before answering. "This is good. Thanks. And, I'm sorry, but I can't be of any help where you and Shiloh are concerned. Remy and I never knew our father."

"Oh. He passed away?"

"Yes, but that's not why we didn't know him. Mama refused to tell us his name. Our birth certificates say Unknown."

He looked shocked. "She never told you?"

Jessie looked toward the house, where her sister was busy composing a shopping list. "She did, but not until we were seventeen. He was dead by then." The revelation had been high drama at the time, completely devastating poor Remy. But as usual, Mama made no excuses, offered no apologies. She lived her life the way she wanted and everyone could be damned.

The patio door opened a few inches and a tousled blond head popped out. "The list is done, Jess. Better check it over and see if you want anything." She looked at Cade and smiled. "Hi, Cade. Hey, I was going to call over and see if Shiloh could go shopping with me." She pulled a face. "But it is Sunday. If you're going to church…"

He shook his head. "We haven't gotten back into that

routine, yet. She's still asleep, but it's time for her to get up. I'm sure she'd love to go."

"I'll be ready in half an hour," Remy said, crossing her fingers.

The door slid shut.

"That's why you were checking the oil."

She didn't say anything. She took care of things: her car, her sister, her family. It's what she did. Most of the time.

Cade stood. "More?" he asked, reaching for the pot.

"No, thanks. I'd better take a look at that list. Appreciate it, though. Chili *and* coffee. Two for two."

She swung her legs over the edge of the chaise and readied her crutches. She hated knowing he was watching her. Did he see her as damaged, helpless? That's how the people of her town saw her when she came home from the burn center. That pity was probably the reason she went out of her way to take on every physical challenge she could find. Starting with gymnastics. Burnt skin didn't stretch, but she practiced and practiced—back bends, forward rolls, walk-overs, flips—ignoring the pain, until she could do anything the non-burn victims on her school's team could do.

She took a deep breath and pulled herself up, pausing to catch her balance. She didn't like the feeling of vertigo the pain pills gave her, but she wouldn't be taking them for long. As the swelling went down, she could start weaning off the meds.

"Let me get the door for you," he said.

"No," she said sharply. His good manners undoubtedly were to blame for her crazy dreams. Sexy dreams. "No, thank you. I'm capable."

"No one could ever dispute that." He sounded amused, but he turned and left without touching the door.

Jessie watched him walk across the lawn and mount the stairs two at a time. Being laughed at was almost as unforgivable as pity.

"Get over yourself," she muttered, nearly dislocating her shoulder trying to slide the door while balancing on one foot. Cade was being nice, not trying to cop a feel. What happened the night before was an accident, and the fact that she couldn't put it out of her mind was probably due more to her dismal sex life than any sort of mutual attraction.

She didn't *date*—for want of a better word—men with kids. Period. As the child of a serial dater, she lived through the ups and downs of her mother's passionate, turbulent, confusing relationships. The highs of hoping this Tom, Dick or Harry might be the *one*. The lows of being sent to the store to buy more tissues when he turned out to be simply one of many.

She hobbled to the counter that separated the kitchen from the living room. The house was compact but practical, with bedrooms separated by the common rooms. She heard the water turn off. Remy would need another fifteen minutes, at least, to "get presentable," as their mother liked to say.

Jessie unplugged her phone from the charger and turned it on. She'd been too wiped out last night to stress about whether or not she got reception, so she'd turned it off. Now she checked for messages.

Two. Eerik and Marsh.

They'd arrived back in L.A. safely. Both apologized for deserting her in her hour of need. She snickered softly and shook her head. They were teammates and friends, but she knew better than anyone that the only way to get ahead in this business was by watching out for your own interests. They had jobs to go to tomorrow. She did not. She'd planned it that way.

Not *this* way, but that was hardly their fault.

But it could be J.T.'s fault.

She tried his number. As it had all day yesterday, the call went straight to voice mail. She repeated her earlier message. "Ignoring me only makes you look guilty," she added.

Could he have tried to hurt her? Worse, could she have been that poor a judge of character? She'd definitely blown it where his mother was concerned, but she'd believed at the time she and J.T. started dating their friendship went beyond their connection to Dar. Had they created an even worse problem by trying to humor Dar's fixation on the two of them becoming a couple?

She didn't know, but that situation was out of her hands. Whatever happened to Dar would be settled in the courts. With any luck, Jessie would one day be able to resurrect Girlz on Fire—a mission she still believed in wholeheartedly. It would take time and a lot of money. Money she'd hoped to earn by winning *Kamikaze*.

Stifling a sigh, she worked her way around the counter to the refrigerator and pulled her ice pack from the freezer.

Fifteen minutes later, Remy dashed through on a perfume-scented breeze—her hair a cloud of gold, her simple cotton skirt topped by a pretty, pale green blouse. "I've got the list and the keys," she said, looping her purse over one shoulder. "Call me if you forgot anything. Shiloh's waiting. Behave yourself."

Jessie blew out a raspberry. "Don't forget to use the parking brake if you stop on a hill," she hollered. She'd been planning to take Yota in to have the rotors turned and the brake pads replaced before she left L.A., but there simply hadn't been time.

She picked up the remote but didn't turn on the TV. She wasn't good with downtime. She didn't know a single person in her profession who was. Except for Zane. She'd never seen anyone party until the wee hours of the morning, show up for work, hit every mark without pause then drop into a dead sleep between takes. He claimed to have developed the technique in the military. "You know the adage 'Hurry up and wait'?" he'd once told her. "Nobody waits better than the Army."

On a lark, she tried his number.

No answer.

"What is going on with these guys?" she muttered with a frustrated sigh. *Oh, well.* There was nothing she could do at the moment.

She hit the power button. What does one watch on a Sunday morning? she wondered, idly punching through the menu. She settled on a car race, but left the sound on mute. She watched the silent jockeying for position without any real interest until she saw two cars collide. The lead car spun into the wall and flipped once, landing on its hood and sliding into oncoming traffic.

A knot formed in her throat. Memories of her own crash worked their way into her head. The sound of metal ripping under pressure—a sound that mimicked the screams she remembered from the treatment room where the nurses scrubbed away the dead and dying tissue on her back, igniting the nerve endings like individual leads attached to an electrical probe.

She startled violently a second later when her phone rang. Swallowing hard to get some saliva back in her mouth, she hit Receive. "Hello?"

"Is this Jessie Bouchard?" an unfamiliar voice asked.

"Yes. Who's this?"

"I'm calling from the Pennington County Sheriff's Department. Deputy Miller wanted to know if you could come in and meet with him today."

"When? My sister just left with my car."

The dispatch person hesitated. "Hold on a moment." Jessie waited, trying not to read too much into the request.

"Ms. Bouchard? It's Hank Miller. Is Cade around by any chance?"

"Not at the moment."

"I understand your sister isn't there right now, and I think you should be here when we interview your friend J.T. He was stopped for speeding near Custer.

They just brought him in. If Cade's available, would you mind catching a ride into town with him? We're a little shorthanded this morning or I'd send a car for you."

J.T. had been arrested? No wonder he wasn't answering his phone. "Um, sure. If he doesn't mind. Do you have his number?"

"Yes, ma'am, I do. Hopefully I'll see you soon."

She ended the call and sat a moment. Her gaze returned to the big-screen TV. Emergency vehicles had surrounded the mangled race car. Two EMTs were kneeling beside the squashed window where the driver was trapped.

She could remember only bits and pieces of what happened after her accident. The doctor said that was due to the trauma of her concussion. She rubbed her temple, wincing slightly. Hopefully, this driver, who, unlike her, was wearing a crash helmet, would emerge unscathed.

She hit the off button.

She couldn't wait around to see. She needed to change. And getting dressed, she'd discovered that morning, was no easy task.

CHAPTER SEVEN

"I NEVER TOUCHED those ropes. I'm not good with heights. Ask Jessie, she'll tell you. I'm a videographer, not a stunt person."

Cade looked at Jessie to gauge her reaction to the man's claim. In profile, he saw her lips pressed together, her brow gathered. She'd pulled her hair into a loose twist that allowed wispy tendrils to frame her face. Her baggy tan cargo shorts and loose, outdoorsy-looking shirt—white with silver stitching—were uniformly wrinkled.

She'd apologized for not looking more presentable when he knocked on her door after getting Hank's call. Cade had been planning to meet with his foreman for a couple of hours while Shiloh was off shopping with Remy, but he changed his mind. Getting to the bottom of what happened to her rigging was important. He knew if it were him, the not knowing would be eating away at him.

"Is he telling the truth?"

She turned to look at him. There was a wall of one-way glass separating them from J.T. and Hank, who was conducting the interview. Hank had made it clear that this was not an interrogation and J.T. was not under arrest.

"Sounds like it."

He could appreciate her frustration.

Hank leaned forward to rest his elbows on the gunmetal-gray table. "Two of your friends—Eerik and Marsh—said you were making threats. Something about Miss Bouchard knowing she needed you. That sounds like a spurned lover looking for some kind of revenge."

"No. That's not what I meant. Jessie keeps people at a distance. Even the people closest to her, like me and my mom. She turned my mom—her own business partner—in to the cops without even calling Mom to get her side of things. What I meant was Jessie couldn't start a firestorm then walk away unscathed. Her reputation, for one thing, was going to wind up tarnished. My mother has a lot of friends in the business. A lot more than Jessie because Jessie doesn't think she needs anybody. She's wrong."

Jessie's upper lip pulled back in a sneer. "Yeah, Dar is loved. But she won't be as highly revered when people learn she stole money from Girlz on Fire."

The man, her ex-boyfriend—lover?—went on. "If Jessie had talked to my mother first, all this could have been cleared up. Yes, Mom made a mistake and borrowed from the company without telling Jessie, but only because Jessie made big promises she didn't come through on. Mom *covered* for Jessie after Jessie blew it in Japan. Her mother died. We got that, but you don't immediately turn around and attack someone who has been like a second mother to you a few months later. That was crazy. Unhinged. I wouldn't put it past her to sabotage her own stunt for the sympathy."

Jessie came out of her chair and flew at the window, fists ready to pound her way through the glass. Cade got there first, catching her wrists. Her weak foot gave out and she fell against him, struggling and twisting. "Let me go. He's insane. Why would I do that? He's trying to spin this away from his mother. And himself."

The door to the observation room opened and Hank walked in. Cade let go of Jessie's hands. She spun about and took a step back, colliding with him. A muffled grunt of pain made him take her elbow, giving her time to catch her balance. He could feel her fury and frustration, but to his surprise, her voice was composed when she said, "There is no way in hell I would risk getting injured to make a point. Sympathy sucks. Just ask anybody who's been on the receiving end. His mother should know that, too, but apparently she enjoys playing the victim."

Hank closed the door and waited for Jessie to sit before he said, "He gave us permission to search his car. We didn't find anything resembling a lubricant. The lab won't have the results for us until sometime tomorrow, but I don't have anything to hold him on."

"He could have ditched the bottle. He's not an idiot," Cade said, glancing at the glass wall. The man was sitting perfectly still, hands folded on the table, his head down. His body language said he was unhappy. Because he'd been caught? He certainly hadn't displayed any concern about his ex-girlfriend.

"Yeah, I know. Running away is suspicious behavior in my book. He's had twenty hours, more or less, to work on his story. That means he's still a person of interest. I'm going to tell him he needs to stay in the area until we've had a chance to talk to the other missing stuntman."

"Does J.T. know where Zane is?"

Hank shook his head. "He says no. I asked to examine his cell phone but he claims to have lost it. Said he bought a cheap disposable one yesterday to call his mother. Plus, he said he'd planned all along to drive back to California for some project he said you knew about."

"He might have mentioned that. We haven't been close for a long time for obvious reasons." She looked at Cade. "Can we go now? My ankle is starting to throb."

"Of course."

Hank stepped into the hallway and waited while Jessie maneuvered sideways on her crutches. "Thanks for coming in."

"I don't know what happened yesterday. I've gone over and over it in my head. It should have been a simple slam dunk. J.T. felt like the one loose end that didn't make sense, but, honestly, I couldn't see him scaling the tower without someone noticing. I wish I could be more help."

Hank nodded supportively. "We'll keep you posted."

She was bummed. Cade could read that clearly enough. He checked his watch. Shiloh and Remy wouldn't be back for another hour. Shiloh had texted him, asking permission to drop by the mall to buy something. He knew what without asking. A bra. All her friends were wearing them. He'd responded, "OK."

"I need to ask you something important."

She looked at him.

"Where do you stand on root-beer floats?"

One corner of her lips twitched in the most beguiling way. "You drink root-beer floats, you don't stand on them."

He chuckled appreciatively. Quick wit was a sure-fire way to his heart. "Well, I just happen to know a place that makes the best, hands-down, anywhere in the country."

"Are you bragging or inviting?"

"Inviting."

"I'm in."

The Dairy Barn was everything an old-fashioned soda fountain ought to be—plus, it was open seven days a week. He found a parking spot close to the door.

"This is cute," Jessie said, slowly making her way to an open table.

The place resembled a 1950s diner, with bright red vinyl stools at the polished chrome bar. White wrought iron tables and chairs were scattered across the black-and-white checkerboard floor.

"Let me grab an extra chair so you can elevate your leg," Cade said, once she was seated.

A waitress in a Sandra Dee ponytail and popping a

big wad of pink bubble gum came to take their order. Two floats with chocolate syrup.

"Chocolate syrup?"

"Don't knock it till you've tried it," he cautioned, holding out his hand for her crutches. "Let me store these over by the umbrella rack so nobody trips over them."

Her gaze followed him to and from. She couldn't help it. His body type was one of her favorites: lean and lanky with a hip-rocking gait that had her thinking of things she shouldn't be thinking about. And his grin when he caught her staring was enough to make her heart do a few backflips of its own.

He reminded her of a slightly more mature Ashton Kutcher, she decided. She'd met Ashton on set once. He was a real person, despite all the hoopla surrounding his personal life. But he didn't have Cade's blue eyes. Bedroom eyes, her mother would have called them, because more often than not a sexy pair of eyes was enough to open that door where Mom was concerned.

"You asked about my family, can I ask about yours?"

"Sure. Unfortunately, there isn't much to say. Buck, you know about. And Kat, you've met. My mother died when I was eight. And my older brother, Charles, was killed in a training accident. He was a marine. My sister lives on the East Coast. For all practical purposes, she divorced herself from the family—Dad mostly, but me, too, I guess. I didn't even hear from her after Faith died."

"Wow. That's harsh."

He shrugged. "She hated living on the ranch. In fact, after Dad married Helen, Renata—that's my sister's name—ran away from home. She was fourteen. Just two years older than Shiloh," he said, as if doing the math for the first time. "She moved in with a friend until the end of the school year, then she gave Buck an ultimatum. Let her go to boarding school on the East Coast or she'd accuse his new wife of abuse."

Jessie winced. "She obviously knew what she wanted."

"A few years ago, Buck decided to put his affairs in order. He had his attorney call Renata to discuss the matter. She told him she wanted nothing to do with Buck or the ranch. If Buck wanted to give her a share, he could donate the value to her alma mater."

"What about you? You're her brother. And Shiloh is her niece."

He looked away. "Here come our floats."

She figured that was his answer—he didn't want to talk about it. But after the waitress had deposited two of the biggest, frothiest soda-fountain drinks she'd ever seen, he said, "My sister was a lot like Mom. Emotionally fragile but as stubborn as any person you've ever known. She made up her mind that Dad killed Mom."

"Murder?"

"Neglect. Mom died of complications from an eating disorder. I was too young to understand, but I remember some of their fights. Frankly, I think Dad blamed himself, too. Renata used his guilt against him to get her way."

He unwrapped his straw and used it to stir his drink.

"I was kind of a quiet kid. She was a bit of a prima donna. We never really bonded. Then Kat was born. She was the sister I wished Renata could have been. That probably didn't help."

Jessie took a pull on her straw. Her mouth positively sparkled with flavor—sweet, cold, delicious. "Oh, yum," she said, smacking her lips. "This is amazing. Definitely the best I've ever had."

Cade smiled with obvious satisfaction.

They enjoyed their drinks in silence a few minutes, before Jessie's curiosity got the better of her. "And your older brother died, too."

A lock of wheat-colored hair fell across his brow when he nodded. She really liked his hair. She wished she was brave enough to reach out and brush it back. Not that she felt entitled to take such liberties, but it was tempting.

"Your poor dad. And you. That must have been pretty rough."

He nodded. "Charles was a lot older than me. I'm sure we'd have been good friends if he'd lived, but, at the time, I can't remember feeling anything but dread. Buck's response to problems of any kind was to get blind drunk and smack around anybody who got in his way."

A telling revelation, she thought, giving her attention to her drink. Not surprising Cade moved away and started his life somewhere else, she thought. Bing's first husband had been a violent alcoholic. Jessie understood all too well.

"Do you miss Texas?"

"Not yet. I've been too busy. Buck and I had a lot of paperwork to get through to make this official. Shiloh seems to swing from one extreme to the other. She either loves the Hills and plans to make this her home forever, or she misses Texas and her friends and her school so much she thinks she might die. Most days it pretty much sucks to be me," he said, adding a little half laugh to make her think he was kidding.

But she knew the feeling. Lately, it hadn't been too pleasant being Jessie Bouchard, either. His honesty made her decide to share a little bit of her own past. Quid pro quo, she thought. Plus, visiting this soda parlor had gotten her mind off J.T.'s distressing accusation. Stage her own accident. Ridiculous.

"My sisters and I used to call Mama the Queen Bee. Her beauty parlors—Marlene's House of Beauty, One, Two and Three—were her hives. The operators who worked for Mama worshipped her. Some of her customers were so loyal to Mama they became like members of our extended family."

"That's impressive. She sounds like a good business-woman."

Jessie used her spoon to scoop up the last remaining barge of ice cream. She closed her eyes to savor the flavor. When she opened them, she found herself staring into Cade's baby blues. A shiver that had nothing to do with ice cream passed through her body. She licked her lips unconsciously. His gaze followed and lingered.

She inhaled deeply to refocus. What were they talking about? Oh, yes, her mother. Her mother? She never talked about her mother.

"One, Two and Three," she said, mostly to herself. The beauty parlors. "Actually, Mom's real gift was understanding people. She was terrible with numbers. If she hadn't watched, her stylists would have robbed her blind." She fiddled with her straw, her appetite strangely gone. "My sister claims that's why Mama couldn't spend more time with me when I was in the hospital. She had four other mouths to feed, and three hives to tend. So to speak."

"Why were you in the hospital?"

She'd known the question was coming. She'd brought the subject up herself. She couldn't back out of the discussion now. "There was a fire in our house when Remy and I were seven. Mama was out back with her new beau. She didn't realize what was happening until she heard the sirens."

"You were burned?"

She watched his gaze skim across her bare arms. He even looked at her legs. No scars. She was lucky that way.

"I pushed Remy out the window right before a hunk of curtain fell. The back of my nightgown caught on fire. Mama saved my life by tackling me when I started to run, but the material of the gown had already melted into my skin."

He took in a sharp, harsh breath. "How long were you in the hospital?"

"The first stay was about five months, I think. I had to go back a couple of times for grafts and some corrective surgeries as I grew."

He pushed his glass away and reached out to take her hand. "That explains a lot. Thank you for telling me."

She looked at him, baffled. "Explains what?"

His fingers squeezed hers gently but firmly. "Now I know how you got to be so brave."

"*Brave,*" she repeated under her breath. Most people called her foolish.

"How could you be so stupid to temp Fate again and again and again?" her eldest sister had screamed at her after Mom's funeral. "You know Mama hated your job, and you even let that ridiculous job keep you from coming home when she needed you the most."

"Are you ready? I didn't bring any pain pills," Jessie said now.

He jumped to his feet and quickly retrieved her crutches. He paid the bill in the time it took her to walk to the door. The high-gloss floor looked like a stunt waiting to happen and she wasn't in the mood to show off.

They'd barely taken two steps toward Cade's truck when a familiar voice said, "Jessie? Can I talk to you a minute?"

Jessie froze. "J.T. How did you find us?"

"I overheard your friend ask if you liked root-beer floats. I did an online search of places that serve them. This is my third stop. Looks like I got here just in time."

She looked at Cade, then at J.T. "What do you want? Wasn't it enough to try to throw off the sheriff by making him believe we Hollywood types are a bunch of publicity-starved freaks who would rather injure ourselves than miss out on a chance for a viral video clip?"

J.T. had the decency to look ashamed. "That was Mom's idea. I'm sorry."

"Dar told you to say that?"

"Payback. For what you put her through."

Jessie wished she could cry. The hurt was intense, but she used anger to deflect it. "For what she put *herself* through." Her fingers tightened around the rubber grips of her crutches. "I didn't make her embezzle money."

"You made it so she had to, Jessie. To pay the mortgage. To keep a roof over her and Dad's heads. You know she took the bare minimum in salary and then you messed up in *Kamikaze,* plus took off time after your mom's funeral. There weren't enough donations to cover her wages. She sold off some of the equipment that wasn't being used."

"And used the money to gamble with." She didn't know to what extent, but the accountant she hired said Dar had several charges in the tens of thousands to an area casino.

"No. Mom said that was seed money for an exhibition you and Team Shockwave were supposed to put on, but you reneged on that, too."

Oh, my God, Jessie thought. Dar is doing exactly the same thing Mama used to do to get out of taking responsibility for something. She would spin the fact to make it someone else's fault. Once again, it all came down to rest on Jessie's shoulders.

"None of that has anything to do with why someone

tampered with my ropes. And you know me well enough to know I wouldn't have done that."

He looked at Cade and nodded as if he'd asked, not her.

"So who did? Marsh? Eerik?"

He shook his head.

That left only one team member who was in Sentinel Pass that morning. "Zane."

"I didn't see him do anything, I swear. And I'm sure as hell not about to say anything to the cops."

"Why?"

He took a step back. "Are you nuts? Don't you know? Zane is a loose cannon." He looked at Cade, pleadingly. "I once saw him crush some drunk's nose—not break, crush—because the guy was wearing a political T-shirt that Zane disagreed with. He went over, picked a fight, then slammed the guy's face into the wall before the man could throw his first punch."

Jessie had heard that story many times but didn't know if it was fact or hype. "He has a reputation for being volatile, but he's my friend. We're co-captains. Why would he do something to hurt me and jeopardize the team's chances in Japan?"

"I don't know. All I can say is the night before last I was in the hotel bar, nursing my broken heart." He tossed a pointed look at her. "I was trying to work up the nerve to confront you. But when I saw you come in with your sister, I gave up and went to my room."

"And spent the night plotting how to get your revenge on Jessie for dumping your sorry ass," Cade theorized.

J.T. shook his head. "No. I went to sleep. I wasn't even gonna go do the show until Zane started pounding on my door. He said you'd changed the script because you needed a solo for your audition tape. He told me he was taking off as soon as the tower was up and the ropes were in place. He said if I really wanted to impress you, I should take his place and prove to you that you weren't invincible. Everybody needs somebody, he said."

"Why did you run away?" Cade asked.

"I'm not stupid, man. I knew they'd be looking for a scapegoat. An accident is one thing, but when I heard somebody mention the word *booby-trapped,* I started thinking about your rollover. What if that wasn't an accident? I was on that set, too. Sooner or later, somebody was bound to point a finger at me, given your problems with my mother."

Jessie froze. She'd been saying for weeks that something wasn't right about her accident, but nobody was listening. "You think my rollover happened that way on purpose?"

"I don't know what to think. But if Zane's behind either of them—" his voice dropped to a whisper, and he looked over his shoulder theatrically "—then I could be in big trouble for even talking to you. Mom wants me to come home, but the cops said I have to stick around."

"What are you going to do?"

He looked down as if embarrassed. "I met a girl. Last night. In Custer. She told me if I needed a place to bunk, her roommate just moved out. You know how it is, Jess. Mention *Sentinel Passtime* and suddenly everybody wants to be your friend."

Jessie didn't know that at all, but several of the guys on the team bragged about making conquests based on their association with the show.

"And you're telling us you don't have any idea where this Zane guy is?" Cade asked, drawing them back on point.

J.T. pulled a face. "No. I came here to warn you, Jessie. You need to watch your back. I don't know what Zane's game is all about. I honestly can't say for sure that he did something to your ropes, but you need to be on your toes." He nudged her crutch. "And that's not that easy when you're a gimp."

Cade made a low sound that came out like a warning growl.

J.T. took a step back. "I gotta go, Jessie. I'm sorry. Okay? About everything. Mom. Us. *Kamikaze*. I know you didn't throw the game on purpose, but Mom was so pissed off I didn't dare say anything. You know how she gets."

Jessie did. Dar's rages never lasted for long, but they were the only thing about being her business partner that Jessie had had reservations about. Luckily, Dar had never turned that fury on her. Until now.

"And for the record, I didn't ask you out only because Mom pushed me to." J.T. gave her one last lingering stare, then left.

She didn't acknowledge his apology or even say goodbye. They stood beside Cade's truck and watched him disappear around the side of the building.

"Are you ready to go home?"

Jessie leaned heavily on her crutches and let out a

sigh. "Are you sure you want me to? I feel like…what's that bird called? The one nobody wants around because it brings bad luck?"

Cade let out a soft snort. "Get in the car. Do you need a boost?"

"No," she snapped.

His grin told her he'd provoked her on purpose.

They were about ten miles down the road when he said, "Albatross. That bird's called an albatross. They don't exist this far inland."

She looked down. There was a spot of root-beer froth on her blouse. She ignored it, trying to focus instead on why Zane—a man she considered her friend—would try to hurt her.

"I know you don't know me well, but do you think I'm horribly self-absorbed? Friendless? So obtuse I wouldn't even know it if someone close to me tried to kill me?"

"I think you're very likable. You're brave and kind and considerate. And nobody deserves to have violence inflicted on them. Nobody." The rock-solid firmness of his declaration made her look at him.

"What if he's not done trying to hurt me?"

"So far, the guy sounds like an opportunistic coward. He won't come onto the ranch, but I'll put a guy on the gate if that would ease your mind."

"No. That's not what I meant. You've already been super good to me. To Remy and me," she corrected. "But you have a daughter to think about. And a business. I don't want to cause you any problems."

"Then don't leave. That's the best thing you can do at

the moment. I mean that. Knowing Shiloh isn't walking all the way home from the bus stop will be a huge load off my mind. Especially if there's some violent nutcase on the loose. Okay?"

"I can see your point. At least for the time being. But I reserve the right to leave at a moment's notice if the threat changes in any way. For your and Shiloh's sake," she added.

"Okay. On one condition."

"What's that?"

"Don't tell Shiloh I took you to the Dairy Barn without her."

She looked at her shirt again. Then pulled a tissue from her purse, spit on it and began to rub away the evidence. She would live up to her part of the agreement to the best of her ability. That's what she did. Even if her ex-business partner tried to claim otherwise.

They drove the rest of the way home in silence. Cade wasn't sure if Jessie was hiding behind her closed eyelids or if she'd actually dozed off. Not that he blamed her for either choice.

A guy she liked well enough to date accuses her of ruining his mother's life *and* suggests another friend might well be trying to hurt her for some unknown reason. Nobody liked to have their life choices scrutinized under the microscope of hindsight.

He wondered if he'd made a mistake insisting she stay. Shiloh came first, of course. And having someone take her to the bus stop and pick her up after school eliminated the chance that she might become a target.

Maybe living so far out gave him a false sense of security. He'd been surprised to see the gatehouse Buck had built a few years back. "We had some bold and very stupid rustlers in the area," Buck had explained. The building still had a working intercom system.

Maybe he'd add a night watch to the duty rotation. Just until Hank figured out if this Zane guy was an ongoing threat or an opportunist with his own agenda. Either way, Cade meant what he'd said to Jessie.

Stay. Because he took care of creatures—like Sugar, the little raccoon—and people like Jessie who were vulnerable and needed help? Or was it because he'd spent a large chunk of their time at the Dairy Barn wanting to kiss her? Or, more specifically, lick the tiny remnant of root-beer froth off the side of her mouth *before* he kissed her.

He glanced at the dashboard clock. It was still early. The days were getting longer and the weather report that morning predicted it would warm up nicely by late afternoon. Maybe he'd open the pool for his guests.

Correction: his tenants.

The word made him frown. Then he shrugged. He and Jessie were adults. They were smart enough— worldly enough—to keep their rental agreement separate from any sort of social interaction that might come up.

Shiloh, on the other hand, was a consideration he needed to take into account before he acted on the attraction he felt for Jessie. She knew he dated, but usually when he gave in to one of his pals and went out on a blind date, he downplayed the significance for Shiloh's sake. And, so far, he'd never brought any of his dates home for Shiloh to meet.

He glanced sideways at his sleeping passenger. Maybe he might be getting ahead of himself. He didn't know for certain that Jessie felt the same little zing he felt. They'd known each other only a couple of days. But they did have all summer. And there was the pool.

Was he curious about her scars?

Yes. He was curious about her and this fire was certainly a big event in her life. How could he not be?

But just because she got in the water didn't mean she'd show him her scars. There was only one way to find out.

CHAPTER EIGHT

CADE WAS PULLING INTO the driveway when his phone rang. Even before he looked at the display, he figured it was either Remy or Shiloh, since the turquoise Toyota was nowhere to be seen.

"Hi, Daddy, it's me. Remy took me to lunch, and I was wondering if you'd mind if her and me—I mean, she and I—went to a movie before we bought groceries. The new Miley Cyrus movie is playing. It's PG-13."

You're not thirteen, he almost said. But that would have come off as so completely lame and controlling he was glad he managed to choke back the words. "What time does it start?"

"Fifteen minutes. We drove past the theater to check it out before calling."

"Are you sure Remy wants to go?"

He heard her put the question to Remy.

"Sure," she called out. "Beats watching Jessie hobble around, grumbling like a bear with a thorn in its paw."

"Did you hear that, Daddy? I didn't twist her arm or anything."

"Sure. Fine. But tell her I'll pay her back when she gets home. And, by the way, I'm going to open the pool.

You two can take a dip later if—" he paused significantly "—your homework is all done."

"It's done. It's done. Cool. We gotta go get our tickets, Daddy. Thank you."

Jessie had undone her seat belt but was still sitting in the cab of the truck, presumably listening to his side of the conversation. He gave her all the pertinent information, then asked, "That's not a problem, is it? Was Remy picking up anything you needed right away?"

She shook her head. She looked a little bit perkier after her micro-nap. "Bread. Coffee. Peanut butter. Fruit. At the moment, I'm still full from my float, so there's no rush. Are you really opening the pool?"

He got out. "Yeah. Do you know anything about filters and pumps and chemicals? I've been meaning to read the literature Buck left for me, but I haven't gotten around to it."

He hurried around the truck to help her out if she needed an extra hand. She didn't. Not Jessie. She was the most independent woman he'd ever known.

"The control for the cover is inside the pump room," he said, pointing toward the far side of the house. "Do you want to take a look at it with me? Buck said the cover is supposed to be strong enough for a full-grown cow to walk across it."

She started to lead the way. "Bet that didn't come cheap."

He followed behind her and couldn't help noticing that the crutches didn't impede her in any way. That's the mark of a true athlete, he decided.

"He said it was a gift for Shiloh. Kat's boys are pretty excited about it, too."

She opened the exterior closet that also served as a storage shed for gardening tools. The smell of chlorine surprised him because Buck had claimed the pool was the saltwater type. "No chemicals for my grandkids," he'd boasted.

A plastic, ziplock bag containing the instruction manuals and a container of test strips was hanging right where Buck left it. "Apparently, this is the how-to bible." He reached around her to snag it. "Do you know anything about pools?"

"Marsh works for his brother's pool-cleaning company when he's between jobs. I've gone along a couple of times to check out the lifestyles of the rich and infamous. One thing I do know is technology has changed since I was a lifeguard."

He hit the clearly marked switch and the taut black cover began to retract. They moved poolside to check out the water. He was greatly relieved to see clear, sparkling water and not some murky mess. Hiring a pool service had been on his to-do list for much too long.

"There's the thermometer," she said, pointing to a braided rope with something attached to it.

Cade went down on one knee to haul it in. "Eighty. Sweet. The cover must act as a solar blanket, too," he said. "That'll make getting in a little easier."

He nodded toward her protective ankle brace. "Since that's not a cast, do you want to get in?"

She swallowed. "With you?"

"Is that a problem?"

She shook her head, but he could tell she wasn't wildly thrilled by the idea. "If you'd rather not, I understand. I just thought I should check it out before Shiloh goes in." He thought a moment then added, "She can swim, but not that well. If I'm not here to go in with her, I'd appreciate it if you didn't let her swim alone."

She looked appalled by the idea. "The buddy system is a must if there's no lifeguard on duty," she said firmly. "And you want to think about posting a few rules as a reminder. Kids sometimes get caught up in what they're doing and forget that water is dangerous."

He liked it that she didn't trivialize his fears or think him overprotective. His father hadn't agreed. "What doesn't kill you makes you stronger," Buck had said when they discussed the pool. "You didn't have a nanny and you turned out fine."

If that had been meant as a compliment, Cade wasn't buying it. "That's a good idea. If I provide the paper and markers, maybe you and Shiloh could make one up. She likes art." He paused. "She used to like art."

She didn't comment on his addendum. "That's a good way to reinforce the idea. And I'm not talking a lot of restrictions. Simply the basics. No running. No glass near the pool. And no diving in the shallow end."

He nodded, pleased to know she was on his side. "So…are you up for a quick dip?"

She inhaled deeply and slowly let it out. "Sure. Why not? I'll meet you back here in fifteen."

He made it in ten, but she was already in the water. Floating on her back. Whatever reticence he thought he'd detected apparently wasn't due to modesty or

embarrassment about her body. Her swimsuit was a
two-piece bikini. Flame-red with white bands along the
high-cut legs and low-cut neckline. Sexy as hell, but his
gut told him the suit belonged to Remy. Why borrow
her sister's suit? he wondered. Did she forget to pack
one? That didn't seem likely, since they'd discussed
the pool and her unlimited access to it in their email
negotiations.

"How's the water?"

Her feet drifted downward and she spread her arms
to keep herself upright in the deep end. "Perfect. This
is going to be great therapy for my ankle."

"Good." He dropped his towel on the lawn then ad-
justed the waistband of his blue-and-white trunks—
Dallas Cowboys colors. A gift from Shiloh. "Look out,"
he warned. "Cannonball."

He took a running start and launched himself toward
the middle of the pool. He hit with a loud crack. Water
shot up his nose and he came up sputtering. "Damn. I
think I forgot how to do this."

He looked around for Jessie. She'd ducked under the
water and was swimming toward him, as graceful as a
sea otter. She surfaced a few feet away, where the water
was waist-deep.

"Okay," she said, motioning him closer. "Let's get
this over with."

A lump formed in his throat. *This.* He was pretty
certain he knew what she intended to do. "Jessie, you
don't have to—"

She didn't let him finish. "I do, actually. It's how I
prefer it. On my terms."

She executed a half-pirouette, a little wobbly because of her ankle. "Everyone is curious when they hear about my burns. It's human nature."

It took Cade a couple of seconds to make sense of what he was seeing. The smooth tanned skin he expected to match her arms and legs was blotchy red—like a bad birthmark—stitched together with gray-white lines. The texture was dimpled and puckered in places, as if someone had laid a wet rag across her back and allowed it to dry.

The total area was much larger than he'd imagined. The pain this must have inflicted was too great to fully comprehend. *A child,* his brain kept repeating, mutely. *She was just a child. Younger than Shiloh. A baby, really.*

"Does it hurt anymore?" he finally managed to ask, his chest tight.

Her ponytail whipped side to side like a wet paintbrush. "No. Some parts are numb. Sometimes I'll feel a pinch or stinging sensation if my bra strap hits just right."

"May I—" He had to swallow twice to get enough saliva in his mouth to finish the question.

"Touch it? Yes."

She sounded so matter-of-fact, like a teacher presenting some sort of class project.

Her skin was wet, glistening in the bright daylight, which might have served to make the scars look even more vivid and fresh. He tentatively touched a braided-looking ripple near the bottom of her right shoulder blade.

He was relieved to find he wasn't repulsed. "I should tell you. I grew up with an alcoholic father. I don't shock easily."

She turned to face him. "I like you, Cade. I'll be honest, if my life weren't such a screwed-up mess at the moment, I'd be thinking…two single people…mutual attraction…what's stopping us?"

"But…?" he supplied, hearing the unspoken word.

"But my life *is* a mess *and* we have a couple of built-in chaperones to dodge." She kicked her foot out of the water. "No simple task given my current condition."

Two chaperones. Remy and Shiloh.

Naturally, he'd thought about what Shiloh might think if he started seeing Jessie socially, but he wasn't sure why Remy's presence had any bearing on Jessie's love life. They were all adults, right? Unless Remy was merely an excuse.

"So, were you hoping that by showing me your scars I'd be so turned off I'd give your sister a try?"

Her eyes went wide with obvious surprise. She had. He advanced toward her, matching step for step as she hopped into deeper water. "Your sister seems like a very nice person, but I'm not into threesomes. And, honestly? Your back doesn't freak me out. It's a very visual reminder of the pain you must have endured, but we all have scars. Some are simply more obvious than others."

She stopped moving away from him. "I'm not easy." She blanched and added quickly, "I don't mean sexually. I mean, in general. But you have a daughter and I…I have my career."

"So, we keep those things separate."

He reached out to touch the side of her face. "Neither of those excuses is good enough to keep me from kissing you. Got any better ones?"

He looked into her eyes and waited, watching for her answer. Her lips parted…and she smiled. "Not really."

"Good." Then he leaned over to press his lips to hers. Soft and warm. Nice. Very nice. But salty.

As if reading his mind, she pulled back and licked her lips. "You taste like seawater."

Which, apparently, wasn't a bad thing, because she moved closer and kissed him again, lips parted this time, welcoming his tongue to explore and parry. The deeper he explored, the sweeter she tasted. Root beer and ice cream sweet. Jessie Bouchard sweet.

He broke it off because his body started telling him it was more than happy to take things to the next level. Not so fast, he silently cautioned. One step at a time. He didn't know for certain he could pull off a casual, summer fling, no strings attached. But he sure as hell wanted to consider the option.

"Nice," he said, taking a step back.

"It was." She sounded surprised. "You're a good kisser. And here you gave me the impression you were out of practice."

He could tell she was teasing, but he definitely didn't want to talk about his dating disasters of late. He hadn't gone out with anyone since arriving in South Dakota. In part, because he'd come to the conclusion that single fathers of a certain age should never let their friends or family set them up on blind dates.

"I haven't roped for ten years, but that doesn't mean I've forgotten how."

Her grin was so adorable and inviting he had no choice but to do the prudent thing. He sank under the water and kicked hard, surfacing at the base of the built-in steps. It was either get out of the pool now or embarrass himself in the most visible way possible. He walked straight to his towel and quickly wrapped it around his middle.

"Thanks for the swim *and* the kiss," he told her.

"You're welcome. Thanks for driving me to the sheriff and for the root-beer float."

She was floating on her back again. Water droplets sparkled in the dip of her belly button. The two swatches of red and white made him think of a candy cane. *Christmas came early this year.* But he wisely kept the thought to himself. Nothing was a given where Jessie was concerned. He was positive of that.

"HI, BUCK," MATTHEW CALLED out, motioning for Buck to squeeze into the cluster of people gathered around the retreat's version of a campfire—a metal fire pit filled with fake logs and bright orange flames fueled by gas. "Glad to see you."

Buck had had no intention of joining the late-night "spew-fest," as one of the other boarders had called it. "Cathartic as a coronary," someone else had muttered.

The day had been a long one. He'd turned in early

and went right to sleep. Unfortunately, something woke him. A dream. A memory. A deep, sad sigh that was probably his own.

He'd gotten out of bed and stepped to the window, in need of fresh air. He missed his ranch, he realized. This place offered wide-open spaces; they simply weren't *his* wide-open spaces.

From his window, he'd spotted the fire, glowing like the friendly inviting beer sign above the door of his favorite local bar. He missed drinking, too. Not the hangovers. Not the blank spots in his memory. Not the gut-wrenching fear of not knowing how he'd made it home. But he longed for the comforting distraction of other voices, people bemoaning every aspect of their lives in detail that usually shocked him. He even missed the smoke and beer smells that started out slightly nauseating but quickly became familiar and comforting.

Before he could talk himself out of it, he'd grabbed his jacket, donning the moccasins Kat and the boys had given him a couple of Christmases ago. And here he was. And it was too late to back out. "I dozed off after dinner. What did I miss?"

"Campfire talk is fluid," Matthew said. "And like smoke, it disappears into the night sky never to be seen—or mentioned—again."

Buck wondered if that was possible. Maybe. He doubted it. But what did he have to lose?

"What we call our Fire Starter question for the evening is twofold. First, what is your most joyful memory of Christmas? Second, what holiday memory is the one you'd most like to forget?"

Buck made a soft harrumph. "What if they're one and the same?"

Matthew nodded wisely. "We get that a lot."

Buck waited for his turn, not completely certain he'd have the guts to say anything. Some of the shared memories were tragic, some poignant and filled with love. His was somewhere in the middle. It would probably sound foolish to the rest of the group, but when the stranger beside him finished speaking, Buck cleared his throat and spoke.

"For my ninth birthday, I wrote a letter to Santa asking for a horse. I was probably too old to believe in Santa, but my mother was a kind, quiet woman who did her best to make us believe in things we couldn't see—Santa Claus, the Easter Bunny, hobgoblins. Even God."

There was a soft murmur from the others. It wasn't his intention to cast aspersions on anyone's beliefs. But what happened that night pretty much killed any trust in anything he couldn't hold concretely in his hand.

"I didn't get a horse. That wasn't a big surprise, actually. Times were tough. My dad worked construction, and this was in South Dakota. If you didn't have a shell up by the first of November, you could kiss any steady work goodbye. I seem to remember we got an early snow that year. Dad did his best, but times were lean. But," he said, recalling this story was also supposed to be a happy memory, "I did receive a puppy in my stockin' on Christmas morning."

"Oh," several of the female members of the group cried in unison. "How sweet!"

"A wiggly, long-tongue homely stray that *Santa* must have found wandering the streets. I called him Riley— after that TV show *The Life of Riley*. He was street-smart and hungry, but he wasn't mean. You could tell that just by looking in his eyes."

Buck could still see that dumb dog plain as day. He'd had dozens of dogs since then. Ranch dogs came and went. He fed 'em, got 'em fixed, and gave 'em all the shots they needed. But he never felt the same way about any of them as he did toward Riley.

"What happened?" someone asked.

"I had the best day of my young life. The sun came out and the air warmed almost as if God was smiling on us. My brothers and I played outside all day while Mother cooked and baked. Dad went off for some visitin', but he promised to come home early for our feast."

Buck paused. His poor mother. She tried. All of her life, she tried. "Dad wasn't a mean man—unless he got some drink in him," he said, slowly.

He looked around and saw the kind of silent acknowledgments he'd found in AA. "He didn't show up for dinner, but we ate and we pretended everything was all right. My dog stayed under my chair the whole time." He grinned. "'Cause like any kid, I snuck pieces of turkey to him."

He took a deep breath and let it out. "To make a long story short, we boys all slept in the same bed. I was usually in the middle, but I made my brother change places with me so I could keep my hand on my dog."

He rolled his shoulders. "At some point, I musta let

go. Riley went into the kitchen and got up on the table and ate my father's dinner. Every bite. Including half a mincemeat pie. Dad's favorite."

A hushed murmur could be heard over the soft hiss of the fake fire. "What did he do when he got back?" a brave soul asked.

Buck held up his hand to reassure them. "He didn't kill the dog, if that's what you're thinking. But he was mad, and like I said, he had a temper when he'd been drinking. He yanked me out of bed and made me take the dog outside. He found a long rope and he watched while I tied Riley to a tree, then he sent me inside."

Buck could feel his chest start to tighten. He stared into the red-orange flow and said what needed to be said. "I know this doesn't seem possible, but I remember it clearly. I was barefoot when I tied that rope. I was cryin', of course, and Riley licked my face. But some-time in the night, the warmest Christmas on record turned cold. A front dropped in from Canada. We figure Riley was thirsty from all that pie he ate. His rope was long enough to reach the pond. He must have broken through the ice. He managed to get out, but he was wet, and when the temperature dropped, he froze. He wasn't made for the cold, like some Eskimo dog. He was just a mutt. And the best Christmas ever turned into the worst. I never forgave my dad. But worse, I don't think he ever forgave himself."

CHAPTER NINE

"WELL," REMY EXCLAIMED, JUMPING to her feet the moment Jessie entered the waiting room. "No cast. That must mean it was a sprain, just like you said."

Jessie limped forward, nodding toward the nurses' station where she'd already used her credit card to cover the co-pay. Specialists weren't cheap, she decided. Nor did they know everything.

"He said there were no visible breaks, but a couple of the tendons were extremely inflamed. There could be a tear. He wants to watch it closely over the next couple of weeks." He also said if she didn't postpone her training, she could wind up with permanent damage.

"No running?"

Jessie balanced on her good foot and tapped the rubber tips of her crutches together. "Not for a while. And I'm not supposed to drive a stick, either."

"No Yota?" Remy exclaimed. "Bummer."

Jessie shrugged as they started for the door. "I guess it's not a huge deal. You're here and you seem to have connected well with Shiloh. Apparently, I'm redundant."

She did her best not to sound jealous, but her sister

gave her a look. "She's a good kid. I like her. Yesterday just sorta happened."

"Yeah. I know. It's okay. I feel a bit useless at the moment. Can't work out. Can't drive. You know me—a life of leisure is my idea of hell."

Remy didn't say anything. In fact, she was silent the entire time it took them to walk to the Land Cruiser. Jessie waited until they were both seated before she asked, "What's up? You're too quiet. Did you hear from the Bullies?"

"Yes, but that's not the problem."

"So…what is?"

"Cade walked Shiloh to the car this morning and he mentioned that his sister was looking for help."

"What kind of help?"

"Her husband is opening a new dental clinic. It was supposed to be up and running a few months ago, but I guess his license got hung up or something. I don't know, but he's in a pinch right now, and Cade thought I might be interested."

"Are you?"

Remy put the key in the ignition but didn't turn it. "Yeah. Why not? I know you already paid the rent for the whole summer, but we still need groceries and gas. Bringing in a regular paycheck would be my contribution. Do you have a problem with that?"

"What about Shiloh?"

Remy smiled eagerly. "I could drop her at the bus stop on my way to work and you could pick her up in the afternoon. I haven't discussed it with Cade, but I'm sure if he has a car with an automatic transmission, he'd let you use it."

She wants me to ask Cade to borrow his car? After the way I ambushed him in the pool yesterday?

Not only had she borrowed Remy's bikini instead of wearing her own sleeveless neoprene body suit, she'd shown him her scars then kissed him. Passionately.

Technically, he'd kissed her first, but she'd taken it to the next level. And she'd liked it. Probably too much. She'd spent the rest of the day and most of the night worrying that she'd inadvertently become the kind of woman who didn't feel complete unless she had some man following after her like a dog in heat. In other words, her mother.

"Remy, do you think Mom was ever happy? I mean, really, truly happy?"

Remy's jaw gaped in a way that would have made their mother shake her head in dismay. "What does that have to do with anything?"

"I just wondered. We haven't exactly talked about what happened."

Remy fastened her seat belt, then started the car. "Well, whose fault is that?"

"I'm asking now. So, answer my question."

Remy turned to look over her shoulder as she backed up, slowly and carefully. She might get lost easily, but she was a very cautious driver. Jessie had to give her that.

"I can't. No one can. You know as well as anyone that Mama had her highs and lows. She'd be on top of the world when she first fell for a new beau. Things would be good for a few months, a year, maybe. Then…she'd lose interest. Or something he did would become an unbearable problem. Or—" she lowered her voice in a way that told Jessie how much it pained her to mention the fact they both knew "—the man's wife would find out and the drama would begin."

Jessie never understood why their mother seemed to favor married men, but unfaithful rogues were the sort she picked. All too often.

They drove in silence for a long while, but about a mile from the intersection that would take them back to the ranch, Remy pulled over. "Tell me what you want me to do," she said, shifting in her seat to face Jessie. "If you need my help getting around or you don't think I should take this job, say so. Otherwise, I'd like to buzz over to Sentinel Pass now and talk to Jack."

What could she say? *No. Don't leave me alone all day with our sexy, single landlord—the guy I've been fantasizing about since day one. Because if you're not there to chaperone, I might start something for the simple reason that it would feel good. And I'm bored.* And if that didn't sound like something their mother would do, Jessie didn't know what did.

"Fine. Go get a job."

Remy snorted. "On that positive note…I think I will." She stomped on the clutch but didn't shift into gear straight off. "Unless you're in pain. Is that why you're so grouchy?"

"I'm not in pain."

"Oh. So, you're just grouchy because your middle name is Oscar."

Jessie stuck out her tongue, but she smiled, too. Remy had always been able to cajole her out of a dark and stormy mood—even when Jessie was in the hospital and Remy could speak to her only on the phone.

Two hours later, when Remy was happily seated in front of Jessie's computer, emailing her good news to the Bullies, Jessie slowly, carefully, strolled—sans crutches—to Cade's. The orthopedist had cautioned her against rushing her recovery, but he'd added, "Most of the athletes I've worked with in the past are pretty intuitive about their body's needs. Your ankle will tell you when you've done too much."

Jessie agreed. She wasn't going to take undue risks but pushing the envelope was simply part of her nature.

She tested the give and take of her calf muscles while she rang the bell. Still stiff.

Cade answered the door, his surprise obvious. His jeans were dusty and his light blue denim shirt had a couple of suspicious stains on it. Blood? "Jessie. Hi. You're back. I just got off the phone with Kat. She said Remy's going to work for Jack. Wow. That was fast."

"Yeah, I know. Can I come in?"

"Of course. Sorry. I got called out early this morning to help deliver a foal. There's a fresh pot of coffee brewing, if you're interested."

"Sounds good. Thanks."

He opened the door and stepped back to give her room to enter. "Where are your sticks?"

"At the house. I'm starting to wean myself off. A few minutes here. A few more tomorrow."

"That must mean your ankle isn't broken. I'm glad."

From the front door to the kitchen island was probably no farther than the distance from her parking spot to her apartment door, but she was visibly limping by the time she sat. She stealthily dabbed at a trace of sweat above her upper lip when Cade's back was turned.

"So, when's Remy going to start at Jack's new office?"

"Tomorrow. We were just there. It looks like the makings of a reality TV show—a combination of *Hoarders* and *Extreme Makeover*."

His low rumble of laughter did very pleasant things to her girl parts. Very pleasant. And watching him move around the kitchen with surprising grace for a guy in cowboy boots was a bonus. The man did have a great butt.

He set a big ceramic mug in front of her. "Poor Kat has been spread too thin trying to do everything."

She picked up the cup but didn't drink from it right away. "You do realize Remy will need to use my car to drive to Sentinel Pass every day, right? Jack's flexible about what time she gets there, so she figures she can drop Shiloh at the bus stop. But I'll have to borrow a car in the afternoon to pick Shiloh up."

He carried his mug to the stool beside hers. "No problem. Buck's truck is in the garage."

"Is it an automatic, I hope?"

He leaned around her stool to look at her foot. "Is a clutch off-limits?"

She nodded.

"Well, we're in luck. Buck's S-10 is a gutless gas hog, but it does have an automatic transmission. The keys are by the back door. It's all yours."

She blew on the steaming, fragrant brew. "Great. Thanks. I told Remy I'd drive Shiloh tomorrow because Rem wants to get an early start. Is that okay?"

"Of course. Is that the only subject you're here to talk to me about?"

Her heart did its little jumpy thing that made her throat tighten. "What else?"

He turned so his knees touched her stool.

"I thought you might be mad at me."

"Why?"

"I don't know. Because I didn't call you last night. I picked up the phone a couple of times, but I wasn't sure what to say."

Jessie knew the smart thing would be to talk this out. Define exactly what he expected to get from a short-term, here-today, gone-tomorrow relationship. But she was more of an action kind of girl. A bored action kind of girl.

She pushed her palms against the counter to make her stool swivel. His knees bracketed hers. "I could pretend to be mad, so we could kiss and make up. Or…" she said, trying to keep from grinning like a fool, "we could skip the mad part and try that kissing thing again. I really liked it."

She also really liked him. How much or for how long was still under debate, but enough to risk getting shot down if he wasn't in the market. Yesterday's kiss had implied he might be, but she knew all about morning-after regrets—her mother had been famous for them.

He carefully set aside his cup then reached for the arms of her stool to haul himself closer. This gave him a slight height advantage, but she didn't mind. She tilted her head up and waited.

She was expecting a polite, let's-take-things-slow approach. Wrong. Cade made it abundantly clear that he knew what he wanted—and he wanted her.

Not surprising, he tasted like hot coffee. She knew because his tongue went straight for all of her trigger points that made other parts of her body stir to life. How long had it been since she'd been kissed like this?

Forever, a seldom heard from portion of her mind answered, urging her to gobble up as much of this wonderful sensation as she could get. No questions asked.

She reached under his arms to splay her hands across the broad width of his back. The texture of his heavy cotton work shirt felt real and substantial. She liked that, too. And his muscles were bunched and coiled from keeping his upper body poised above her.

She wasn't ready for him to stop, but he did. He pulled back enough to look into her eyes. "I sat with a bunch of actors at Kat's wedding. They were all talking about motivation. I spent a lot of last night wondering how far you plan to take this and why."

"Why?" she repeated, genuinely baffled. "There has to be a reason."

He returned to his chair. "There usually is."

"You're looking for something deeper than 'it feels good,' I take it."

He threw out his hands and nodded. "You told me yesterday that you're not easy. So, I have to assume you don't sleep around or have brief, meaningless affairs with men you barely know. If you're interested in taking what we both have to admit is some pretty strong sexual attraction any further, I need to know what's in it for you."

She sat back, drumming her fingers on the arm of her chair where Cade's hands had been a moment earlier. "Well, if you must know," she said, hoping she wasn't going to regret being completely honest, "yesterday in the pool was a test. I've met men who thought they were attracted to me, but when they saw the whole me, the scarred me, they changed their minds."

His look turned intense but he let her continue without interrupting.

"They didn't always come right out and say they were repulsed, but they often didn't stick around long after they found out, either. So, over the years, I've developed what you might call a litmus test for losers."

He silently repeated the phrase. "Did I pass or fail?"

She took a big breath. "C-plus, maybe. We shared a nice kiss, there was a little circuitous groping, you didn't gag or anything. But—" she paused for effect "—you took off in a hurry and you didn't call last night."

He made a snarling sound. "I knew you were mad."

She reached out and brushed the backs of her fingers across his cheek. He hadn't shaved that morning. She found the slightly unkempt look very sexy. "I'm not mad. I'm not even hurt. A kiss is a kiss. And you're right about the mutual sizzle here. I feel it, too. But I understand completely if you're not interested in taking things further. Really. I do."

He gave her a look she'd never seen before. His brow crinkled in a serious scowl and his eyes narrowed to an intense squint. "That might well be the most insulting thing anyone has ever said to me. And believe me, when you grow up with a drunk in the house, there's no limit to the depth and breadth of the insults."

She blinked. "What part of what I said was insulting?"

"That wasn't just a kiss. It was a step. If the road feels right and you get a sense from the other person that you're moving in the proper direction, you take another step. And another. But—" he raised his hand to keep her from interrupting "—one person or the other might need to pause a moment between steps to sort out all the other things in his life. Or her life," he added pointedly.

She had been the one to bring up Remy and Shiloh.

"You're right. I shouldn't compare you to anyone."

He relaxed visibly. "No more grading on the curve?"

She'd been disappointed by men a great many times in the past. Was he really that different from the men who'd tried to get past her scars and couldn't? They might be able to block out the distraction long enough to have sex with her, but eventually they'd go searching for someone whole.

"I'll try."

"Good."

They each reached for their mugs at the same time. Jessie was pretty sure that meant they were done kissing for the moment. Unfortunately.

"Any news from Hank?"

She swallowed fast. She'd forgotten that she planned to bring Cade up to date. "The lab thinks the slippery stuff on the rope was petroleum jelly. Not traceable, but also not the act of some vandal tossing a soft drink at the tower."

"Also not the casual sort of thing you could have done without anyone noticing if *you* were trying to sabotage the thing yourself," he said, proving how in tune he was to her thought process.

"Exactly."

"Somebody needs to find that Zane guy."

"I agree. It's killing me not to be able to hop in Yota and start a grid search." She made a face. "I still haven't been able to come up with a single plausible reason why he'd do that to me, but he's the only one who could have."

"You'd know his bike if you saw it?"

She sat up a little straighter. "Of course. What are you thinking?"

He stood and held out his hand. "I was planning to take the afternoon off. How 'bout I give you a little tour of the Black Hills? Remy will pick up Shiloh, right?"

She stood, wincing slightly from the pins-and-needles sensation in her sore foot. Her circulation wasn't back to normal yet. "Uh-huh. She wants to explain about her new job so Shiloh doesn't get her feelings hurt."

"That's very nice of her. I appreciate that. But that means we have an entire afternoon. Are you game?"

Was she ever not game? "Let's do it."

CADE KNEW A GOOD EXCUSE when he saw one. Did either of them think they'd stumble across the elusive Zane, who may or may not be the saboteur? He didn't think so, but Jessie had agreed to spend time with him. And that made this exercise more pleasure than work.

"So, here we are in downtown Sturgis," he said, playing up the role of tour guide. "You're lucky this is May, not August."

"Why?" she asked, looking around at the few short blocks of the main drag. "Oh, wait, I remember. There's a big motorcycle rally here."

He nodded. "Your friend would blend in a little too well, I think."

He drove toward the most popular of the campgrounds that swelled to unbelievable numbers for a few short weeks each year. The place was mostly empty now. No gleaming chrome skull in sight. "Let's check out Deadwood. Does this Zane character like to gamble?"

She didn't answer right away.

He turned to look at her. "What?"

She startled slightly. "Our team performed an exhibit in Monaco last year and Zane missed it because he was in the middle of a hot run at one of the casinos." She frowned. "You know, now that I think about it, he's missed several events lately. Maybe that's why I wasn't surprised when he didn't show up for the Sentinel Pass gig."

"Why do you put up with that?"

She shrugged. "We're a team. If one of us is off our game, the others take up the slack. Usually."

A hint of sadness in the last word made him ask, "But not always?"

She looked out the window instead of answering. Just when he was certain she wasn't going to say any more on the topic, she told him, "Last year in Japan, I didn't do as well as I should have. I had a very 'disappointing' performance," she said making halfhearted air quotes.

"What happened?"

"The night we arrived in Tokyo, I had a call from Remy telling me Mom's kidneys were shutting down. When I left, Mom was on dialysis and doing pretty good, so this was a big change. Her doctors moved her up on the donor list. A list I'd failed to join before I left."

He wasn't sure he wanted to know why, but she told him. "If I'd had invasive tests and blood draws, I would have compromised my body. I knew going into this competition it was all or nothing. I gambled. Took a chance that Mom would remain stable until I got home—hopefully with my share of the million dollars in prize money in my pocket."

A million dollars? No wonder her team was disappointed that she didn't do better. "What happened in the games? Why did you…um…"

"Fail?" she supplied. She tapped the side of her head. "Ask any professional athlete, they'll tell you that at least half of any sport is mental. My head wasn't in it. My mother was dying. I felt guilty. The Bullies were calling constantly, leaving messages at the hotel, texting. Remy's the only one who didn't beg me to come home."

"Why?"

"Twin sense. She guessed what I was going through. Plus, she trusted me to do the right thing."

"You got tested?"

"It wasn't easy. Or cheap. Even in as cosmopolitan a city as Tokyo, there were language issues. And insurance issues." She shuddered. "I had a blood test. They took more vials than I imagined they'd take. Did that contribute to my not being able to climb the exact same wall I flew up the day before in practice? Don't know. But I washed out, and my team finished in the bottom half of the field."

She blinked and looked at her lap. "Mom died the next day. While I was on the plane. Somewhere over the Pacific."

Her tone was flat, but he felt the emotion she was trying to hide. "I'm sorry."

She flashed him an obviously fake smile. "The good news—if you want to call it that—is that I wasn't a match. Turns out my blood is full of antibodies and creepy stuff from my many transfusions and skin grafts. If they'd tried to give her my kidney, she would have died anyway."

He blew out a low breath. Damn. He didn't know

what to say, but he knew she wasn't the type to share this sort of personal insight with just anyone. He felt privileged, touched. And moved. He wanted to stop the car and hold her in his arms until she cried every one of those tears he knew—*he knew*—she had never shed.

But he didn't. They weren't at that place in their relationship.

Hell, he couldn't say for sure they even had a relationship, but he was beginning to think he wanted one. Maybe even a serious one. But he was pretty certain the same wasn't true for Jessie.

CHAPTER TEN

JESSIE CLOSED HER EYES AND sank under the water. She held her breath as long as she could while reviewing what had happened between her and Cade today.

She'd told him her big secret. Her most painful regret. Her failure as a daughter, and some might say a human being.

True, in the end, she couldn't have saved her mother. But the fact she didn't try harder, didn't willingly shine on the whole *Kamikaze* thing and rush home, made it pretty clear to everyone that she was a terrible person.

And no amount of excuses. No rationalization. No quid pro quo in the world made her decision okay.

The fact that Cade hadn't booted her out of the truck and made her walk home said a lot about him as a man. A kind, nurturing, forgiving man.

No wonder she liked him.

If she were more like him—more normal—she might even consider letting herself get involved with him. For the summer, of course. Not for…um…ever. That was so not her style.

With a huge exhale, she surfaced, swam to the side closest to her little house and levered herself out of the pool to sit with her feet in the water. The late-evening breeze had turned chilly, and when it blew across her wet hair and skin she started to shiver. She was about to reach for her towel when a small shadow separated itself from a bigger shadow and rushed toward her.

Her heart stopped for a fraction of a second until she realized the shadow was actually a small, furry body. Sugar. The infant raccoon had for some unknown reason seemed to have formed an attachment to Jessie. And her delicate little black-gloved fingers somehow had managed to reach inside Jessie's heart and latch on.

Jessie picked her up and cuddled her close. "Hey, sweetie pie," Jessie said, anticipating a cold, pokey nose in her ear.

True to form, Sugar rose up on her hind legs and quickly checked out Jessie's head, face, hair and ears. Jessie's wet hair obviously confused the little beast, but after a few seconds of sniffing, Sugar must have decided Jessie was still Jessie. She burrowed under Jessie's chin, rolling to her back.

"Oh, you silly thing," Jessie said, blowing softly on the raccoon's fine fur. "How could anyone not fall in love with you?"

Her voice sounded louder than she'd intended. The words seemed to hold significant import that made her want to take them back. From everything she'd ever observed, falling in love made stunt work look like child's play. She truly didn't think she was that brave.

She turned her chin to look at the second floor of the big house where a yellow light glowed bright against the dark silhouette of the night sky. Cade. Working late, she guessed.

If she were brave, she knew exactly whose name would be at the top of her list of potential lovers: Cade.

CADE SQUINTED AGAINST THE brightness of his laptop's screen. He wasn't a neophyte when it came to computers, but he didn't want to take the time to figure out how to adjust the screen brightness. He was on the hunt at the moment, and his gut told him he was getting closer to finding out more about the elusive egomaniac who called himself Zane.

The man's website was filled with so much bull, Cade had given up hoping to find a concrete, truthful fact—he wasn't completely convinced this was the jerk's real name. One thing Cade had found interesting was a cache of videos. Most were of Team Shockwave and many featured Jessie.

Watching her perform was nothing at all like he'd expected. For one thing, she almost always seemed in complete control of the situation, no matter how dicey it looked on camera. The only time that assessment didn't apply was when she filled in for Zane on a stunt that involved a car chase. He'd seen the YouTube version, but this clip included text that explained the stunt's intent. The vehicle she was driving had been rigged for a front-tire blowout, which was supposed to cause the driver to overcorrect, slide and, eventually, turn over. What actually happened was a bizarre roll-over flip that had Cade's heart pumping and armpits tingling with fear.

He played it twice, each time wondering how anyone survived, but the video included footage of the rescue team extracting her from the crushed car body. In true Jessie form, she'd waved to the camera as they pushed her gurney toward a waiting ambulance.

She'd claimed the rollover wasn't her fault. That meant it had happened despite her skill and planning. He sat unmoving for a good ten minutes, trying to decide how he felt about her career, which appeared to include an inherent danger that in many ways rivaled his late wife's job.

Finally, he'd clicked off the page and resumed his hunt. Jessie wasn't his wife, his girlfriend, his significant other. He had no right to criticize her. Period. If their fledgling relationship went any further, he'd give the question of her career choice more thought.

If. At the moment, he wouldn't have put money on either outcome.

He returned to his home page and opened a new search. Jessie had mentioned that Zane was ex-military. Maybe he could find some sort of lead through that avenue.

A dead end, he decided a few minutes later. He was poised to click on another link when his phone rang. He quickly answered it so the sound didn't wake Shiloh, who was asleep a couple of doors down the hall. "Hello?"

"Hi. You weren't in bed, were you?"

Kat.

He closed the lid of the laptop and got up from his father's big, comfortable leather armchair—Cade's favorite piece of furniture in the house. "Nope. I was doing some work on the computer. What's up?"

"Nothing, really. I thought I'd see if you have plans this weekend."

He thought a moment. "No. Not really. Why?"

"I want to invite my family and me to a barbecue-slash-pool party at your house."

Cade chuckled. "Oh, you do, do you? What am I barbecuing?"

"How 'bout bison burgers? My treat, of course, since you're supplying the grill…and the pool." Her laugh sounded a bit self-conscious. "Remy told us you'd opened the pool, and when the boys heard that, they were practically out of their minds with envy."

"I don't blame them. The water's great. As much as it pains me to admit this, Buck did good where the pool is concerned, and your boys are welcome to use it anytime."

"Including this weekend?"

Cade walked to the window and looked down at the pool, absently wondering if his renters might be interested in joining the fun. A movement—a black silhouette, really, backlit by the blue-green glow of the underwater light—caught his attention. He looked a moment longer to be sure it wasn't Shiloh. No. It was Jessie.

"Cade?"

"What? Oh, sorry. I was checking my calendar," he lied. "Completely open. What time do you want this shindig to start?"

They discussed logistics a few minutes longer, then hung up.

He stood at the window, debating. He didn't need an excuse to talk to Jessie, but he also didn't need to go outside to deliver an invitation that could be asked and answered via text.

But texting lacked the personal warmth of a face-to-face exchange, he decided. And since when was warmth a bad thing?

He shoved his feet into his oldest pair of boots and hurried out the door. *Let her still be there*, he silently wished. *Let her...*

She was sitting on the side of the pool, a towel draped around her shoulders. She seemed to be having a one-sided conversation with someone.

Sugar. The raccoon kit, he realized. The little animal had developed a real attachment to Jessie—much to Shiloh's consternation.

"Hey," he called out to avoid startling her.

She turned toward the sound of his voice. The moon was faint, but the glow from the windows where her sister apparently was watching TV and the blue-green underwater spot cast her in such a flattering light she looked like a mermaid carved from marble.

The raccoon leaped from Jessie's arms and went scurrying toward its remodeled dog crate, which had been moved to a spot below Jessie's window—because that seemed to be Sugar's favorite place in the whole world.

Jessie stood, carefully putting her good foot under her first. She hopped a couple of steps to catch her balance, but within a second or two, she was facing him, towel tucked firmly around the tops of her breasts.

"You're up late."

He was, considering he'd started his day well before dawn. But he didn't feel the least bit tired. Not now, anyway. "I saw you from my window. Thought you might like some help with the cover."

She wiggled her finger. "Nope. My finger's in good shape. I think I can flip the switch without help."

He chuckled, acknowledging his extremely lame excuse.

"I wanted to see you."

"Oh," she said. "In that case, would you mind getting the pool cover for me? I need to get out of this wet suit. But don't go away. I'll be right back."

"I'll be here."

The cover completed its course with a loud thunk. Cade squatted and turned the switch to the locked position then clicked off the underwater light. With the glow from the pool extinguished, it took a few seconds for his eyes to adjust, but the moment they did, he felt Jessie materialize beside him. Even in the dim light he could see she'd changed into baggy gray sweats. Her feet were still bare.

"Dark, huh?"

"That's a serious understatement," she said, looking skyward. "Wow. I know L.A. is famous for its star sightings, but it can't hold a candle to this place."

The clever pun and honest awe made him reach for her hand. "If you think that's something, come with me."

Her fingers closed around his as if they'd been

holding hands all their lives. "Let me warn you, if what you're going to show me involves etchings, I've seen them before and wasn't impressed."

Humor. Damn, he liked a woman who could laugh at herself.

"No etchings. I promise."

"Okay. Let me grab my flip-flops." Shoes on, she was ready.

Now that his night vision had kicked in, he could pick his way through the damp grass without worry of bumping into something painful. He grabbed two oversize towels from the clothesline as they passed. "When I was a kid, I used to sneak out of the house to come up here," he said.

At the edge of the lawn, he hesitated. "It's a bit uphill but it's not far. Can your ankle handle it?"

"If I can use you for a crutch, it shouldn't be a problem." She tightened her grip in a reassuring way.

The knoll wasn't much to look at by day—most people probably never gave it a second glance. But at night it was like a miniature observatory. He spread out the towels, side by side, then helped her to sit.

He quickly joined her, then dropped backward, linking his fingers behind his head. Jessie copied him, their elbows touching. She went still, her breathing barely audible. After a good minute of silence, she made a soft "Wow."

He stared, unblinking, trying to recall the constellations he'd memorized from a book he'd checked out of the school library. His brother once told him Buck knew the names of all the star formations, but Cade had never been able to talk his dad into joining him here. A fact that still brought a small, familiar ache to his heart. Maybe he needed to make that happen once his father returned.

"Shiloh and I came here wearing snowmobile suits and winter boots the first week we moved in. The winter constellations are different, of course."

"Remy and I loved Greek and Roman mythology when we were kids. We had a homemade telescope out of soup cans. It would have been so great to have a parent who was into that, too. Mom definitely wasn't that kind of person."

He shifted sideways, lifting up on one arm to rest his head in his palm. "What kind of person was she?"

She didn't answer right away. He sensed she was searching for a politically correct answer.

"Busy," she finally replied. "Keeping three beauty parlors going while raising five daughters *and* maintaining an active dating life was no picnic. You know?"

Did he ever—and he was talking one kid. Five? The thought shook him to the core. Or, maybe being a widower was worse because his skill set was less hearth-and-home oriented. He'd been a complete and utter mess right after Faith died, but he'd done his best to keep his focus on Shiloh and her needs. He got the impression that wasn't the case where Jessie's mother was concerned. Mrs. Bouchard might have put her own needs ahead of her daughters' welfare. But neither Jessie nor Remy seemed too screwed up—despite Jessie's non-traditional job choice—so the woman must have done something right.

Before he could say as much, Jessie turned on her side, too. Their faces were a foot or so apart. Close enough for him to smell the minty freshness of her toothpaste. "Can I tell you something I probably shouldn't tell you?" she asked.

"Sure."

"You're the first single dad I've ever…um…lusted after. Too blunt, huh?"

Blunt, yes, but also honest, with a side of vulnerability. How could he resist that?

"Well, this is a first for me on a number of levels, too. But I'm okay with that. Are you?"

Am I? Jessie asked herself. *Yes, but…*

Any reservations her brain had prepared to raise disappeared the moment his hands splayed across her back and he moved an inch or two closer.

She waited to see if his explorations faltered. True, he'd already seen her in a bikini, but this was different. This wasn't a little friendly groping. This journey was leading somewhere. Possibly to a place where they both were naked and sweaty and exploring each other's bodies without fear.

His hand dipped to the base of her spine and a moment later his fingers slipped under the hem of the loose sweatshirt she'd thrown on…without a bra. When his hand settled atop the worst of her scars, she held her breath. He stopped kissing her, pulling back slightly to give her a chance to change her mind or call the whole thing off, she figured.

She didn't. Because she knew what would happen.

He'd feel the ridges and uneven texture of her skin and remember what he'd seen yesterday. He'd congratulate himself on being brave then quickly move on to the normal parts. That's how the men she'd slept with in the past handled her deformity.

"I know this is probably a dumb question," he said, his fingers lightly skimming her tragic skin, "but I need to know. Does it bother you when someone touches your scars?"

No one had ever asked that before.

"It's not physically painful, of course. Most of the nerve endings got fried or buried under the scar tissue, but there are spots that get sensitive in certain weather or when I've been sitting in the wrong position too long. I've been told it's like an amputee's phantom pain."

He opened up a bit more space between them. "Would you let me look at you?"

"In the dark?" She glanced around, realizing for the first time that there was more light from the stars and the sliver of a moon than she'd thought.

He nodded.

Oh, hell, why not get the inevitable over? The sooner he got this sympathy thing out of the way, the sooner they could fool around. If that was still on the agenda. So far, this seduction wasn't going anything like the encounters she'd had in the past.

She rolled to her belly, crossing her wrists on top of each other to make a resting spot for her forehead. She breathed slowly, the way she did in a yoga relaxation pose. She closed her eyes, listening to the night sounds: crickets chirping, a bullfrog in the stock pond doing his best to impress his sweetheart and the very distant hum from trucks on the highway. The only smell to reach her nose was from the fabric softener Remy had used in the wash.

A shiver passed through her from head to toe when he pulled up her shirt. "Cold?" he asked, his voice a low, sexy rumble.

"Not really."

He laid both of his hands on her. She could feel each fingertip, as if she were the piano keys and he was the player. He moved boldly, firmly—a blind student studying in Braille for an important test.

The flesh she'd long termed *dead* tingled in a way that went straight to her core. His touch was intimate but not sexual. And yet, she was more turned on than she could remember being in a long, long time.

She crossed her legs at the ankles, ignoring the twinge of complaint from beneath the tightly wrapped bandage. Her thighs squeezed against each other and her womanly core went moist and hot as she imagined those clever, sensitive hands dropping lower.

He bent over to lay his cheek on a beribboned spot between her shoulder blades. Her doctors had tried three times to improve the grafts in this area, lifting skin from her thigh and the inside of her arms but that particular section refused to heal right.

When he rubbed his nose against the exact place of her worst anguish—a hot spot that had taken forever to heal—she stopped breathing. A rush of emotion— something harsh and savage—tore through her, bringing back memories she'd worked hard to forget. Kindly nurses who did their best to fill in for her absent mother. Worried, serious doctors who probably thought they were talking over her head when they whispered about their young patient's emotional disconnect.

This spot might have been invisible to the world, and yet, somehow, Cade found it.

"Stop." Her cry sounded too much like a whimper in her opinion, but it worked. He moved back immediately, giving her the room she needed to flip over.

The cool air made gooseflesh prickle across her exposed belly. She held out her arms to him. "I need you to kiss me."

He obliged without hesitation, placing his hands on either side of her head and lowering himself close enough for their lips to touch, but not providing the full-body contact she craved.

She wrapped her arms around his neck and drew him closer, wishing there was a way to crawl through him to come out whole on the other side.

That, she realized, was the sort of power she felt within him, the magic they created together.

She'd never felt an urgency quite this strong. *Desire.* Such a bland word to describe such a powerful force. She grappled with his shirt, needing to feel his skin against hers. His heat. His perfection.

Getting out of her loose sweats was nothing, waiting for him to take off his pants, pure agony. She used the time to clear up the questions that needed to be asked. "Protection?"

"Celibate for ten years."

Not me. "The blood tests I had done in Japan showed

I was healthy." *Even if I wasn't a match for Mom.* "And I've been on the pill since I was eighteen."

Their green light shone brighter than any star in the sky, but apparently Cade needed more. After shedding his pants, he returned to lie beside her, naked and aroused, but he didn't make a move to hold her. Not right away. Instead, he ran the back of his hand gently across her cheek, as if making certain she was real.

Did he need something else from her? Words of love? Promises of a commitment of some sort?

Don't make me lie to you, she whispered silently.

He must have heard because he was the one to say, "This is just tonight. Here and now. Nothing more. Right?"

She nodded. Living in the moment was as Zen as it came with stunt people. You never knew what the next stunt might bring. Here and now was the one sure thing. She'd made that her mantra for a long time. Tonight would be enough.

CHAPTER ELEVEN

CADE WASN'T WORRIED THAT HE couldn't perform. He was a normal, healthy male. His only fear was he might hurt her—physically. The woman had been hanging upside down from a tower a few days earlier. Now, instead of making love in one of the many soft, comfortable beds in either of their two houses, he had them naked on a towel on the ground. That nearly unmanned him. He was a heartbeat away from suggesting they head inside when she took his hand and placed it on her breast. Her nipple was hard. Just like him.

"What about your ankle?" he asked.

He could see her mischievous grin in the starlight. "It's not like you have to chase me. The only pain I feel at the moment is a deep ache. Here," she answered, moving his hand to the cleft between her legs. She opened for him and he had the answer he needed. She wanted him. He wanted her. Maybe life really was that simple.

His fingers explored her nest of curls much as they had her damaged back—testing, feeling, probing. She inched closer, her back slightly arched. He timed his entry to the second he took her nipple in his mouth. Her moan fired his need all the more.

He made a judgment call. Now.

Keeping his full weight on his knees and elbows, he moved to the top position. Missionary style. He'd never understood the name. Why? Because the man was praying he could satisfy his partner before he completely lost his mind and his control?

He was pretty sure that was one battle he was destined to lose. At least where Jessie was concerned.

Luckily, Jessie applied herself to sex the same way he'd observed her throwing herself into each stunt she performed—with her entire being. The sounds she made were his guideline, his lifeline. Together, they moved like dancers who had danced this routine a thousand times. They crested the biggest, most powerful wave at the exact same moment.

He collapsed mindlessly, his focus—what was left of it—captivated by the delicious afterglow. An occasional high-pitched whine of a mosquito buzzed past his ear, but thankfully none landed. Or if they did, he was too blissed out to notice.

He did, however, notice when she shifted slightly—as if realizing a rock or something was poking her. He immediately rolled to one side, pulling her with him.

"That was incredible," she said, snuggling closer with a small shiver that brought back his guilt about not planning this better.

He found her sweatshirt and used it to cover her back.

As his body returned to normal, the magnitude of what they'd just done—made love in the open—struck him. His senses went on high alert. Nobody was around to hear them, to know what they'd done, but he rarely left the house after Shiloh went to sleep. What if she woke up and he wasn't there?

"Are you regretting this already?" she asked, apparently picking up on his growing tension.

He nuzzled her nose with his own and kissed her. "I will never regret this. But I'm not in the habit of leaving the house with Shiloh in it alone."

"Are you afraid she'll wake up and come looking for you?"

The question struck him as naive. "No. I'm afraid she'll wake up, realize I'm gone and jump on the internet. We've been arguing over inappropriate social-networking behavior lately, and short of banning her from the computer completely, I'm a bit frustrated and perplexed about how to handle this issue. Any suggestions?"

She sat up and pulled on her top. "Me? Nope. Sorry. I teach a few yoga classes at Girlz on Fire—I mean, I did—but I have absolutely no parenting skills." She laughed—her tone strained. "And what do you expect given my role model?"

"But your older sisters have children," he said, a little surprised by her hands-off attitude. "Remy mentioned a niece Shiloh's age."

She leaned across him for her pants. "True. But our older sisters had more of a traditional family structure than Remy and me. The Bullies knew their daddy. Mama didn't divorce him until shortly before Remy and I were born." She wiggled into her pants then added, "And, of course, Bossy, Bing and Rita are married."

He heard something uncompromising in her tone—
or was it fear? "I've never met a single parent—by *single*
I mean mother or father, married or not—who claimed
to know everything there is to know about raising kids.
Some of it you make up as you go."

She shrugged. "I'm in show business, remember?
I do my best work from a script. When you ad lib in
stunts, people get hurt."

She got to her knees. "I'm going to start physical
therapy tomorrow after I drive Shiloh to the bus. I
should really get to bed."

He needed to go, too, but he felt a little uneasy. He
sensed some undercurrent between them that hadn't
been there before he brought up Shiloh and his worries
about her current social-networking addiction.

He scrambled to his feet and helped her up. "If
you wait a second, I'll give you a piggyback ride," he
offered.

She looked at him, unsmiling. "This was nice.
Crazy nice. But don't try to read anything too hearth
and homey into it, okay? I'm only here for the summer.
Even if my ankle isn't healed enough to participate in
Japan, my life—small and strange as it may seem—
is back in L.A. And as much as I like your daughter,
believe me, I'm doing Shiloh a favor by not pretending
to be the motherly type. Are we clear on that?"

No. Not even close. But she didn't wait for his answer.
She touched the side of his face with a gesture that implied regret and left.

He stood there. Alone. His arms filled with towels

that still retained a hint of their heat and the scent of their lovemaking.

Was he confused? Yes. Annoyed? Uh-huh. Sorry he'd had sex with her? Not for a second.

Was he content to leave things between them like this? Hell, no. Whether she liked it or not, they'd forged a connection. He could understand her reluctance to get involved for the long-term—hell, she hadn't even met Buck. But he'd be damned if he'd let her hide behind her mother's apparently ineffectual parenting skirts.

He started toward the house, the chill of the night seeping past the afterglow of their crazy-good sex. He shook his head and sighed. Man, he thought, if anyone deserved to be relationship gun-shy, it was him. He'd grown up with Buck for a dad, after all.

Cade could vividly remember his father and step-mom arguing. Inevitably his father would start stomping around in his big cowboy boots. Chairs would suddenly sprout wings and fly across a room. Cade would disappear—under a bed, into the far reaches of a closet—anywhere he could pretend to be an island of serenity in the midst of a hurricane called Buck.

Fortunately, he'd learned early in his marriage to Faith he couldn't be provoked into those sorts of arguments. He might get upset, angry or deeply frustrated, but he never turned into his father.

Maybe, just maybe, he could help Jessie see that she wasn't predisposed to be a clone of her mother, either. If he was upset at all, his ire was directed at Mrs. Bouchard. Where was this woman when her daughter needed her? Where was that Old South network of family he'd always heard about? The Bullies would have been in their teens when Jessie was hurt. Why didn't they do more? And what about any aunts, uncles or grandparents? Someone should have been by that poor little girl's side to hold her hand and comfort her when her mother couldn't be present. And if, for whatever reason, her mother chose to be a single parent, why the hell hadn't she made some sort of effort to provide a father figure for her daughter?

Wasn't that, in essence, why he moved back to the Black Hills? Yes, he welcomed the chance to be his own boss and make amends with his father, but he also wanted Shiloh to be around Kat, to learn womanly things from her and go to her with questions Shiloh might feel strange asking him.

Jessie's mother had failed her daughter, in his opinion. Naturally, he couldn't say that to Jessie. No kid wanted to hear his or her parent criticized. That even held true for Cade where Buck was concerned.

He paused at the corner of the house and stared at the pool a moment. As he'd told his sister, Buck's instincts had been spot-on where this was concerned. He was looking forward to hosting a party this weekend and actually felt sorry Buck wouldn't be here to attend it. His father would have treasured the validation. And, now that he was sober, maybe everyone else could have a good time, too, without worrying about the ticking time bomb in the room, waiting for that last, incendiary whiskey to set him off.

Cade shrugged and resumed walking. No, on second thought, why risk it? Buck was where he needed to be and Cade was getting along fine without him.

"I ASKED HIM."

"Good girl, Kat. Your brother needs to get shook out of his safety zone now and then. Always has."

Kat's chuckle made Buck feel warm inside. He might have screwed up six ways of hell where his other kids were concerned but somehow Kat had turned out better than Buck or Helen had any right to hope.

"I think you're wrong about Cade, Dad. He's extremely generous. And rock solid. You should have seen the way he came to Jessie's rescue the other day. My brother only knows one mode—hero."

Buck cocked his head to think. *Hero.* Not a word anyone would ever associate with him. Maybe he'd done better than he'd thought by the boy. "Are you telling me you think there might be something going on between Cade and this girl?"

Kat's laughter echoed off the walls of his small, monklike room. "*Girl?* Dad, Shiloh is a girl. Jessie is a successful, sought-after stuntwoman," she said, emphasizing the last word clearly. "She's also beautiful in a very ungirly way and from what Shiloh tells me, Jessie doesn't take you-know-what from anybody—your son included. He'd be crazy not to fall for her, but, at the same time, she's made it clear her career comes first."

"Like Faith." The daughter-in-law Buck never got to know.

Kat's sigh didn't sound overly worried. "Maybe

superficially. But trust me, Dad, Jessie isn't anything like Faith."

The tension in Buck's shoulders relaxed a bit. Maybe he'd give that yoga class a try after all. It didn't hurt that the instructor was a lovely, silver-haired lady with a kind smile.

"Good. I'll leave it in Cade's hands, then. Thanks for taking my call tonight, Kat. I was a little homesick."

"Dad, you know how I feel about your self-imposed exile. Mom would be rolling over in her grave if she wasn't in an urn on my mantle at the moment. She was as much to blame for what went wrong in your marriage as you were. Divorces happen. Get over it."

He chuckled softly. "Sounds like a bumper sticker I saw the other day. All right, I'll try to forgive myself. Now, you go tend to that husband of yours so the D-word doesn't happen again."

"Never," she vowed. "Not me and Jack. We're the real deal. It just took me a couple of tries to get it right. 'Night, Dad. Sleep well."

Buck turned off his phone and smiled. He might not have been a good husband, but Kat was proof he wasn't a total screwup as a father. If she could forgive him, maybe there was a chance his son would, too.

"How was it?"

Jessie nearly dropped her coffee mug—the one that said Cowboys Rock. She'd almost forgotten today was her sister's first day on the new job until she turned and saw Remy walking toward her, completely dressed and ready to head off to work. "How was what?"

"Your swim last night?" Remy said, grabbing a banana from the bowl of fruit on the counter. "I tried to stay awake to make sure you didn't drown or something, but I was so tired I crashed."

"Oh. It was fine." The truth. The swim was completely unremarkable. Her interlude with Cade, however, was something she still hadn't wrapped her head around. And didn't plan to share with her sister.

As she peeled the banana, Remy said, "I had a dream about you and Mama."

"A nightmare, huh? I'm sorry."

Remy took a bite and chewed a moment. "It wasn't a bad dream. It simply made no sense. You were standing off in the distance and Mom was calling to you. Over and over. I don't know if you were ignoring her or you couldn't hear for some reason."

"That makes perfect sense. She always said I never listened to her. Are you sure it was me?"

"Of course it was you. You think I don't know my own twin? Besides, she said your name. She said, 'Jessie, I'm sorry.'"

Jessie hated those kinds of dreams. They seemed too simple. Too pat. She wasn't even completely certain her sister didn't make them up as a way of manipulating her family.

"So," she said, changing the subject, "is that what you're wearing to work?" Her sister was a skirt-or-dress sort of girl, not jeans and a ratty T-shirt.

"Kat texted me last night. This is a work detail. She said to dress grubby. This is the grubbiest I've got. She also said we're invited to a barbecue and pool party on

Saturday. I wonder what we should make. Something Cajun?"

Jessie shrugged. "That's your department."

Remy shook her half-eaten banana at Jessie. "You can cook every bit as well as me, Jess. You simply pretend you can't. You have to admit that's one thing Mama did right with us girls."

Jessie didn't argue the point—it truly didn't matter whether or not Marlene Bouchard taught her daughters how to make moist cornbread. Mom hadn't been around when Jessie needed her and that was the one thing Jessie remembered above all the other lessons Mom might have preferred she point to as her legacy.

Remy squinted at the clock on the microwave. "Ooh. I've gotta dash. I need to stop for gas on the way." She looked at Jessie and made a face. "What happened to Miss Awake-at-the-Butt-Crack-of-Dawn today? You need to get dressed, girlfriend. Take it from someone who tried and failed. That school bus driver doesn't respond to a flirtatious smile. She doesn't wait for anybody," she called, racing out the door, purse in hand.

Jessie was moving a little slowly this morning. Probably because she'd spent way too much of the night worrying about whether or not she'd made a mistake. And the fact that she was stewing over—not celebrating—her fabulous encounter with Cade bothered her all the more. She'd made a pretty good effort to live her life the way she wanted without apology or fear. Until lately.

She managed to make it to the garage on time and was ridiculously disappointed to find Shiloh waiting by herself. No Cade.

"Where's your dad?"

Shiloh shrugged. "He leaves before the sun comes up some mornings. But he always has breakfast sitting out for me. Fuel for the brain, he calls it." She made a face, but she looked proud, too.

"He's right. I get up, do yoga, then eat." The only person on their team who didn't join the others for breakfast when they were at an event was Zane. He claimed to follow a secret dietary regimen that he planned to take public someday and make his fortune.

Shiloh got in the passenger seat and fastened her seat belt without being asked. Jessie backed out slowly, getting a feel for the truck. Although big and ungainly looking, the truck drove like a luxury car, but she quickly figured out it had the get-up-and-go of an oxcart. They'd been ambling along the gravel road for about five minutes when Shiloh said, "How come you don't have a boyfriend?"

"Who said I don't?"

"Remy. She said the last guy you dated turned out to be a schmuck. I like that word."

"Me, too. But J.T. wasn't completely to blame. We sorta went out to make his mother happy."

"Are moms supposed to do that? Set you up with boys? What if you don't have one? A mom, I mean," she quickly added.

The slight panic in her voice made Jessie want to reach across the bench seat and give her a one-arm hug. She didn't. "No, no, no. Believe me, mothers can mean well and think they're helping, but ask Remy how much our mother helped her high school romance." She felt a little guilty bringing up the subject, which had been terribly dramatic and traumatic at the time, but obviously Remy felt no hesitation when it came to gossiping about other people's lives so turnabout was fair play.

"I will. She's funny. She talks a lot about your family and growing up in the South. My English teacher would probably say Remy doesn't have all her filters in place."

Jessie had to press her lips together to keep from laughing out loud.

"Your career is really important to you, right?"

Jessie nodded, wondering where this was taking them.

"Would you ever consider giving it up if you were in love and the guy asked you to?"

Jessie was afraid to think what that might mean. Had her dad said something to Shiloh about Jessie's career? Or was this a holdover from Shiloh's mother's job and tragic death?

"Well, I'd like to hope that wouldn't be an issue. If the guy loved me, too, he wouldn't want to change me, right?" But Jessie knew from experience that was an altruistic dream relationship. The problem came up all the time when you worked in a profession that was widely considered a man's job.

Changing the subject, she asked Shiloh, "Do you know how to drive?"

"Sorta. Ranch kids learn things like that early, but I've never driven out on the road. Liability, Dad says."

"I'm sure he's right. But I don't see why you couldn't

practice on the way home from school every day. Practice makes perfect, right?"

"You'd let me? Really?" Shiloh cried, her voice shrill with excitement. "OMG. I can't wait to tell Hunter. I—I mean...my friends."

Hunter. A certain friend has a name.

Jessie nosed the truck toward the shelter that had been built to the left of where the private road intersected the highway. A row of mailboxes, presumably belonging to houses across the road from the ranch, angled off in the other direction. They were a few minutes early, but the terrain was flat enough that Jessie could see a bright yellow vehicle a mile or so away.

She killed the engine. "I don't have a problem with you driving, but since this is your grandpa's truck, I will have to ask your dad's permission. I don't see why that would be a problem. Your driveway seems like a pretty safe place to learn. The worst that could happen is you'd get turned sideways in the gravel, but you'll be fine if you take it slow. You have to learn sometime, right?"

"That's what Grandpa told Dad, but Dad said it was up to him to decide when that was." Her expression looked far from optimistic.

"Hmm," Jessie said, hearing the roar of the bus motor approach. "Maybe we'll try the Jessie Bouchard method, then. Assume the answer is yes until you hear a no."

Shiloh clapped excitedly. "Really? Oh, Jessie, you're the best. Thank you. See you after school."

Moments later, her young charge was safely aboard

the bus, waving through the dusty glass. Jessie waited until the bus was out of sight before attempting a three-point turn to head to the ranch. Her ankle was throbbing by the time she parked and walked into the house.

She realized she'd forgotten to take her pain medication and was on her way to her bedroom when she spotted a flashing light on the answering machine. The phone line was in Buck Garrity's name.

Oh, well, she thought, *it's not for me.*

She'd barely taken a step when the phone rang. As far as she knew, the only people who had this number were friends or family interested in talking to Buck and more than likely knew he was out of town for the summer. But the flashing light prompted her to act. If someone had called more than once, maybe something was wrong. Maybe the caller was Cade.

"Garrity Ranch, Jessie speaking."

Silence.

"Hello?"

She could hear someone breathing. A crank call this early in the morning? Maybe a robocall gone bad, she thought. She started to hang up the receiver when a voice said, "You lucky bitch. That must mean the wrong twin was behind the wheel."

CHAPTER TWELVE

THE LINE DISCONNECTED WITH a menacing snap.

A shiver raced down Jessie's spine as adrenaline coursed through her body. Remy had grabbed Jessie's Girlz on Fire ball cap on her way out the door. From a distance they'd be indistinguishable.

Whoever this caller was, he'd done something to Remy, thinking he'd reached his real target: Jessie.

She snatched up the keys and raced back to the truck. As she hauled herself into the cab, she heard a voice call out, "Jessie, wait. Where are you going? Can we talk?"

She frantically rolled down the window. "There was a call on your dad's line. I think something's happened to Remy. Something bad. I have to find her."

Cade charged across the driveway. "Move over. I'll drive."

She didn't bother protesting. Her ankle was throbbing. She hadn't had a chance to grab her pills. She needed his help.

"Who called? What did they say?"

"A man. He said something about the wrong twin being behind the wheel. Remy drove my car this morning and she was wearing my ball cap."

"Why didn't he call your cell?"

She fastened her seat belt. "Maybe he thought he'd reach Remy. To tell her I was dead or something," she answered, grabbing at straws. The panic she'd initially felt blossomed into a really bad feeling.

"Did you recognize his voice?"

She shook her head. "No. The sound was distorted. Like one of those voice-altering devices you see in the movies."

Movies.

"It was Zane."

"How can you be sure? You said it was altered."

She grabbed the armrest to keep from sliding across the bench seat into Cade when the truck fishtailed on the gravel. He drove like a pro, making every turn exactly the way she would have if this was a choreographed stunt.

"Zane has always bragged about stealing props from sets that he worked on. Little things that wouldn't be missed. He called it *gleaning*. One of the things he mentioned came from a spy movie," she said, meaningfully.

"Got it." Cade swore under his breath. "Does Remy have her phone with her?"

Jessie pulled hers out of the pocket of her sweatshirt and hit Remy's number on speed dial. The call went straight to voice mail. "She doesn't leave it on because service is so sketchy around here. Do you have Jack's number? Maybe this is a false alarm. If she made it to work safely…" *Please God. Please let her be okay.*

Cade flipped up his little belt holster and handed

his phone to her. "Number's listed. It's a dead zone through here but you should have service as soon as we get on the highway. Do you know which way she took to Sentinel Pass?"

"No." Jessie opened the phone and found the number. "I only know the way we took to the clinic. Is there another road?"

He nodded. "A shortcut. Less traffic but very winding, and—" He hesitated before continuing. "It has some serious drop-offs. If she went that way, we're going to need backup."

Jessie gulped. They'd reached the same spot she'd left a few minutes earlier. Cade turned onto the shoulder of the road and waited. "Try Jack."

She hit the button, silently urging the call to go faster.

"Hey, brother-in-law, what's up?"

"Jack? It's Jessie. Cade and I are trying to reach Remy. Is she there?"

"No. I called the house a little bit ago to see if she was coming. Is something wrong?"

The red flashing light. She should have listened to the message. "Maybe," she mumbled, filled with dread and guilt. She'd felt safe at the ranch, protected from the whims of Fate—a nebulous and dangerous trickster that seemed to have it in for her. She'd let down her guard and something bad had happened to someone she loved. This was her fault.

Cade took the phone from her trembling fingers and hit the speaker button. "Jack. We don't know what's happened, if anything, but we need to find Remy. Do you know if she planned on taking the cutoff?"

"I think so, yes. But she said she had to get gas."

He nodded. "Okay. We're taking off. We'll keep you posted."

"I'll head out from here," Jack told them. "She's driving the big blue boxy car, right?"

Cade looked at Jessie. "Yota. The car's name is Yota."

Jessie sat forward, her gaze searching the sides of the road—even though logic told her any sort of attack would probably come on a lonely stretch of road, not a busy highway.

"Tell me more about this Zane character."

"He comes across as laid-back, but he's actually very ambitious—some of the past members of our team have called it delusions of grandeur. Physical training is his passion, and yet he's been known to disappear on a weeklong bender. Then, if any of us go to a bar after work for a drink or two, he calls us slackers."

"That's a bit hypocritical."

She agreed. "Zane is smart, but sometimes he gets stuck on a whacko philosophy or belief and can't let go. When my mother first got sick, he went on and on about how certain foreign governments were plotting to kill us—one burrito at a time."

"How did he take your losing in Japan?"

Horrible. Mean-spirited. Uncharitable. Could that be his motivation? Revenge? But why now—nearly a year after the fact? "After Mom passed, he put on a huge show of sympathy. Sent a giant spray of flowers to the funeral. But right after I fell and sank us in the competition, he called me every name in the book." Loser. Cheater. Human dog dung.

Cade shrugged. "Maybe being nice was a way to throw you off the fact he was plotting some sort of payback."

Maybe. Another thought struck her. "Remember when you asked about his gambling habits? It just hit me. Marsh and Eerik were telling me Zane bragged about making a haul on an online site a couple of months ago. Gamblers only talk about their wins, right? Never their losses."

He put on the blinker and they pulled into a gas station. "This is the last one before heading into the hills. Seems like the place she'd use. I'll ask the attendant if he remembers seeing her."

Jessie opened her door. "I'll save you having to give him a description." For once, she was glad she and her sister looked alike.

"Excuse me," Cade said, cutting in front of the guy waiting in line to pay.

"Hey," the stranger complained.

"It's important," Jessie said. "We're looking for my sister. We're afraid her car's broken down somewhere between here and Sentinel Pass."

The customer continued to frown, but he stopped complaining to listen to Cade and the clerk.

"The woman we're looking for is blonde. She was wearing a hot pink ball cap with her hair in a ponytail."

"She looks like me, only prettier."

Cade gave her a sharp look but before he could say anything, the twentysomething clerk snapped his fingers. "Yeah, sure, I know who you mean. She was hot. Came in right before pump five went ballistic."

He shook his head. "Talk about crazy. The alarms went nuts. The fire department showed up even though there wasn't a fire."

Several other people in line started talking. "We saw that," one lady said. "What happened?"

The kid shrugged. "My manager thinks somebody tampered with the pump. Not sure how, exactly, but, boy, what a mess." He pointed through the window to the island of gas pumps to the right of the counter. "Took fifteen minutes to turn off the alarms and reboot the computers. Some people were pretty mad, but your sister was real nice," he added.

Cade and Jessie looked at each other. A diversion. The kind of thing an ex-Special Ops guy would know to do.

"Do you remember which pump she used?" Cade asked.

"She was driving a turquoise-blue '71 Land Cruiser," Jessie put in.

The kid grinned. "Hellacool. It's a classic. She said it was her sister's." He pointed to the bank of pumps behind them. "She was at number twelve, I think. Opposite side. Why?"

"She's not answering her cell and we're afraid she might have gotten lost. Thanks for your help," Cade said, shaking the young man's hand.

"Good luck," several of the people in line called as Cade and Jessie hurried back to the truck.

"So," Cade said once they were on the road again, "your buddy did something to the gas pump that got all eyes looking one way so he could do something to your car."

Jessie's thought exactly. Hearing her suspicion articulated so perfectly made her nerves kick up a notch. "But how would he know she'd stop at this station? And when?"

Cade looked at her, his expression severe. "He followed her. He must have been casing the ranch for days, waiting for his chance. And our name is above the gate. That would explain how come he called Dad's house phone. Alphabetically, Buck's name comes before mine."

He cursed low but fervently, undoubtedly troubled by the idea of Zane keeping an eye on the comings and goings of all members of his family—including his daughter.

The road Y'ed to the right and traffic fell off a mile or so later when the road began to climb and the terrain changed to pine and aspen forests.

Cade eased up on the gas. He didn't want to add to Jessie's obvious fear and concern, but this stretch of road had a bad reputation. He hadn't been around when it happened, but he'd heard the story of Mac McGannon's ex-wife. She'd missed a curve and her car wasn't found for several weeks—her dead body in it.

"At least your car will be easy to spot," he said, grasping for any sort of positive note.

Jessie didn't acknowledge his comment. Her back was to him, her gaze glued to the road and ditches.

His phone, which was sitting on the seat between them, began to play a ring tone Cade recognized as his brother-in-law's. Jessie grabbed it and hit the speaker button. "Hello?"

"Jess. It's me. Jack just drove up. I'm about five miles outside of Sentinel Pass. Two people stopped to help within a minute of my pulling over, but neither of them had a cell phone. One of them drove into town to send for a tow truck while the other one hung around to make sure I was okay. Mac—the first guy who stopped—wanted me to go with him, but I refused to leave Yota alone and unprotected."

Cade kept driving but he saw Jessie blink rapidly, a sure sign she was choked up. "What happened?"

"Two flat tires," Remy answered. "Front and back on the same side. Can you believe that? Mac thought maybe I ran over something, but we couldn't see any nails sticking out. I'm really sorry, Jess, if this is something I did."

Jessie made a snarling noise. "It's not your fault, Remy. And screw Yota. You should have gone with Mac. Cade and I will be there soon...." She let her voice trail off as she looked at him for confirmation. He held up both hands to indicate ten minutes. "Under ten. Do you know if Mac called the cops?"

There was a moment of silence, then Remy said, "Yes. Mac says his first thought was this was somehow related to your fall."

"I didn't fall. I—"

Cade bit down on his lip to keep from smiling. Her response was so Jessie. And he couldn't help loving her for it even though the situation was nothing to laugh about.

She shook her head. "Never mind. Are you sure you're okay?"

"Yeah. I'm fine. Mac says it's a good thing I'm a slow driver. If I'd been speeding—the way *some* people drive, I might have flipped."

Cade and Jessie looked at each other. She knew he was thinking the same thing she was.

"Your tires are shredded, Jess. And the rims might be ruined, too. Sorry. It took me a mile or so to find a shoulder big enough to pull over safely."

"I don't care about the freaking tires, you dork. Or the rims. I'm just relieved you're okay. I'm hanging up now before we lose the signal. See you in a few." She started to close the phone but changed her mind, adding, "I love you, Rem. You did good."

She set the phone between them then turned in her seat to look at Cade. "This proves my rollover wasn't an accident, doesn't it?"

"Looks like a definite possibility. Was Zane on the set that day?"

She shook her head. "No. He called in sick. My agent said Zane asked for me to fill in for him. I thought he was throwing me a bone since he'd been so hostile in Japan."

"Well, I think you need to let someone in the studio know what's going on here. The guy's a menace and whatever his motivation, I think it's safe to say he's stepped beyond simply trying to teach you a lesson."

"I can't believe he'd go this far. He was my friend. Why?"

"I don't know, but apparently he doesn't have any qualms about incurring collateral damage. What if Shiloh had had the day off and was riding with you? Or what if Remy overcorrected and crossed into oncoming traffic? Any number of innocent bystanders could have wound up dead."

"My God, you're right," she said, her tone hushed. "Shiloh could have been—" She sat up straight, gaze forward. "Remy and I will move into a motel as soon as we get back to the ranch. I can't leave here until he's caught. I refuse to run away like some sort of coward, always looking over my shoulder, but I will not put you and your family in jeopardy a minute longer."

Leave? His grip on the wheel tightened. "That's not what I meant. If you think I'm letting you take this guy on alone, you don't know me very well. When you mess with a Garrity, you mess with trouble."

"I'm not a Garrity," she argued.

"Shiloh has been riding in that vehicle every day for a week, right? If Remy had missed the bus and stopped for gas…who knows what would have happened? The point is, just because you're his target doesn't mean you have to be his victim."

Her shoulders went back and her spine stiffened. "I'm nobody's victim."

That's my girl. "Then help me figure out a way to find him. Neither of us is the kind of person who sits around waiting for something to happen. Let's draw him in—at the time and place of our choosing, and then let the police do their job."

She looked interested but didn't jump on the idea. "I'd never forgive myself if something happened to Shiloh. It would be safer for you both if I went away."

Safe being a relative thing. He wouldn't be able to sleep at night knowing there was a nutcase out there trying to hurt Jessie. "The kids don't have school on Friday. Remy can take Shiloh to Kat's. Sentinel Pass is as safe as it gets."

"And what will we do?"

He knew what he'd like to do. With her. In his king-size bed.

He cleared his throat and forced his brain back to the very serious business at hand. "We'll lay a trap."

Jessie pointed ahead to a grouping of cars on a pull-off that probably provided a highway department storage place for salt and gravel in the winter. A tow truck and a sheriff's patrol car were on the scene, lights flashing.

Jessie hurried to the group of people standing to one side. She barely even limped, Cade noticed. Force of will and adrenaline, he guessed.

Cade was glad to see his old buddy Hank.

Hank motioned with his chin to talk to Cade privately while Jessie and Remy embraced and rehashed what had happened.

"It took a while to get this Zane character's records from the military," Hank said, his tone filled with disgust. "Turns out he wasn't Special Forces. He washed out of Rangers in his early twenties and bounced around a couple of brigs until his enlistment was up. Disappeared after that. Half a dozen arrests, mostly for assault. Bar fights gone bad. The person who got the crap kicked out of him usually dropped the charges or failed to show up at arraignment. Points to intimidation but nothing we can prove."

Jessie joined them. "I told Remy to go to work with Jack. You were done with her, right?" she asked the deputy.

"Yes, ma'am. We're lucky here. No harm, no proof of foul. Yet," he added with emphasis. "I asked to have the tires sent to our lab. Looked to me like someone messed with the stems. But I'm no expert."

Cade listened while she filled Hank in on what they'd learned at the gas station. He shook his head. "This dude is a pest. I don't think I'm premature in calling him a stalker, Ms. Bouchard. He's got it in for you. If you want, we've got a kid on staff who is part computer geek. I'll have him take a look at the rollover video you told me about."

Jessie nodded intently. "What do you want me to do?"

"Stay out of his way."

Cade had been turning this problem over in his mind ever since they left the gas station. "My hired men are always begging for overtime. I'll put on rotating shifts at the main gate and set up a patrol to cover the fence."

Hank looked skeptical. "That's a big ranch you got there, Cade."

"It is, but we're a small village. No stranger could get close without somebody noticing. Jessie and I were talking about sending Remy and Shiloh to stay with Kat for the weekend. If nothing happens by Monday morning, we'll move to Plan B. Whatever that is," he added ruefully.

Hank looked at Jessie. "That makes you bait, Jessie. Are you comfortable with that?"

She inhaled deeply. "I trust Cade's instincts. He knows the land. I know Zane. As long as there's no chance of collateral casualties, I think we'll make a good team."

She trusts me. And whether she knew it or not, that meant the stakes were now a whole lot higher.

"HEY, DAD, IT'S ME, CADE. Just a quick message. Some things have been happening around here you should know about."

Buck was lying on his bed, looking at the ceiling, checking his messages. He'd left his phone in his room while he attended his first yoga class. He'd enjoyed the pace—even if he felt as graceful as a snapping turtle on ice.

After a slight pause, his son's message continued. "One of the women who moved into your house— Jessie—seems to have become the target of a stalker. He's most likely the reason she injured her leg, and now he's made another move against her. Did something to her car. Nobody was hurt, but that's the same car Shiloh has ridden to school in for a week."

Buck's heart rate spiked momentarily until Cade added, "No worries. Shiloh's fine. She was on the bus when all this went down, and I'm sending her to Kat's this weekend. In fact, Kat just called. She said she and Jack decided to take Shiloh and Jessie's sister, Remy, with them to Denver this weekend to pick up a load of Jack's office stuff, instead of doing the pool party we'd planned. I wanted you to know what was going on."

Buck appreciated that. He probably didn't deserve his son's generous inclusion considering the way he'd left Cade high and dry with a lame, poorly expressed excuse. But now, with some time and distance under his belt, Buck was feeling less panicky. He was almost positive he could return home without feeling the overwhelming urge to escape into a bottle of booze.

"And listen, I called our insurance agent and double-checked to make sure we're covered against malicious mischief. Hopefully, it won't come to that."

Buck figured that was the end of the message and he started to close his phone when he heard Cade add, "And, Dad, just FYI, I'm pretty much head over heels where Jessie is concerned. Yes, it's fast, and she's made it clear she isn't sticking around here after her rental agreement is up, but that's how it goes sometimes, right? I'm only telling you this because I think I finally understand why you married Helen. You weren't trying to screw up your family like Charlie claimed. You were in love. I get it now. Talk to you later."

Buck walked straight to his tiny bathroom and leaned over the sink to splash water on his face. His son had forgiven him. Cade. His *living* son. There were ghosts that still needed to be appeased, but at least Buck knew now that he *could* go home again. When the time was right.

CHAPTER THIRTEEN

"I FEEL LIKE A COWARD FOR RUNNING away."

Jessie hugged Remy fiercely. "You're doing your part by keeping Shiloh safe. Neither Cade nor I could focus on Zane if we had to worry about you two. Are we clear on that?"

Remy nodded. Her weekend bag was packed and waiting by the door. Since Yota was still in the shop having its brakes redone—a timely precaution, the mechanic had assured her, not another sort of tampering—Kat was stopping by to pick up her two guests.

"The Bullies took a vote. They think we should get in Yota as soon as it's fixed and come home."

Jessie shook her head. "Oh, really? So, they'd rather I bring my psycho stalker to their backyard than let Cade set a trap and end this here? That's big of them."

Remy made a face. Then suddenly burst out laughing. "I don't think any of them thought of that."

"Listen," Jessie said, holding out her arms for a hug, "I'm not crazy about this idea, either. I feel like an idiot walking around with a big fat target on my back, but Cade thinks in terms of containment. Set up on the high ground and wait for the bad guy to come to you."

"What if he doesn't come?"

Jessie wasn't sure, but Cade had pulled her aside a few minutes ago and asked her to pack a bag, too. "I need you in the main house for the weekend. There's an alarm system and a second floor." *And two wonderfully strong arms to sleep curled in,* her mind had added.

"I don't know what's going to happen, but Cade and his crew have been busy. It'll be okay, Rem. I'm sure of it."

Shiloh dashed up, a pair of earbuds hanging around her neck and a barrel-shaped backpack slung over one arm. "The gate called, Remy. Kat should be here any second." She turned to Jessie. "I wish Dad would let me stay, Jessie. I'd kick some stalker butt."

Jessie laughed and looked at her sister. "Who does that attitude remind you of?"

"You." Remy grinned.

She might have said more, but a large SUV pulled into the driveway and honked. Remy picked up her bag. "Be safe, Jess. And call me when you catch the bad guy."

"Yeah," Shiloh called, hurrying toward her aunt and uncle, who had gotten out of the car and were talking to Cade. "Me, too. And take a video if you get the chance. I wanna post it on the Net."

A video? That reminded her, she'd never looked at the clip from her tower demonstration. Maybe she would.

She waved from the doorway but didn't go out to join the others. Her ankle was better, but walking any distance took a toll. In his very first email to her about renting the house, Cade had mentioned an empty barn suitable for her training. She'd never even checked it out, since her accident had precluded any sort of physical training to date. But part of Cade's plan included setting up a workout area in the barn and having Jessie walk there several times a day.

"Routine," he'd told her. "That's what will bring him in."

She wasn't sure she believed that, but she'd do her part—including packing a bag to take to Cade's. She went to her bedroom and pulled the duffel she always used from the closet. It felt heavy and she wondered what she'd forgotten to unpack.

"My camera," she exclaimed, pulling out the small black object.

She turned around and sat on the bed, pulling a pillow from under the covers to rest against the headboard. She checked the battery—still charged. Then she leaned back and pushed the replay button. To her surprise, the footage didn't start with the day of the climbing tower exhibition.

"Oh, my God," she exclaimed softly. "I forgot I recorded this." Her face-to-face with Dar. J.T. had accused Jessie of not giving Dar a chance to defend herself, but he'd been wrong. Or lied to.

"Dar, what happened? Tell me you didn't steal this money. My accountant says you filed a tax return that doesn't make sense. I know we took in more money than you're showing because I personally handed you checks worth twice this much."

"Your accountant is an idiot," Dar said, pacing the small confines of their Girlz on Fire office. The building had been a warehouse and still resembled one, except for the half-dozen interior walls that housed their offices, a storage room and the bathrooms. "You know me, Jessie. I'd never do such a thing."

Jessie wanted to believe her, but the truth was right there in black-and-white. "If you'd married J.T., we wouldn't be having this conversation," Dar alleged. "He loves you. He's always loved you. Even when you broke his heart. And if you had married him, you would have been family. Family sticks together. Through good times and bad. And these are bad times, Jessie. You should know that."

"He doesn't love me, Dar. We're friends."

Dar turned on her. "He still would have married you if I asked him to. He'd do anything for his mother. Just like you'd do anything for yours. Just like you threw that *Kamikaze* game."

"I didn't." Jessie heard the shock and mortification in her voice. This woman had been a second mother to her and yet was accusing her of cheating.

"I bet it all on you winning, Jessie. And when you lost, everything we built here together went down the drain, too. So don't you point the finger at me, little girl. You're the reason Girlz is done. You and you alone. You picked your worthless whore of a mother over me."

Jessie braced herself for the sound of the door slamming. She wished now that she'd slapped Dar as hard as she could. That's what she'd wanted to do, but she didn't because in the back of her mind she knew her mother would have been shocked and mortified by her lack of manners.

"Manners," she said softly, snickering. "Oh, Mama, where did good manners ever get us?"

But deep down Jessie knew. Slapping Dar probably would have landed her in jail. "Thank you, Mama," she mumbled, fast-forwarding the tape to where the conversation had continued when Dar came back into the office.

Jessie hit Play and Dar was talking. "...borrowed a little bit from Girlz On Fire. Not a lot. Just enough to keep my head above water. I planned to pay it back after I sold my house, but you know what happened to the market. This wasn't my fault, Jessie. I'm a victim here. Me. And you're trying to hurt me. After all I've done for you. How could you?"

Jessie had been more wounded by Dar's defection than she could put into words. All those years of friendship, mentoring and mutual sacrifice trashed in an instant.

And though it made no sense, she'd felt vindicated in a way. She was glad she tried to help her mother, even if what she did came too late and was of no real help at all. They'd probably never know if the blood tests or the worry were to blame for Jessie messing up in the competition, but she no longer felt bad about not making enough money to give Dar.

The greedy witch.

According to Remy, Jessie was still mourning. And making poor choices based on her unresolved issues.

Was that true? Jessie didn't think so, but nothing was quite as clear at the moment as it had been before Zane decided to turn into some kind of deranged stalker.

"Jessie," a voice called from the other room. "You ready?"

She sat up, letting her feet fall to the carpeted floor. "In here. I'm packing. What exactly does one take to a trap?"

"Workout clothes, of course."

"Workout clothes?"

He held out his hand. "Come on. I'll show you."

She handed him her camera instead. "I forgot I had this. Do you want to see what Remy filmed?"

He gave her a hard look. "Do you?"

She liked that he put her state of mind ahead of what was happening—or not happening—with Zane. No evidence that he was anywhere around the area. No phone calls. No threats. Jessie might have thought she'd imagined the whole thing if not for a call from the sheriff telling her the tire stems had been injected with acid. They'd eroded through the many layers of rubber to cause both tires to burst at nearly the same time. Another accident that was no accident.

"I think we should see what it looks like. I was in no position to take in what was happening around me. Maybe she filmed something that could help us catch Zane."

"You're right," he said. "Let's sit and watch it together."

She hit the play button, glad she'd watched her argument with Dar alone. But it bothered her that she'd forgotten filming the encounter.

"Something wrong?"

She pushed aside the question for examination later. "No. Maybe. I don't know. Let's deal with this first. Here we go…"

The setting was the first thing that hit her. She'd forgotten how small the tower looked from a distance—bright and garish. A child's toy, really. And she'd wound up injured from it. Talk about humiliating. Is that what Zane was going for? She wished she knew.

"There you are," Cade said. "Getting ready to begin."

She recognized her hesitation when J.T. joined them. He'd been a surprise addition that made no sense. A distraction. She hit Pause and went back a few seconds. "Look. In the crowd. We were all focused on J.T., but there's Zane."

Cade leaned closer, squinting. "You're right. I recognize him from his website photos."

Remy was doing a good job of following the action, but once Jessie knew to look for Zane, he was easy to spot. Right up to the moment when she started her climb.

"He's leaving now. There," Cade said, pointing toward the far side of the screen.

"He didn't wait around to see if I fell because he knew I would."

Cade took the camera from her hands and turned off the power, then he pulled her into his arms for a hug. "That was brave. And now we can place Zane at the scene. I don't know if that will mean anything to a jury once we catch this bastard, but we have it."

She accepted the comfort he offered without comment. She didn't feel brave. She felt incredibly stupid. How could she have trusted Zane blindly? What did she really know about him? Apparently, nothing. She was a fool.

Cade kissed the top of her head then got up. "Come on. Remy said you need to be exercised."

Jessie pulled back. "I'm sorry, what? I'm not a horse, you know."

He grinned. "Oh, did I say that wrong? Maybe she said, 'Jessie needs to exercise.'"

Jessie rolled her eyes. "Where are we going to do this exercise?"

"Follow me, my lady. Be prepared to be impressed."

They left her duffel by the back door, where Sugar promptly tried to climb inside it. Cade shook his head but didn't scold her or try to shoo her away. He simply took Jessie's hand and started toward the far side of the house, beyond their stargazing knoll.

The path had been trimmed, she noticed. And the area around the barn looked tidied. She'd admired the huge, rustic building from afar. "Dad retired this barn when he built the new, modern one. And, frankly, that was the right thing to do. This place is still used for storage, and I think Buck used to host parties in here because I found a pile of beer cans tossed in the corners. We hauled off a few old engines and some worthless tools, and now it's all yours."

He opened the walk-in door and turned on the lights then stepped out of the way, allowing her to enter first. She stepped inside and looked around. "Wow. It's big."

And surprisingly clean. It still smelled like a barn—dusty, machine parts and animal smells she couldn't quite place. Not unpleasantly so, thankfully.

"You brought my mats in," she exclaimed.

Stretched side by side on top of a large, slightly faded Oriental wool rug were her purple and teal yoga mats. "Mac grabbed them for me from Yota and gave them to Kat. I wanted to surprise you."

She was touched. "Thank you. I'd been thinking it was time to start stretching out, but it's not the same without your regular equipment, you know?"

He didn't answer. Instead, he walked to a chrome table that looked like something a butcher might use. A very modern MP3 player was plugged in. "Is that my iPod, too?"

He nodded. "Remy gave it to me. She said you have special music you like to listen to when you're exercising."

She kicked off her running shoes and stepped onto the space he'd created for her. "This is really amazing, Cade. I feel as if I should be teaching a class to pay my way."

He held up one hand. "Me. I'll be your student."

The sexual undertones in his voice made her swallow. "I'm sorry to tell you this, but I don't date my students." Mainly because the people she'd taught were bitter teenage girls who started out thinking yoga was a boring waste of time…until their second or third lesson.

"Who said anything about a date?" he joked, sitting on the mat to pull off his boots.

She'd never seen anyone do yoga in jeans, but she was so happy to see her mats and music, she didn't care if he was in a full set of armor.

She turned on the player and found the file she wanted. Peaceful but not boring, she liked to think. When she turned around, her mouth fell open. "Oh."

Cade had removed his jeans and was wearing skin-tight yoga shorts, black and sleek. He'd lost his Western-style shirt, too, in favor of a clingy dark blue T-shirt. "I had no idea you were such a chameleon."

He rubbed his hands together. "All part of my disguise," he said, glancing around as if someone were watching him. "I figure Insane Zane is perched in a tree somewhere beyond our fence with a high-power spotting scope. He's going to watch you trek back and forth a couple of times a day. Your limp is so much better he's going to know his earlier attempt to hurt you failed. Which, of course, means he'll finally snap and fall straight into our trap."

"You do know he could be halfway to Aruba by now, right?" She chose a mat of her own and sat, legs crossed.

"He's not."

He copied her pose across from her.

"Let's start with a complete breath."

She described the method of breathing she'd learned so many years before—in the hospital. An enlightened, progressive nurse had helped Jessie deal with the pain using her mind and focused breathing instead of drugs—some of the time. "Draw a full breath from deep in the diaphragm. Fill your lungs from the bottom up. Let your belly relax and expand like a balloon. Hold the air in, shifting the muscles in your abdomen like a belly dancer. Up and down, then exhale, forcing the air out completely."

She wasn't a formally trained yoga instructor, but she'd been studying the practice for many years. Some classes she'd attended were highly structured. Her approach was not. She liked to move from pose to pose as her subconscious suggested, spending as much time as necessary on whatever muscle group needed attention.

This time, she consciously selected poses she thought her student—and her damaged ankle—could handle, changing positions with a slow and deliberate pace.

"Wow. This is harder than it looks," Cade said, struggling to keep his balance in the extended leg-stretch pose.

Jessie got up and walked to his mat to help position his body to take advantage of his center of gravity. "Sink back on your haunches, keeping your upper body as straight as possible. Use your core muscles to maintain your balance."

He wobbled a bit, but she lined him up by bracing her hands on his shoulders. His muscles were thickly roped from his very physical job. She could picture him shirtless, fixing a fence in the hot sun. Sweaty. Tanned. Gorgeous.

She swallowed hard. "Focus," she said, her voice huskier than she would have liked.

She returned to her mat, but the image of Cade's

chiseled derriere in yoga pants would not leave her brain. How was she supposed to lead a yoga class when her mind was stuck in Hot-for-Cade overdrive?

Bad Jessie. Lust was not one of the principals of yoga.

"Let's come into standing," she said, out of habit shifting to her left leg to allow her right foot to swing out and down. Her full weight was only on her left foot for a few seconds, but that was long enough to send a nasty reminder through her body. Damn. Her ankle was better and getting stronger every day. She needed to keep her mind on her goal and not get distracted by hunky cowboys.

"Lower yourself to the mat, bottom first."

Normally, she'd move through the squat gracefully. Not this time. She plopped backward, landing hard. There was no disguising her muffled, "Uff."

"Are you okay?" Cade asked.

"Fine. Obviously out of shape, but I'm getting there. I'm actually surprised by you. Most men aren't this limber."

"I have a good teacher." The look he gave her was complimentary, but there was a hint of teasing, too. And sexy. She was reminded that although they had something serious going on, the fact remained that they were alone for the weekend. If no stalker showed up, they could spend the entire time in bed.

A good idea, except for one thing. She wanted it a hair too much. Nothing had been resolved between them, formalized, recognizing for sure that Cade accepted the inevitable. Her life was not in the Black Hills—not long-term.

"Since *prana*—another word for *breath*—is key to life *and* yoga, let's work on fire breath and fire wash. These are both good for stress," she said pointedly.

She heard Cade give a soft chuckle but she didn't acknowledge him.

"Place your hands on your knees and lean forward. Now, we're going turn our belly into a billows. Breathe in and out through your nose in short, staccato breaths. Like this."

She demonstrated, exaggerating her form so her student could get the idea. Cade watched but obviously wasn't trying to copy her. She realized he was looking at her much the same way she'd been looking at him a few minutes earlier.

She felt flustered and overly warm and completely out of sync—not at all the way she normally felt when she was doing yoga. Damn. The man was quite possibly even more dangerous than Zane. Her former friend might have managed to turn Jessie's life upside down, but Cade somehow turned her emotions inside out.

Cade watched his teacher reach skyward and take a deep breath. He knew he was supposed to be concentrating on learning her calm, elegant technique, but the truth was, he simply liked looking at her.

And he was pretty sure the end goal of yoga did not include being turned on. Unfortunately, he was also pretty sure that baking cookies in church would probably be a turn-on for him if Jessie was leading the demonstration.

He liked her. He was totally, utterly infatuated. Did guys get infatuated? He didn't know. What he did know was he couldn't stop thinking about her.

He copied her inhalation and let out his deep gulp of air with a huge sigh. She told him he was supposed to keep his mind empty—turn away any and all outside thoughts. An impossible task, he decided. Images kept popping into his mind. Shiloh waving as his sister and her family pulled out of the driveway. Jessie looking grim and perplexed as she watched the video her sister had shot. Her surprise and pleasure at seeing his father's old barn converted to a yoga studio of sorts.

People didn't do enough for her, he decided. She was the doer. The one who took care of others. This was his chance to show her that it was okay to let down her guard. Hand that task to someone who cared, who wouldn't let her down.

"Ohm," she hummed on her final exhale.

Cade couldn't bring himself to try that. He was too self-conscious. Tugging on a pair of his brother-in-law's workout shorts was strange enough. Chanting was definitely out.

She turned to look at him. "Not bad for a first time."

Their first time was burned in his memory for good. He was ready for a second time. And a third.

"I'M AFRAID MY FAMILY NEEDS me and I'm letting them down. Again. That's my modus operandi."

Buck hadn't planned to spill his guts to Matthew. The man certainly hadn't asked him for that plaintive, pathetic outburst when he accidentally bumped into Buck. But that's what happened when a socially inept reformed drunk is asked, "How's it going?" by a friendly, kindhearted soul.

"Ah. You're there, my friend. You've arrived."

Buck shook his head. "What? Where?"

"Your happy place."

Buck laughed out loud. "You weren't listening, Matthew. I'm not happy. I'm a miserable, self-serving screwup and there's a good chance I'm screwing up again simply by being here."

Matthew took a step closer, his smile unchanged. He pressed his hand flat against Buck's chest, directly above his heart. "I meant the inner you has arrived," he explained. "When you came here, you were outwardly calm and composed, albeit somewhat sad and serious. You were looking for answers from outside, but the real answers you sought were tucked deep inside. And now you've found them."

Buck pulled back, horrified. "The answer is I'm a self-serving screwup?"

Matthew shook his head, his smile even bigger. "No. Your answer is you care about your family so much you'd leave this place of safety and dive into their lives to try to help. Does that sound self-serving, Buck?"

No. He had to admit it didn't.

"Wait, my friend. Sleep on it. Your family is learning to navigate without you. We both know that is a reality that will face them someday. Just as you've been teaching yourself how to live without them, without their worries, their needs and demands on your energy. We all learn in different ways, Buck. But time is by far the best teacher."

Buck took a deep breath. He felt calmer now. Almost as if a veil of grace had fallen over him. Matthew was right. Buck wasn't there, yet. He needed to stay until he truly understood that his happy place would be a part of him forever.

CHAPTER FOURTEEN

"I DON'T THINK I LIKE Plan A," Jessie said, looking at Cade from across the table. He'd cooked them two of the buffalo burgers Kat had dropped off for the barbecue he was no longer hosting.

"Why?"

"It's boring. And it depends on someone else acting first. I hate to wait. I can't simply sit around waiting for Zane to show up and try to kill me, Cade. That's not my style."

"Well, then, what do you suggest as a Plan B?"

"What if we call him out, so to speak, on a couple of the social-networking sites? We both agree the man is ego personified. I could put the clip of the video Remy took and tell everyone that the person who tried to hurt me failed."

"Do you really think he's spending a lot of time online at the moment? I'm not knocking your idea—trust me, I'm not wild about feeling trapped in my own home—but I think he's smart enough not to burst in here because his feelings are bruised. The guy might be obsessive, but he's not dumb, right?"

She drummed her fingers on the countertop. "Not by a long shot. Which is partly why I'm so confused. I mean, until he messed with Yota, which made every-body realize my car could have reacted exactly like my rollover, he'd basically gotten away with trying to kill me. Why? We don't know. But everybody called it an accident and most people were happy to blame my driving ability. The whole thing would have gone away—even if I'd been killed. With the climbing tower, he still could have talked his way out of any charge if he'd stuck around. But now everybody is looking at him as a suspect. If he somehow manages to outsmart us, I might get hurt or be killed, but he's going down, too. How could he possibly expect to get away with this?"

Cade shook his head. "I don't think he cares any-more. Sometimes you reach a point where you have to win—at any cost."

"By win, do you mean successfully kill me?"

He threw out his hands. "If that's his goal. Maybe he planned to disable Yota so he could snatch you. He might even have settled for Remy if Mac hadn't stopped to help her."

Jessie pushed her plate away. "This was good. Thank you, but I've suddenly lost my appetite."

He rose to carry their plates to the sink. She needed to pace. That's how she worked out things that were troubling her, but the yoga had been taxing enough on her ankle. She'd had to ice it again before dinner.

She took a sip of wine. The light fruity taste was refreshing. "What if I died? Very publicly? Very the-atrically."

The plate in his hand clattered to the counter. "I beg your pardon?"

"It was Remy's idea. She told me she had a dream last night that I was on fire." She spotted the look of abject horror on his face and quickly added, "It's okay. I was fine. She said she knew it was a stunt. There was a crew around me to put out the flames. I pretended to limp. I fell and it looked as though I died, but, of course, I didn't."

He shook his head. "I don't get it."

"I think I should leave. Fly home. I have friends in the business. People who would help me create this stunt and release the clip and—" She stopped. "Bad idea, huh?"

"Yeah. And the answer is no. If he sees you leave, he'll follow. I don't want to see what this guy will do if he decides to improvise."

She gave him that point, but Remy's dream had bothered her on several levels. Fire was not her friend and she didn't want to think what might happen if Zane decided to smoke them out—literally. "I couldn't live with the guilt if you lost this beautiful home because of me."

He wiped his hands on a towel, then walked to her chair. "Jessie, you don't have to prove to me how brave you are by facing your worst fear. I'd let him set fire to every freaking building on this ranch before I'd put you through that."

"I'm not afraid."

"But I am." He took her hand. "I'm afraid of losing you…"

The words held an import Jessie was terrified to examine too closely. She pulled her hand free. "Well, then, what do you suggest?"

"I think we should go to the movies."

Her mouth dropped open. "What?"

He picked up a newspaper that she'd seen lying on the counter. "What do you prefer? Chick flick or action adventure?" He gave her a wry look. "No-brainer, huh?"

"We can't just—"

He lowered the paper. "Live our lives? Why not? The guy is a cowardly opportunist. You're his obsession. You, Jessie. Nobody else. He's not going to blow up a crowded theater just because you're inside it."

She had to admit he had a point. So far, all of the bad things that had happened were focused entirely on her. She was the only one who got hurt. Even when he booby trapped Yota, he'd admitted that he'd gotten the wrong twin by mistake. "Does this mean you're asking me on a date?"

"Yeah. I guess it does."

Jessie snatched the paper out of his hands. "*Chick flick?* Please. I'm an animated-kids'-movie kind of girl. Don't you know anything?"

He was too startled by her quicksilver change of heart to laugh but his own heart did that funny leaping thing he was beginning to associate strictly with her. That's when it hit him.

I love her.

He swallowed hard. The rational part of his brain was shouting, "Too soon." But a far more fatalistic side—maybe the young boy who would cradle baby Kat in his arms when the fighting and hollering got too much—knew love didn't ask permission or make logical, time-sensitive choices. Love happened.

He hadn't expected to love Kat—the child his father seemed to adore above his other three children—but he did. He hadn't expected to love and marry Faith, but once she flashed that Look out, cowboy, here I am smile his way, he was a goner. And now he was in love with Jessie.

He'd told his father he was head over heels a few days earlier. How odd, he thought, sharing that private thought with a man he didn't trust when he hadn't even admitted the truth to himself.

"Damn," he muttered.

She looked at him. "I'm teasing. I'm actually not that picky. I like most movies. It doesn't even have to be great. Just keep me entertained for a hundred and twenty minutes and I'm a happy camper. But animated movies are my favorite. And there's a new one playing that I've been dying to see." She snickered. "No pun intended."

She flattened the paper and nudged the Entertainment section closer to Cade, pointing to a familiar logo with her finger. "And it's even playing in Spearfish. Here are the times."

She looked so hopeful. So real.

"Let's go. I'll set the alarm and let the boys in the gatehouse know when we're coming back so they don't shoot first and ask questions later."

"It's okay. Really," Jessie said the moment they'd cleared the lobby of the theater. "Don't be embarrassed."

Cade blinked against the setting sun as the hundred

or so small children who had shared the theater with them swept past like shiny fish avoiding two large rocks in the stream.

"It was a kids' movie," he said, his tone genuinely perplexed. "Nobody is supposed to cry in kids' movies."

She'd been incredibly touched when she spotted him brushing away a tear at one point in the movie. Touched and a little envious. "Somebody told me modern production companies realize they can't make enough on ticket sales to kids alone, so they layer in subliminal story lines for adults. Humor that an eight-year-old misses makes you and me laugh out loud."

He nodded.

"Same with the heart-tugging stuff. There's always some aspect of the script that gets you. Right here," she said, tapping the center of his chest.

"Is that a slam?" His eyes were narrowed but she could tell he wasn't any more serious than she was. She felt relaxed. And strangely content.

"No. It was a joke. Remy always cries in G-rated movies, too."

"But not you."

She cried. On the inside. And in a darkened theater she didn't have to worry about her feelings showing on her face. The rest of the time she had to be strong—for Mama's sake.

Weird. Where did that thought come from?

"Are you okay? Seriously. You still look a little blue."

"No, I'm good. Let's go home."

Home? That didn't sound right, but she decided not to correct herself. The ranch was *his* home. And hers... for the moment. And even while she'd enjoyed the escapism of the movie, she'd spent a good portion of the time worrying that Zane had found his way past the guards, dismantled the alarm with some techno-gadget lifted from some recently filmed spy movie, and was now lying in wait.

It was pitch-black by the time they got home. Watching Cade get out of the truck to talk to the guard at the gate made her feel safer than she'd ever felt in her life. She didn't understand the feeling, given the uncertainty of their current situation, but she liked it. She also liked Cade. A lot.

Liar.

The voice—hers? Or her sister's? She couldn't be sure—did not lie. What she was feeling was a whole lot more than *like*. There was a good chance she was in love with him, but how could she know for sure? Her mother's problematic, convoluted love life was at least three chapters short of a romance novel, according to Remy. *What chance do I have of getting this right?*

And her mother wasn't the only one who never seemed to pick the right guy. Bing was on hubby number two. Bossy had been married forever to the same guy but, according to Remy, he strayed and she stayed. No one could figure out why. Rita had so many kids she couldn't leave her husband. They seemed to have an okay life, but was that love? Jessie simply didn't know.

Even poor Remy, who believed in love wholeheartedly, couldn't be considered a poster child for that elusive destination known as Happily Ever After. The boy she'd loved with all her heart had been lost to her forever thanks to their mother's careless ways. Love was scarier than any stunt Jessie had ever tried.

If what she felt for Cade was love, it didn't match any of the goofy descriptions her sisters used to describe the word. It sure as hell didn't originate in her heart; it seemed to come from deep in her bones and grow in intensity the more she was with him.

Yes, she liked the person he was—strong, genuine and focused on what counted most. Family. Integrity. But *like* was the pretty words on the outside of a greeting card. *Love* was the juicy, heartfelt, handwritten scribbles on the inside. *Real. Kind. Fearless. Heroic. Good. Humble.*

He embodied all those things and she was starting to realize those were things she'd always secretly craved but had been too afraid to acknowledge as possible to find in a mate.

"No sign of trouble," he said, getting into the truck. "We checked in with the other sentries and they all said the same thing. Maybe Zane decided to sit this one out."

"I hope so, for everyone's sake. I really feel stupid about bringing all this drama and expense into your life. I'll pay you back."

He didn't speak until he pulled to a stop at the end of the driveway and he'd turned off the engine. Then he turned to loop one arm across the back of the seat and face her. The motion-sensor light above the garage doors had come on, but for some reason he'd decided not to park the truck inside.

"Let's get something clear," he said. "This is my fight, too. This asshole brought his agenda to me and mine. My home. My employees. My daughter. And my woman."

"I'm your woman?" She tried to laugh. "That's a bit old-fashioned. Or should I say Old West?"

He shrugged. "You can say anything you want. I won't apologize for being politically incorrect. You're a woman in my life who I care about a great deal." He paused. "Oh, hell, I might as well put this out there. I love you, Jessie Bouchard. I'm sorry if that freaks you out or scares you away and you split tomorrow, but I—"

She cut him off midsentence by throwing herself into his arms, her lips pressed to his. The kiss started out messy and awkward because she'd forgotten to undo her seat belt, but only for a second—until he reached between them and released the latch. Then his arms closed around her and he pulled her tight against his chest. They both were breathing hard—as if they'd been racing from opposite ends of a football field to meet at the fifty-yard line.

"This is new territory for me. I feel like I'm in the middle of a dangerous stunt with no script and no net. I don't know how I got here and I don't know what will happen next, but…"

His low, sexy chuckle made a zing of desire trip-wire

through her body. "I can answer that. I know what, when and where."

"You do?"

He opened the door and got out. She didn't want to be separated from him even for the amount of time and space it would take for him to walk around the truck, so she climbed over the console and slid across his seat to drop to her feet beside him. "What?"

He kissed her again, one hand pressing against her low back. There was no missing his arousal. "This."

"When?"

He scooped her into his arms and closed the door with his heel. "Now."

So much for me hating to be carried, she thought, using the proximity to outline his ear with her tongue. "Now is good."

They entered the house through the side door. He set her down when the alarm system started beeping but lingered long enough to kiss her—hard, wet and full of promise.

He quickly punched in the code then turned to her. "Where were we? Oh, yes." He dipped down to pick her up but she stopped him with a hand pressed flat against his chest.

"You lead. I'll follow. I'd rather you saved your strength for what I have in mind."

He grabbed her hand and led the way through the kitchen to the stairs, pausing so Jessie could hang up her backpack on a hook by the door. As they climbed the stairs, Jessie inhaled deeply, tasting each and every scent as a confirmation that she was home. Truly home.

He paused at the tops of stairs to kiss her again. "This isn't going to be like the last time, Jessie. No hiding out in the dark. There will be lights. Candles at the very least."

She lifted her chin, determined not to show fear. "I'm okay with lights, but no candles."

His expression turned pained. "Sorry. That was—"

She put her finger to his lips. "Candles are distracting. You have to remember to blow them out. I want to focus completely on us. Nothing else. No past. No crazy lunatics. No worries."

She hoped. Perfection was something to strive for, right?

His smile was all Cade. It lit up his vibrant blue eyes and made her heart expand in a way she'd never felt before. "Okay." He turned toward the master bedroom but stopped. "Oh. And there will be a bed. Did I mention that?"

She laughed. "I like beds. So, stop talking. Let's do this."

This, Cade thought later, turned out to be so much more than he'd pictured it being. *This* was new, novel and life-changing because the woman making love with him was a different Jessie. A Jessie who felt comfortable enough to ignore her scars, who trusted him enough to play.

"First one naked gets to pick the position," she said, slipping under his arm like a minnow the moment he opened the door to his room.

He stood, arms akimbo, shaking his head. "Are you always competitive in everything you do?"

She wiggled out of her shorts and kicked them aside. "Always." Next, she stripped off her shirt. Facing him in her bra and panties, she put her hands on her hips, too. "Does that scare you?"

He let out a hoot and starting pulled off his clothes—to hell with the buttons. "Petrified. Wanna feel?"

She let out a squeal and sprang to the bed like a gazelle—or a gymnast. But after a couple of uneven bounces, she dropped to her knees. Somehow she managed to lose her underwear in the process, making him the half-dressed loser. But Cade could honestly say he'd never felt more like a winner.

"You are so beautiful," he said, shaking his hands so his shirt fell to the floor. He peeled off his jockey shorts and joined her on the bed, on his knees, too. Two supplicants praying for the same thing, he hoped.

He didn't kiss her right away. Instead, he ran his nose across the top of her shoulder, making a slight detour toward her chest. Her breasts were small and firm. They fit her frame perfectly, and her hard-as-pebbles nipples let him know her body was ready to be touched, tongued and pleased.

Her hands gripped his shoulders for balance and leverage as he moved from one breast to the other. Her knees were parted to give her greater balance, and he felt her hips move in a grinding motion when he put his lips around one nipple and sucked.

"Oh, nice," she said with a low, breathless groan. "You're the devil incarnate."

He looked up. "It's hard to suck and laugh."

"But not impossible." She gave him an impish wink. "Let me show you how it's done."

She scooted back, her lips and tongue mapping a downward course. By the time she got to his groin, his thighs were quivering with anticipation. He sank back, toes tucked under him.

She rubbed her cheek and chin across his penis until he thought he might explode, then she took him into her mouth. His brain couldn't catalog all the sensations bursting across the plain of his mind, so he stopped thinking and simply experienced a turn-on that was turning him inside out.

"If I'm the devil," he panted, struggling for control, "what does this make you? A witch? Because you…I… wait…no…ah…" He stopped speaking because he needed every ounce of self-control and focus to ease away from the brink.

Jessie let out a triumphant chortle. She'd forgotten what point she was trying to make but that didn't matter. What did count was the fact her heart felt huge, her emotions a vast reservoir brimming with love and hope and glee. This landscape was all new, exciting—even scary. But she wasn't really afraid, because she wasn't alone.

"Come with me, Cade. Now."

He didn't answer with words, but he gave her what she asked for—and more. "We have all night, remember?" he said in a throaty whisper as he arranged the big, puffy pillows the way he wanted them. Then he helped her recline like some sort of film noir siren.

All the better to watch, she realized, as he copied her maneuver, his tongue and lips blazing a trail downward. He paused to toy with her belly button before exploring her nicely trimmed triangle of curls. Waxing wasn't a conceit when you routinely had your photo taken while playing volleyball on the beach, right?

His hand felt heavy, possessive. A part of her knew that this was more than sex. If she let this—made this—happen, she would truly be his woman. That knowledge added to the excitement, she had to admit.

His fingers parted her curls and he nuzzled a path to the place she couldn't wait for him to touch. Everything about this day—the good and the bad—seemed to culminate in an emotional eddy, pulling her through the mists to a place she'd never visited before. Trusting Cade as her guide freed her to feel things she'd never let herself feel before. The word *orgasm* simply didn't cover the quaking vibrations that ripped through her thighs, converging on her inner core. She grabbed for the light—the taste of pleasure that had never tasted so sweet. And when it came, she gave herself over to the feeling with complete and uninhibited abandon.

"Oh, oh, *O. M. G.*," she panted, a puffing pause between each letter.

Cade looked satisfied until he got to his knees and moved toward her. His fully aroused anatomy made her realize the fun was only beginning. "Dessert!" she exclaimed, making a keep-it-coming motion with her hands.

"The main course, sweetheart."

She didn't care what it was called. Her body was

primed and ready, as she proved when he entered her. *Completion.* That was the word she'd been looking for—maybe her whole life—and never found. Until now. "Perfect," she whispered, her hands on his shoulders.

She saw the look of pleasure on his face change to one of need. She wrapped her legs around him, forgetting that her ankle was not a hundred percent. The sharp bite of pain distracted her for a moment, but the coursing sensations she'd experienced a few minutes earlier returned, blocking all thoughts of pain and pretty much everything else. All that mattered was Cade and finding that wonderful, perfect release.

The explosion that rocketed through Cade's body and brain was very possibly the best he could remember. She fit him perfectly. She picked up his rhythm as if they were humming the same song. He wished he was a poet or singer with some means to tell her how much he loved her.

But words were not his friend. He'd told her he loved her and she stuck around long enough for him to prove it, but her words back had been lukewarm at best.

"I think I might love you, too."

Might?

Might?

He might well hate that word. But he knew he couldn't rush her into a relationship. He couldn't change Jessie into a domestic partner any more than she could turn Sugar into a house cat.

"Will you sleep with me tonight?" he asked, not

taking anything for granted. There was a guest room in the place if she wanted her space.

They were still melded together, like one body with eight limbs and two heads. He'd read about that once in a book his father left open. Plato. Buck had explained that according to Plato this was how humans were originally—whole and so happy and content they ignored the gods, who punished them by cutting them apart and setting them off as individuals doomed to spend eternity searching for their other half.

"I'm not going anywhere," she said, her tone sleepy and satisfied.

"Good." He shifted enough to take his weight off her, but he wasn't ready to let go completely. "As I said, the night is young, but I am old."

"You are not," she said, giggling. "You're forty-two. Your daughter told me so. I'll be thirty-three in August." She looked up. "Wow. You really are old. No wonder you need a nap."

He could tell she was teasing by the glint of laughter in her eyes. He took a deep breath, taking in the smell of her hair on his pillow. He could see himself sleeping with her every day for the rest of his life. A dream, maybe, but if Plato was right, he'd found his missing half.

Proving that to Jessie might take a while. All night and then some.

CHAPTER FIFTEEN

JESSIE OPENED HER EYES, instantly awake. She didn't know what woke her. A dream? A memory? She couldn't remember, but she knew from experience she'd be tossing and turning for hours if she didn't get up and move around to dissipate the wasted adrenaline in her system.

She could barely make out Cade's sleeping form. He'd turned off the lights right after he asked her to stay with him. She hadn't hesitated to say yes. She wanted to make the most of this brief interlude, no matter what it cost her in the long run.

And the cost could be extreme.

Having someone tell you he loved you and admitting that you had similar feelings was a huge step—relationship-wise. And probably an unwise step if you were someone like Jessie.

She carefully slid out of bed and picked up the clothes she'd worn to the movie. Not the best for working out, but good enough, she decided, pulling on her shorts and top.

The air temperature was cool, telling her several windows must have been left open. Further assurance of their safety. The door might have an alarm but the second-floor windows, at least, provided a welcome cross-ventilation.

The open windows also provided enough light to make her way downstairs. She located her backpack where she'd left it hanging on a hook by the door and pulled out her phone and MP3 player.

Her phone served as a flashlight to avoid turning on any switches. Cade had shown her the home gym his father had installed years earlier. Older, clunky machines that reminded her of stylized dinosaurs. Not her type at all, but the stationary bike seemed like a safe choice, if her ankle didn't object.

Before she gave it a try, she decided to check her messages and texts. The only one that interested her was from Hank, her friendly neighborhood sheriff's deputy.

"Darlene Feathering's husband was arrested on tax fraud. Might give her up in return for deal."

Give her up? How? She was already pleading her way out of the embezzlement charges against her. What did Roger Feathering have on his wife? Jessie wondered.

Dar's betrayal hurt, but Jessie was done mourning the loss of another woman who only pretended to love her. Screw them all.

She knew there was no changing the past, but there was one question she would have liked to ask her mother before she died. "Did I do it, Mama?" she said out loud. To no one. To the blank white walls and the dusty, unused exercise equipment. *Would someone please tell me whether or not I put that candle in the window?* She didn't remember getting up and finding the matches. Her doctors said it wasn't unusual to forget details surrounding a trauma. Jessie could remember going to sleep. She and Remy had been planning to go to the bridge the next day. That was the last thing she could recall until waking up to find their bedroom ablaze.

Would her question have been answered if Jessie had pulled out of the competition the moment her sisters called to tell her Mom was dying?

Probably not. According to Remy, Mama went downhill fast and the pain meds kept her under a thick layer from which she never completely surfaced. But Jessie probably would always wonder and wish she had a do-over.

Shaking her head, she plugged in her headphones and clicked on a playlist called Work Out 2—middle of the night. The first song always made her smirk. Rick Springfield belting out "Jessie's Girl." She would silently lip-sync or—if she was completely alone—belt out the words, changing the last to *guy*.

For the first time, she had a face to go with that name.

Smiling, she decided to keep this workout short. Maybe she'd make just enough noise while getting back into bed to wake up Cade for a little middle-of-the-night fun. But first, she'd finish what she started. Because that's the kind of girl she was.

CADE WOKE INCREMENTALLY. He tried to hold on to his dream but it fell away in big chunks like a brick wall crumbling around him. He'd been with Jessie in a strange house. Loud music coming from the basement had made the boards under their feet vibrate, the amplified bass thumping like a heartbeat.

One minute she'd been at his side, the next she was gone. He'd dashed from window to window looking for her. At the last window, he couldn't get close enough to look because it was on fire. A perfect rectangle of heat and snapping flames, too perfect to be real.

"This is a stunt," he murmured out loud. "Pretend."

But the heat felt very real and his panic grew when he spotted a figure in a padded suit streak across the room and dive, headfirst through the window. A second, smaller figure started past him. He grabbed an arm, an elbow.

"Jessie," he cried. "Stop. Don't do this."

But when the person turned to look at him, he realized it wasn't Jessie. It was Shiloh.

He opened his eyes, his heart racing.

He rolled over, reaching out to touch Jessie.

She was gone. The messy sheets the only sign she'd been there.

A sour taste in his mouth made him spring out of bed and walk into the bath. A small night-light shaped like a buffalo—a gift from Kat to Buck, Cade would bet his bottom dollar—provided enough light for him to brush his teeth. He used his hand to cup a drink of water, then braced his hands on either side of the sink and looked in the mirror.

"What are you doing?" he asked his image. "You invite a woman who is the complete antithesis of what you want and need in a mate to move in. You fall flat-out crazy in love within seconds of meeting her. And now you're talking to yourself in a mirror. This is nuts."

His image laughed.

Nuts, maybe. And his dream served to remind him that he wasn't in this relationship alone. He had Shiloh to think about. But he wasn't as worried about her as he probably should have been. His daughter had a good head on her shoulders, and after this teenage, drive-your-dad-batty phase passed, they'd be back on track. His sister was right. Kids had dreams and ambitions that changed all the time. So did full-grown men.

If Jessie was his second chance at love, he was going to do everything in his power to make this thing work. And that meant giving the person he loved room to be the person he loved. He'd spent too damn much time and effort trying to get Faith off a horse, instead of celebrating her drive and talent and dreams. He wasn't going to make the same mistake with Jessie.

"I wonder how much it costs to fly to Japan," he thought idly as he returned to the bedroom. If her ankle was strong enough for her to participate, he'd find a way to get there. Shiloh, too.

He quickly pulled on a pair of swim trunks—the kind that looked like beach-bum shorts—and grabbed the same undershirt he'd had on earlier and raced down-stairs.

"Jessie," he called, expecting to find her raiding the refrigerator.

He looked around, noticing her bag was missing.

"Where the hell is she?" he muttered, walking to the sink for a glass of water.

As the glass filled, he looked outside. His dad's house was black, but he thought he detected a flicker of light coming from the barn.

Would she have gone to the barn to do yoga? In the middle of the night?

No.

Unless she was having second thoughts about telling him she loved him. Regrets, maybe? Doubts? Jessie was the most emotionally tentative person he'd ever met. She could probably talk herself out of loving him in half an hour or less.

He set down his glass and marched to the door. That wasn't going to happen. He was prepared to make whatever accommodations that needed to be made to fit her career into their lives. Once they got this nutcase off her back.

He stopped dead in his tracks when he saw the red flashing light of the alarm. How could she have gotten out without disarm... "Oh, right," he muttered. "Shiloh."

His daughter must have given Jessie the code, which meant Jessie could disarm the device, open the door, then rearm it in the few seconds it gave you to punch in the code.

He was in such a hurry to find her he almost tripped over a scuttling shadow.

"Sugar," he exclaimed, backtracking a moment. He went down on one knee and held out his hand. "I know you're nocturnal, but is there a way you could do your thing without causing bodily damage?"

She took a small, nonmalicious nip at his fingers. He wasn't offended. He understood. "Yeah, I know. I'm not Jessie. Sorry about that. We'll stop and visit on our way back."

Then he took off at a slow lope. In a way, he hoped Jessie was doing yoga. He'd heard about a kind that involved sex. He didn't know the first thing about it other than its name, but he figured they could make it up as they went. He smiled, seeing the faint light coming from under the door. He yanked open the door and stepped inside.

"Jess?"

The place appeared empty. The only sign anyone had been there recently was a familiar red can sitting a few feet away. A gas can. There were three or four of them in the shop. He took a step closer.

The smell of gasoline was powerful and fresh. His instincts went on high alert.

He turned to run and found his way blocked. A man he'd know anywhere. Zane.

"Bummer, dude. You got here too soon. My surprise still needs work." He raised his arm in a friendly gesture. Cade had been preparing for combat. He hadn't expected a Taser. The charge swept through his body like fire on steroids.

He flew backward, his legs giving out as the electrical charge rendered him paralyzed. His head hit the ground hard, but luckily the rug he'd brought in for Jessie's yoga managed to keep him from passing out.

Zane stood over him for a few seconds, obviously enjoying Cade's inability to move, much less speak.

"I was hoping Jessie would come first. She's the type, you know. Never ever follows a schedule. Refuses to obey a direct command. She is so in need of a little comeuppance. And I'm just the man to give it to her." He cocked his head and grinned. "Guess you're gonna have to watch, man. Sorry about that."

He walked away, laughing.

Cade's brain seemed capable of thought despite his body's complete and utter short circuit. He had no idea how long it took for the effects of a Taser to wear off. He tried moving his fingers and toes.

Maybe. Is that my toe moving?

His heroic plans fell apart the moment Zane returned—with several zip ties.

BUCK OPENED HIS EYES INTO complete darkness.

It took a few seconds for the thunder of his racing heartbeat to die down before he knew for certain he was alive. He sat up in bed, rubbing a tender spot on his chest.

Lord. He had no idea what he was dreaming about, but something fearful gave him an unwelcome adrenaline rush. His armpits were damp from sweat. His fingers tingled. And his mouth was so dry he felt as though he'd been walking the Sahara for a week.

He got out of bed and headed for his restroom. He should have been used to a midnight pee by now, but he wasn't. He'd started to settle into normal sleep patterns the past few days. No bad dreams...until tonight.

He checked his phone out of habit on his way back.

Nothing. No reason at all for this uneasiness that had settled deep in the middle of him.

He wanted to call Cade. Granted, a stupid thing to do in the middle of the night. The boy would think Buck was drinking again. Drunken calls had been a fairly common occurrence for most of Cade's twenties. That pretty young daughter-in-law of his—Faith—told him off in no uncertain terms more than once.

He was sorry she was dead. Not because he thought she was the be-all and end-all of wives. She wasn't. And she hadn't been that great of a mother to Shiloh, either—more worried about her fame and reputation than providing a stable solid home for his granddaughter. But at least Cade had seemed happy when he was married.

His son was the marrying sort—just like Buck. And until Cade's last phone call, Buck would have said he was the slow and deliberate type when it came to picking a wife. Something had changed. Someone had changed him. Jessie Bouchard. Buck was dying to meet her.

Dying.

He didn't like that word. Tried not to use it. Shouldn't be thinking about it at this time of night.

His mouth filled with a bad taste.

He picked up his phone again and hit dial before he could change his mind. If he woke up his son, so be it. At least he'd know Cade was okay.

The phone rang and rang and rang. No one answered.

He tried Cade's cell number. It went straight to voice mail.

He knew the gatehouse number and punched it in, his finger shaky. Cade's message had warned of potential trouble. *If he's put on extra help...* "Garrity Ranch."

Buck didn't recognize the voice. Worry made him bark, "This is Buck Garrity. Where the hell is my son?"

"Sir? What? Sorry, Mr. Garrity, I can't talk right now. We've got shots fired out by the buffalo. I just called it in. The sheriff will be here soon, but I can't get hold of your son. He isn't picking up. I'm on my way there now."

Buck surged to his feet. He didn't bother saying goodbye. He walked to his closet and started tossing clothes into his bag. He might have questioned his worth when it came to being a father, but one thing he never doubted was his usefulness in a fight.

It was time to go home.

CHAPTER SIXTEEN

JESSIE STOPPED PEDALING TO drop forward over the handlebars of the old-fashioned machine. A raw sob escaped from her throat. Frustration, not pain. The truth hit her after less than thirty minutes into her workout. She was not going to Japan.

Not this summer, at least.

Her ankle was healing, but nowhere near quickly enough to be able to compete at an international level. She'd known that from the start, but like everything in her life, needed to come to grips with the reality of her situation at her own speed.

She pulled back, half laughing, half fighting tears, of all things. "Jessie is as hardheaded as my neighbor's pit bull," Mama used to tell people. "Only, she's a lot sweeter on the inside."

Jessie pushed her hair out of her face and sat, immobile, thinking. The orthopedist wanted to start her on a long-range rehabilitation program. "We have some excellent physical therapists in the area, but your needs are pretty specific. A true sports-medicine therapist might be better for you. If you reinjure this ligament before it's completely healed, you'll be looking at surgery," he'd told her.

She hadn't been ready to listen to him. She hadn't wanted to leave for some reason.

Some reason? One reason. Cade. *Okay, two. Shiloh, too.*

She got off the machine and walked to the bench where she'd left her phone and sat, drawing her right ankle across her knee. The bruising was gone, the swelling was mostly back to normal, but the strength simply wasn't there. She probed the tendons and wiggled her toes. Not perfect, but strong enough to carry her through the activities of a normal person. She could probably even return to stunt work—if she picked her jobs carefully.

But admitting that *Kamikaze* was not going to happen meant she also needed to address the issue of Girlz On Fire. Without the prize money she'd planned to win, there was a good chance she'd never be able to rehabilitate Girlz anytime soon.

She grabbed the plastic water bottle she always carried and heaved it across the room. It hit the wall with a solid thud and rolled under the treadmill.

"Damn," she swore. There had to be another way. Grants, maybe. A giant fundraiser, perhaps. This wasn't a glamorous charity—angry girls with attitude did not become media darlings—but there might be a way to keep the dream alive if Jessie used her head instead of her physical aptitude.

Jessie knew herself well enough to know that she wasn't cut out for the bookkeeping side of the business—hadn't she willingly handed over that part to Dar without any oversight whatsoever? But she knew people. The stunt community was strong and generous and supportive.

She couldn't make this happen overnight. It would take work, but she could reshape the dream and maybe even expand to other places…like here. Shiloh was a perfect example of a young girl who easily could have become a victim if she hadn't had a father willing to do whatever it took to protect her until she found her footing in this world.

At the beep from her phone she picked it up and looked at the display. A text from Cade? *Seriously?* She smiled, thinking it would say something about coming back to bed. She was ready now. Her ducks were lined up and swimming in the same direction again. She could relax and be happy in his bed, his arms.

Come 2 barn.

"The barn?"

Alarm bells went off in her head like a Fourth of July fireworks show. Zane. Somehow he'd lured Cade out of the house and ambushed him. She had no idea how, but that didn't matter. She needed to get help. Swearing under her breath, she shot to her feet.

She didn't bother going upstairs to check on him, because she could see from the foot of the stairs that the alarm had been turned off. She dashed to the house phone and called the front gate. She needed to alert the guards.

The call went through but no one answered. She said

a silent prayer that whoever was on duty hadn't been bushwhacked, too.

She started to punch in Hank's number when her phone beeped again.

Hurry. Need you. Now.

Damn. Was this for real? Was she overreacting? No. The one thing she knew about Cade for certain was he'd never put anyone he loved at risk. If he wanted to arrange a tryst in the barn, he would have walked her there to make sure she was safe.

She scrolled down to Hank's number and pushed Call. "Yeah? What?" a sleepy voice growled.

"Sorry, Hank. Jessie Bouchard. We have a situation. Cade's not in the house. I've gotten two suspicious texts and nobody is answering at the gatehouse."

"I'll call it in. Stay put. Someone will be there soon." He hung up, sounding wide-awake.

But there was no way in hell she could follow his order. Cade was in trouble. It was her fault. She'd brought this mess to his doorstep and she wasn't going to risk his life by playing it safe.

She opened the door. She had her hand on the porch light switch but changed her mind. She didn't plan to make this easy for Zane. Two could play commando.

The moment she stepped outside, Sugar scampered up the steps to greet her. The little beast seemed agitated. She was shivering, but that could have been from the stiff wind that seemed to have blown up. "Hello, sweetie," she said, picking up the raccoon. "It's a bad night, baby girl. Time for you to go into your crate."

She closed the door on the plastic carrier and hurried away. She pulled up her hoodie and dashed from the edge of the patio to the wooded knoll where she and Cade had made love. She could feel a twinge in her ankle from walking over uneven terrain, but she ignored it.

Using her phone as a flashlight, she checked every so often to make sure she didn't trip over anything. The temperature was a good fifteen degrees cooler than when they got home and the sky was a muddy color— too black to call gray, despite the moon's attempt to break through the layer of fast-moving clouds.

She shivered in her thin sweatshirt, pausing a second to zip it all the way to her neck. *Cade will warm me up,* she thought. A promise and a hope.

A thin blade of yellow was visible beneath the walk-in door, but she wasn't dumb enough to march straight into a trap. She edged around the side of the building, praying for another entrance. She found it. A drop-down trapdoor apparently used to funnel hay or feed or something into a trough.

The opening wasn't large. No way in hell Zane could have gotten through it, but she would crawl through even if she had to strip to her bra and panties. She grasped the wooden toggle that apparently kept it from falling open, then slowly, quietly lowered the door. The rusty hinges protested but she spit on them and gradually got the door open.

She tried hard to listen, but the rush of the wind

blocked any sound beyond a distant noise she couldn't quite make out. Sirens, she hoped. Sirens. Hank.

She dropped to one knee and hunched over her phone to shield it from view and tapped in one word: *barn*. If anything happened to her, he had to know where to look. Then she stowed her phone in her pocket and climbed—good foot first—into the breadbox-size opening.

She needed every bit of her upper-body strength to lower herself into the barn without making any noise. She didn't for a minute underestimate Zane, who may not have actually served in Special Forces but had convinced himself he was an American ninja.

Once both feet were on the ground, she flattened her back against the wall and looked around. The barn was black except for the glow near where Cade had set up her yoga mats. Earlier, he'd turned on the overhead lights to see by. Reality hit a second later. The flickering quality, the yellowish tone… Candles.

She cursed under her breath. She should have guessed. Zane knew her story. He'd seen her back. He went straight for her weakest point—her greatest fear. Fire. The thought struck her that maybe Remy's dream was a prophecy. If she got out of here alive, she was never going to doubt her sister's dreams again.

She couldn't just sit, paralyzed with fear. Cade was here. Somewhere. And she was damn well going to find him. Screw Zane and his twisted threats.

The first thing she needed was to get out of the feed box or whatever this was. She climbed over the edge quietly and dropped to all fours. This spot gave her a clear view to the door. Red plastic containers appeared to anchor the four corners of the carpet Cade had put down. And in the middle of that carpet, lying very still—corpselike—was a body. Cade's body.

She sprang to her feet, instinct warring with caution. But it was too late to play cat and mouse. The mouse she'd been hunting had found her—and he was better armed.

"Hello, Jessie," a familiar voice said as the cold, hard muzzle of a gun touched the back of her neck. She hadn't realized until that moment that her hood had fallen off. Damn blond hair, she thought irrationally.

She didn't move, but she did answer him, trying very hard to appear calm and cool. "Zane. What have you done to Cade? Is he alive?"

Cade moaned, apparently in response to their voices. His head turned her way, his eyes squinting, but she wasn't sure he could see her.

She spun around without warning, sweeping her leg knee-height, the way she'd been taught. The move might have dropped a lesser man, but Zane was a highly trained athlete with self-defense skills every bit as formidable as hers. And he had a gun. Which went off less than a foot away from her head.

The shot went wild, but the ringing in her ears disrupted her focus and equilibrium. Zane's free hand shot out and grabbed her around the neck. "Stupid blonde girl, when will you learn that you can't play this game? You don't belong. You proved that last summer. Remember? You faltered, bitch. And you cost me a pretty penny."

His fingers squeezed, keeping any sound from passing through her lips. He brought his face close to hers and said, "I hated you for that. So, when your ex-partner offered to split the insurance money she had on you fifty-fifty, how could I say no? Accidents happen, right?"

Jessie struggled. She wasn't going down without a fight. The eyes, a voice in her head said. She jabbed with all the force her oxygen-deprived body had left. Her aim felt true even though a black haze blurred her vision, robbing her of seeing Zane's reaction. But he dropped his hold and stepped back, his hands going to his face. His gun must have dropped to the ground, but Jessie's eyes were watering too much to see clearly.

He swore and made a grab for her, but she darted away, her fluid gymnastics training serving her well. She parried left, spun to the right. Graceless and slow compared to her usual form, but fast enough to evade Zane's rage-blinded attempt to catch her.

She couldn't fight him one-on-one. She didn't have a weapon. And she had to get Cade the hell out of the barn. Gas cans and candles told her exactly what Zane planned. Hank was coming and there was plenty of help nearby, but none of that would matter in the least if Zane shot them both and set the barn on fire to provide a distraction so he could escape.

Wits. She could always try outsmarting him.

"You're a stupid, cowardly fool, Zane, hiding behind your little pistol. Where's that big brave Special Ops guy now? Oh, wait, you lied. You're a liar, too. You washed out of the military. They said you were too dumb."

Another shot rang out and a hunk of wood splintered a few feet to her left. She dropped to the ground and made a combat crawl under the shiny new table Cade had set up for her boom box.

The candlelight was working in her favor now. Her hearing was returning and she knew without looking that Zane was searching the far side of the barn. Cade was lying very still but she was certain he was listening as hard as she was. His feet were bound with plastic zip ties, as were his wrists. Getting him out of here was not going to be easy.

Distraction.

Damn. She had only one chance. It was dangerous. Probably stupid. It might cost— She stopped thinking and acted.

She dashed from cover, grabbed the first red gas can she encountered and snatched up the closest votive. Its flame shivered as if it was going to go out, but she carried it close to her body as she returned to her safe spot. She needed a wick. Her shirt. Perfect.

She tugged off her hoodie and pulled her top over her head, gooseflesh erupting over every inch of her bare skin. Cade's head turned her way. She kept her focus on her mission. She didn't know for certain that what she planned would work. All she could do was try.

"Where are you, you dumb bitch?" Zane bellowed. "You can't get out. Well, you can, but your lover boy is going down."

Jessie rezipped her sweatshirt and moved away from the sound of his voice, inching along the outer wall of the barn toward where she dropped in. He was right.

She could leave but getting Cade out that feeder hole would never work. She had to hope their rescuers would break down the barn door in time.

She paused to listen for sirens. None.

Stall.

"You are stupid, Zane," she called once she reached the farthest corner away from Cade. "You know that, right? Dar is in jail, dumb ass. And her husband just had a visit from the IRS. The cops told me Roger is singing like a freaking canary. Attempted murder, Zane. If you were smart, you'd get the hell out of here and run for the border, dude. You're going down, baby."

A chunk of wood exploded above her head. She knew she was trapped, but this time she was armed. Poised to strike, muscles bunched, she listened hard. His breathing gave away his exact position.

She held the candle to the hem of her shirt—the only part sticking out of the gas can. The smell was nearly enough to overcome her; the first crackle as the fire grabbed hold made her hands start to shake. She willed herself to stay calm, keep the memories at bay. *I can do this. I can.*

When she decided he was in range, she stood and hurled the heavy container. He was closer than she thought. He was forced to dodge to the right to avoid the flaming projectile. She saw the look of surprise in his eyes, but that was the last thing she saw. She used his moment of hesitation to vault over the horse stall to her right. She landed hard. Her ankle protested, but adrenaline and abject fear—fueled by the smell of smoke—gave her the extra burst of speed she needed.

She spotted an ax leaning against the wall near an old tool bench. She grabbed it in passing. The wooden handle was splintery and heavy, but all she needed was one good hit to knock away the padlock Zane must have put on the door after he realized she was in the barn.

She lost track of Zane in the smoke that billowed toward the front of the barn, driven, she guessed, by the draft from the hatch door she'd left open. An intense crackling sound told her the leftover hay and straw was providing fuel. The old timbers would ignite soon.

She swung with all her might. A miss. She tried again.

"Jessie. Cut me free. I can do it."

She turned to see Cade struggling to a sitting position. "Cut you?" She looked at the rusty ax. What choice did she have?

She dropped to her knees in front of him and secured the ax blade upright so he could saw the plastic band back and forth across it. "You're doing it. Good job."

Once his hands were free, he grabbed the ax and used it to break the bond around his ankle. She helped him up. He staggered, but once he was stable, he looked around, checking for Zane before he headed for the door.

Once. Twice. Metal on metal. A spark glinted in the low light. The padlock dropped to the ground.

"Yes," Jessie cried. She took one step toward him before an unexpected force yanked on the hood of her sweatshirt, pulling her backward.

Instinct took over. She'd taught her students at Girlz exactly what to do when someone grabbed you from behind. She went limp, falling backward like a sack of feed. Her motion threw Zane off balance. He was pulled forward. One step. Two. Then he met the blunt end of an ax, midchest.

His scream of pain gave Jessie the only warning she needed to roll out of the way as he dropped to the ground. He curled into a ball, writhing and gasping for air.

Cade reached out. "Come on. We have to get out of here."

The fire.

She didn't hesitate. She took his hand and followed, choking on the smoke that seemed to have taken on a life of its own.

She gulped in deep gasps of cold, fresh air the second they made it outside. She could hear the sirens now. A lot of them. Trucks and people, too. She looked up and understood why. Beautiful red-and-gold sparks danced in the night sky. She'd seen this view before. From the gurney that took her to the ambulance that raced her to the burn hospital.

She looked at Cade, who was speaking. She couldn't make out a single word, but she held out her arms and fell toward him, sobbing.

Apparently, her tear ducts weren't melted shut, after all.

Cade held his brave, amazing, sobbing Jesse as tightly as he could. His muscles still tingled and twitched, and it seemed at any moment he'd lose strength altogether.

"It's the boss," a voice called. "Over here. Where's the ambulance?"

Six men rushed up to him. "Boss, you're hurt. What happened?"

Cade pointed toward the door. "One man. Inside. Dangerous. Might have a gun."

The men looked at each other.

"Hank is coming," Jessie said. "I called him."

And as if beckoned by their thoughts, the man materialized through the smoke. Hank didn't hesitate to call for backup. "Fire trucks are rolling. This doesn't look good."

"We know what to do," his foreman said. He took off at a dead run, shouting orders. "Get the animals in the new barn outside. Roust the day crew. We need all hands on the water pumps and hoses. Let's go, people."

Cade sagged slightly.

"Hank," Jessie cried. "Help."

The deputy rushed forward to flop Cade's free arm around his shoulders. "What a pair you make," he said, looking at Jessie.

Cade looked down. She was limping badly.

"Yeah, well, it's better than a gunshot."

"Huh?"

Cade barely listened as she filled in the details he'd mostly missed. His brain wanted to participate, but his recovering muscles captured all his attention.

"Shock," he heard someone say.

"No," he said. "He Tasered me."

With that announcement, the EMTs eased him onto the gurney and started checking his vitals. Rubber-coated fingers pried up his eyelids and flashed a bright pencil-tip strobe of light back and forth.

"We're taking him in," one of them murmured.

He wanted to stay, to be at Jessie's side when Zane was carted away. He tried to rise from the stretcher.

A warm, familiar hand gripped his. "Cade. Relax and let these guys do their job."

He opened his eyes. Jessie.

"I'll call his sister. She's in Denver with his daughter. I'm sure they'll want to come home right away."

"Tell Shiloh not to worry. I'm fine."

Jessie leaned close and pressed a quick kiss to his lips. "Braggart."

He was still smiling when he was loaded into the rear of the ambulance. There was so much he wanted to tell her. Important stuff, like he'd never expected to love anyone again but the feelings he had for her redefined love.

As the EMTs were preparing to close the doors, Jessie climbed in. Now was his chance. Now he could tell her everything.

She squeezed his hand. "I know, love. I know. You can rest now. Everything is being handled. I'll keep an eye on things until you get back." She hopped out and the ambulance headed in the direction of the hospital.

Until you get back.

He was pretty sure she said that.

But he wasn't sure what she meant. Why did her eyes look so sad when she made the promise? And why did that sound like goodbye?

CHAPTER SEVENTEEN

TO JESSIE'S IMMENSE SURPRISE, she discovered her phone in the pocket of her hoodie. She was bleeding, filthy and she smelled like a bonfire, but she had her communication device. "Bizarre," she mumbled from her perch on the back of the second emergency vehicle.

The three EMTs were not the same ones who'd transported her the first time. These guys actually listened to her when she said she was fine. "My ankle is an old injury. I'll keep it iced tonight and hobble into the ortho doc's office tomorrow."

While they'd agreed not to take her to the hospital, they had insisted on observing her and measuring her lung function over the next hour. Fires equaled smoke inhalation. She got it. She knew the drill, all too well.

She started to take a deep breath but felt a cough coming on, so she let it out and panted shallowly while she called her sister.

"Jessie? What time is it? What's wrong?"

"Our trap was a huge success," she said, speaking as lowly as possible. She didn't want anyone to hear exactly how stupid they'd been. Zane was a maniac. She'd completely underestimated him—mostly because she hadn't grasped his motive. Jessie vaguely remembered

Dar talking about mutual insurance policies in case something happened to either of them. "So Girlz doesn't suffer," she'd claimed.

But Jessie couldn't recall ever seeing one or signing anything. Whatever the dollar value, it must have been huge.

"Zane showed up. He's in custody."

Hank hadn't hesitated for a moment. After escorting Cade and Jessie to the waiting gurneys, he'd plunged fearlessly into the barn, shoulder to shoulder with the first firefighter he could buttonhole. Together they dragged Zane to safety.

The man was obviously injured and couldn't draw a deep breath without hacking up a lung, but he was the last to be seen by the paramedics. First, Hank read Zane his rights and made certain he answered with a gasping, "Yeah," followed by a long stream of curse words.

She didn't know where either man was currently.

"That's good," Remy said, her voice a hushed whisper. "Hold on a minute, Jess. Let me get to the bathroom so we can talk. Shiloh and I are sharing a room."

Shiloh. Oh, God, how was she going to face Shiloh when she was nearly responsible for making the little girl an orphan?

"Okay," Remy said, coming back on the line. "Tell me what's going on. Everything. I can hear it in your voice. Something happened."

Jessie sagged against the open door of the ambulance and spilled her guts. Everything. Including her conclusion that her career was going to be on hold for who knew how long. She looked at her ankle, which was swollen to twice its size.

"Oh, no," Remy cried. "I'm so sorry. But the important thing is you're both okay, right?"

"Yeah," Jessie concurred halfheartedly.

"I'll wake up Kat and Jack. We'll be there as soon as humanly possible. What hospital did they take Cade to?"

"Same one I was in."

"Jessie," Remy said sharply. "It's late. You're traumatized and in pain. You need to go to bed and let Cade's people handle things. I mean it. Go to bed. The world will look brighter in the morning."

She turned to face the beautiful, dazzling red-orange flames devouring the handsome old barn. Her fault. Her ego. Her foolish belief that she had even a tiny bit of control over her destiny.

"Okay," she said softly. "See you when you get here. Oh, wait, Remy. Do you remember the name of the garage that is fixing Yota?"

Remy didn't answer immediately. "What are you planning?"

"Since I'm not going to Japan, there's no reason for me to stay here, right?"

Remy said the name but she added, "Do not—I repeat—*do not* make an impulsive gesture, Jessie. I know how you think, and I can tell you, whatever you're planning, don't."

Jessie laughed. "I'm planning to go to bed."

"Oh. Okay. Do that. But nothing else."

"Good night, Remy," she said, closing her phone.

She wouldn't make promises she couldn't keep. That seemed to be the point of this life lesson, didn't it? She'd promised to win *Kamikaze* and donate the proceeds to Girlz. When she failed to do that, Dar decided to cash in on a life-insurance policy using Jessie's job to make her death look like an accident.

"Damn," she muttered, slipping off the back of the ambulance.

She couldn't face returning to Cade's bed without him, so she hobbled to the guesthouse and dropped like a hot, stinky rock on top of the covers. She closed her eyes and was out, just like that.

JESSIE SLEPT FOR WHAT FELT like days and when she rolled over and opened her eyes she found a white-haired giant standing beside her bed. She levitated off the bed, scrambling backward even as her brain decided that she actually knew this person, even though she'd never met him.

Buck.

He was Cade's father.

He tilted his head to one side and smiled, gently. "You must be Jessie. Looks like that party in the barn was a doozy. Want some coffee? I just made it."

Then he left.

Her heart rate slowly dropped to normal. She looked at the clock beside her bed. Nearly noon. Crap. She'd planned to be gone by now.

Of course, she didn't have a car, but she'd remedy that soon enough. If Yota wasn't ready to go, she'd rent one.

"Shower first," she called to the man she assumed was still in his house.

She stood under the hot water until her sore, over-taxed muscles finally loosened up. Then she dressed in jeans and a T-shirt. She didn't know where her shoes were, but she'd find them while she packed.

She glanced at her reflection for a second, then opened the door and walked to the kitchen to face what she was certain would be the first of many inter-rogations. She had a lot to answer for, but when hadn't she?

BUCK COULDN'T REMEMBER ever wanting to be rich. He worked because that's what a man did. He was smart enough and lucky enough to amass a pretty sizeable fortune. Only on rare moments, such as waking up in the middle of the night in California and wanting to be back in South Dakota as fast as possible, did his money play a factor. It was times like this that he was happy to burn through however much it took.

He'd arrived before the last of the fire trucks rolled out his gate. He'd stepped from the limo he'd hired to meet his jet at the airport and talked briefly with the engine commander. Buck heard the whole story and was given the number for the sheriff's deputy in charge of the investigation.

Hank Miller was an old friend. He shared what he knew willingly. The saga made Buck's heart race. He couldn't care less about the barn. All that mattered were his son, his granddaughter and the people under Cade's care. Cade was doing fine and would be released later that day. Their staff was all fine. No injuries. The bad guy was in custody.

The only person no one seemed to know for sure about was Jessie. Like Baby Bear in the children's story, he returned home to find Goldilocks sound asleep on his bed. Sooty tear tracks told him all was not well.

"I'm Jessie Bouchard," she said, limping toward him after her shower.

"Nice to meet you. My son told me you and your sister were staying here. I probably shouldn't have burst in like this, but nobody was in the big house. I was concerned."

She shook his hand then walked to the counter and poured herself a cup of coffee. "No problem. How did you get here so fast? I thought you were on the West Coast."

"Learjet. Damn fast. I'd buy one if I knew how to fly it."

She snickered softly. "Beats driving."

He didn't ask the obvious. She'd tell him when she was ready.

"Do you want the long or the short version?"

"Already heard the long one from Hank. Gimme the short."

"A teammate of mine—someone I considered a friend—decided he'd make a fortune by killing me. The money was supposed to come from another ex-friend who embezzled from our company then hired a hit man so she could collect on the life insurance I stupidly let her take out on me. Dumb, huh?"

"Eh," he said with a shrug. "We trust people. Some of them turn out to be snakes. It happens."

Her slightly bloodshot eyes opened wide.

She might have said more but his phone jingled in his pocket. "'Lo?"

"Dad. You heard the news, right? Cade, this huge basket of flowers is for you." Kat had always been one to carry on two conversations at once. You had to pay attention or you'd never know if she was talking to you.

"Yeah. Men never get flowers. What's with that? You must be at the hospital," Buck said.

"We are. Cade is fine. He's not happy to be here and keeps trying to get out of bed, but Nurse Ratchet is bound and determined to keep him here until his doctor signs the proper form."

"Good for her. Listen, Kat, I'm home now. And if Cade's being released soon, I won't bother heading into town. I'm having coffee with Jessie at the moment."

He heard his daughter share that information with the people she was with. "Dad, Jessie's sister Remy wants to talk to her. Can you give her your phone?"

"Can and will." He held out the phone. "Your sister."

He refreshed his coffee, trying not to eavesdrop too obviously.

"I know."

"Yes."

"Okay."

"Maybe."

"Tell her goodbye for me. And I'll call Cade from the road."

She hit End and handed him the phone.

"You're leaving."

She nodded. "Yes. My ankle is pretty jacked up. I'm canceling all of my upcoming jobs. I need R & R. Remy and I inherited our family home after our mother passed. I figure that's a cheap place to recuperate."

All logical, well-thought-out arguments. But none was the reason she was leaving.

"My son cares for you. Deeply."

She rinsed her cup under the faucet. "Your son is a wonderful person. Probably the best I've ever met. He's also a great father."

"In other words, you love him, too," Buck said, cutting to the chase. "Then why are you leaving?"

She walked to the far window and pulled back the drapes. "Did you see your barn when you drove in?"

"Pretty hard to miss."

"It would still be standing if not for me. I'm cursed or something. I'm like a firebug. This is the second structure I've managed to level in my lifetime."

He joined her at the window. "I can't speak to the first, but according to the fire investigator, my barn was booby-trapped. The initial fire could have been put out relatively quick, only this whack job planted a whole bunch of little incendiary devices all along the outer walls. Is that your fault, too?"

She didn't answer right away. "I'm the reason he came here. He was looking for me. Trying to kill me."

"Doesn't sound like you had any say in that matter."

She turned away. "It's complicated." She paused in

the doorway leading to her bedroom. "Is there anyone around who could give me a ride to my car? It's in someplace called Hill City."

Buck weighed his options a moment. Cade might never forgive him, but maybe, just maybe, Buck could find out what was really bothering this poor girl if he volunteered to drive her.

"Since my truck made it through the fire fine, I'd be happy to give you a lift."

"Thank you. I'll get my things together and meet you outside." She paused. "Oh, wait. Would you do me a favor and let Sugar—the little raccoon in the pen on the veranda—out after you get home?"

He heard a tremor in her voice, but she didn't stick around long enough for him to ask any questions. This woman was hurting. Deep down in a way that had nothing to do with physical pain.

Oh, son of mine, you're gonna have your hands full convincing this one she's worthy of your love. But I wish you luck. The good ones are always worth the effort.

CADE KNEW WHAT JESSIE WAS going to say even before he pushed the button on his cell phone. "Hey," he said, leaning back against his small, ineffectual hospital pillow. "I wondered if you were going to call. Or come see me."

"I can't."

"Why not? Need a ride?"

"No. Your father just dropped me off at the Hill City garage. I'm sitting in Yota as we speak. I'm two new tires and a brake job poorer, but at least I'm road-worthy."

He scowled at the ceiling. "And that's important because…"

"I'm going home."

There. The truth. How had he known it was coming? The look of despair in her eyes the night before? Maybe.

"L.A.?"

"No. I'll have to go back there sometime. All my stuff is in storage, but I don't expect to be working for a long time."

Her ankle. "You sacrificed your body to save my life."

She gave a raw little chuckle that didn't sound happy. "I was fighting tooth and nail to save my own hide. Burns are not my friend, remember?"

How could he forget? Last night must have been pure hell for her. The fear, the memories, the potential horror of going down that road again. "Don't go, Jessie. Please. Not yet. We need to talk, face-to-face."

She let out a long, raspy sigh that served to remind him that she'd refused inhalation treatment. One of the paramedics had told him so. "Ah, well, now you know the truth about me. I'm a coward. Physical challenges don't scare me, but emotional quagmires I avoid like the plague. It's better this way, Cade. Trust me. We had fun. It was…amazing. But your dad is home now. You don't need me anymore."

"You're wrong, Jessie. I might not need a renter or a babysitter, but I—I meant it when I told you I love you."

She was quiet for so long he thought the call had been dropped. Then she said, "I know, Cade. Me, too. But it wasn't the ever-after kind of love. That takes a special sort of person, and I'm not one of them. I hope you'll find someone better. I have to go. I love you. I do. Goodbye."

"*I love you? Goodbye?*" he repeated, nearly hurling his phone across the room. What the hell sense did that make?

He grabbed his call button and stabbed the little nurse symbol as hard as he could. He wanted out of this bed, this room and this hospital right this minute. The love of his life was leaving and he was stuck in bed in a bare-ass hospital gown.

Half an hour later, he faced his greeting party—Kat and Remy and Shiloh—in the main lobby when his strong-willed nurse, who reminded him in some ways of Jessie, wheeled him to the door.

He decided to get the subject out in the open the moment Kat pulled out of the parking lot. "She called. She told me she was leaving."

Remy reached across the seat to squeeze his shoulder. "I tried to talk her out of it. But I'd like to go on record as saying I think this is less about you than it is about our mother, her death and what happened when Jessie was a girl. The fire brought back a lot of memories. None of them good."

He was willing to give her that, but running away

never solved anything. Wasn't he living proof of that? He'd turned his back on his family and missed out on whole chunks of his sister's life. He barely knew his father, but that was going to change—even if Buck was the one to deliver Jessie to her car.

"As far as I'm concerned, she left with her heart in pieces, Cade," Kat said, her fingers gripping the steering wheel as if it might jump out of her hands and run away. "I'm a woman. I know these things. She left because she thought she was doing the right thing for you."

"How could leaving be good for me?"

She put a finger to her mouth and pretended to think a moment. "Hmm...let's see. Oh, right, because of her, your barn is now a smoldering shell. Because of her, you got Tasered and your daughter had to go stay with relatives for her own safety. Should I go on?"

He snarled. "Damn. I hate it when you're right. But none of those things makes any difference. She should know that."

"How? Did you tell her specifically that you would love her no matter how bad things got?"

"Not in so many words."

Kat looked in the rearview mirror. "Shiloh, are you taking notes? Men have no clue what women in love need to hear out of their mouths."

Cade made a face, which made his daughter laugh. Kat did not find it amusing. "You are so juvenile. Do you want to win her back or not?"

"Can I? She sounded pretty sure this was over."

Kat glanced at Remy. "Remy and I both agree that

Jessie is the kind of person who requires proof of commitment." She held up her hand where a sparkly diamond rested. "If you want Jess back in your life, you'd better be prepared to cough up a rock *and* prove to her that you are in it for the long run."

He took a breath. "I can do that." He turned in his seat and reached out a hand to his daughter. "But I'm not the only one who counts here. Shiloh, you've been surprisingly quiet since all of this happened. Tell me what you think."

"Last night…when we heard about the fire, I was really mad at Jessie, Dad. I blamed her because the guy who set the barn on fire followed her here."

Cade nodded. "They did catch him, though. He's not a threat to any of us anymore." Cade had had a long conversation with Hank when the man showed up to take Cade's statement. Apparently, Jessie had sought Hank out first, seeking permission to leave. Since Zane was not getting out of jail for a long, long time, and the case against him was pretty much ironclad, Hank had given her a green light.

Shiloh nodded. With her hair in a ponytail, she looked so much like Faith, he could hardly breathe. Until she smiled. "I know. And Aunt Kat and I talked on the way back. A friend of hers had some bad things happen a while back. The guy died, but it took her friend time to figure out that he was to blame, nobody else. This wasn't Jessie's fault. I wanted to tell her that. I tried her phone, but she must not have it turned on."

He'd called several times, too.

"So, what do we do now? Hang out and wait for her to come to her senses?"

Remy let out a low groan. "Oh, no. Bad idea. With Jessie, you need to get in her face and make her say the words."

"Okay. I can do that. As soon as I get hold of our insurance company…" He stopped and began to grin. "Wait a minute. Buck's home. He can do all that."

Cade pulled out his phone and hit speed dial number one. "I'm going after her, Dad. I need you to hold down the fort, so to speak. Can you do that for me?"

"I thought you'd never ask," his father answered. "And it's good to hear you calling me *Dad*. By the way, I happen to know an excellent pilot. Let me know when you're ready to leave."

CHAPTER EIGHTEEN

CADE LEANED PAST HIS sleeping daughter to look out the window of the plane. The South looked like the South even from a bird's-eye view. He could almost taste the humidity in the air and the chicory in the coffee.

They'd be landing soon.

In the end, they'd passed on Buck's offer of a jet. Cade decided it wouldn't be fair to go without Shiloh. She had a test she couldn't miss, and Remy felt obligated to fulfill her obligation to Jack and Kat to repay them for all their help. So, although he was champing at the bit, his travel plans were put on hold until the following Friday.

Luckily, Cade's pal Mac had a friend who happened to have a plane. William, their pilot, seemed like a friendly guy, who, according to Mac, had an interesting love story of his own to tell.

Cade didn't ask. He was too worried that his own story might well grind to an unhappy ending the moment they landed and drove to the Bouchard home.

Remy, who was peacefully sitting in the seat across the aisle from him with her eyes closed and her hands folded in her lap, kept insisting that they were on the right path.

"You love her and she loves you, Cade. The rest of the details are simply details. Everything will work out. I saw it in my dream."

He wanted to believe that, but he also knew he might wind up looking like a fool in front of the whole world. Well, the part of the world that mattered to him. His daughter and his family.

His father, for his part, seemed to be holding fast to some sort of West Coast inner equanimity that Cade couldn't understand. Buck had been surprisingly blasé about the loss of the barn. "It was a waste of space. I think our next one should be solar. What do you think?"

"I don't think we need another barn, but we might be able to use a yoga-slash-gymnastics school."

Buck had chuckled. He hadn't axed the idea, proving to Cade that his father truly had changed. "You're different, Dad. That spiritual retreat really worked, huh?"

They were alone, sharing a midmorning cup of coffee the day before Cade left. "Everybody should take the time to look back. Most of us don't. We're so busy moving forward, trying to keep out of the way of the wrecking ball that seems to be chasing us around. If I'd ever stopped long enough to look over my shoulder, maybe I'd truly have seen and appreciated how fortunate I was.

"I loved two women in my life, Cade. I lost your mom by not paying attention. And I'm sorry for the way I shoved Helen down your throat. I was only thinking of myself. I was so damn afraid of being left with you kids after your mother died, I panicked. But the strange thing is I loved her."

"I know you probably won't believe this, Dad, but I grew to care for her, too. Charlie hated her, but Helen always was nice to me. And she trusted me with Kat when she was a baby. That meant a lot to me. It might be why I wanted to be a father someday."

His father seemed lost in thought, so Cade continued. "We've all made our share of mistakes, Dad. I don't know how things will work out with Jessie. I'm asking a lot of her. I'm not sure how she'd maintain a stunt career while living in the middle of nowhere. But I feel alive when I'm with her—not just living."

Cade knew he was leaving with his father's blessing. Now he simply had to find the right words to convince Jessie that he was the right man for her.

"We're landing in two minutes, Cade," a voice over the intercom said. "Make sure everyone is buckled in nice and tight."

He shook his daughter's shoulder. "Shiloh, wake up, honey. We're here. It's time to go get you a new mom."

JESSIE WAS SITTING ON THE porch of her family home, which she and Remy had inherited. The Bullies each had received a beauty parlor. The drive south had been punctuated by crying jags, a bottle of aspirin and the recent addition of a dog. Ridiculous, she knew, but she'd found a forlorn-looking, mixed-breed Catahoula hound at a rest area. Abandoned, she'd guessed, since the poor beast was malnourished with no tags. His blue eyes reminded her of Cade, and when he licked her face, she was a goner.

On her lap rested the old diary she'd hidden under the stoop. She'd remembered the diary her first night home. She'd been sitting in this exact spot, swatting mosquitoes, when it came to her. The next morning, she got down on her hands and knees and went hunting.

Some of the pages were mildewed. And the handwriting was that of a ten-year-old. She'd started it in the hospital where she was having one of her many skin grafts performed. The process was grueling, but for a child who was growing at a rate that far exceeded the stretching ability of her dead skin, she had no choice.

She'd never thought of herself as a romantic, but this young Jessie had very strong opinions about who constituted her soul mate.

He will be stronger than me.

He will be nice but not pansy-ass.

Remy would have been mortified that Jessie used a bad word to describe the love of her life…if she'd known about this book. She didn't because Jessie hadn't wanted to hurt Remy's feelings. Requirement number three was why. *He will like me best.*

Everyone liked Remy. Not everyone liked Jessie. Including their mother.

"Why can't you be more like your sister?" was a familiar refrain around the Bouchard home.

The day Jessie answered, "Because I'm too much like you," was the day she and Remy left home for Nashville.

But despite their butting of heads and the unresolved

feelings Jessie held over being left alone in the hospital, Jessie had loved her mother.

Funny, it had taken a second fire for her to remember all those things she'd forgotten about the first. Such as how the fire started. If she closed her eyes, she could picture watching her mother walk into her bedroom carrying that tall white taper, safely protected from the wind by the glass chimney. Mama put it on the night-stand right in front of the window closest to Remy's bed. The twins' room faced the street and had two old-fashioned windows side-by-side, separated by the width of an eight-year-old's shoulders.

When Mama turned to leave, she noticed Jessie watching her. "Go back to sleep, honey child."

She dropped a light kiss on Jessie's cheek then hurried away on a cloud of her best perfume. Jessie knew what that meant. The candle was a signal of some sort for a man.

Jessie pictured the tableau all too clearly. The candle flickering when an errant gust of wind passed over the chimney. She didn't know why she felt the need to move the candle. Was she afraid it might go out and her mother would wait and wait for the man who wouldn't show? Was she worried the flickering might wake Remy? She didn't know, but she knew what happened next.

The antique candleholder was heavier than she thought it would be. The glass chimney was wobbly. Heated wax sloshed over the rim and landed on her fingers. She dropped the holder. The lit candle fell into a pile of dress-up clothes the girls had been playing with that day.

Jessie tried smothering it with a blanket, but that only made the fire spread. Toward the door, blocking their escape route. She screamed and cried for help, but no one came. She shook and shook Remy, who slept like the dead, until she opened her eyes. Then, terrified and frozen in panic, she refused to move until Jessie finally pulled her out of bed and shoved her out the window. Jessie went next. Too late.

Mama had been the first one there after the girls got out of the house. She'd rolled Jessie in the grass and patted out the flames using her bare hands—hands that worked every day to put food on the table and pay the mortgage.

Mama's burns.

How could I have blanked that out? Why didn't she remind me?

The answer had come to her near the Nashville turn-off. Mama did what she did out of love, not guilt. She didn't put that candle in the window to create havoc. She was signaling her lover. Her married lover. What happened next was an accident, plain and simple.

That knowledge changed everything.

Her mother might have set this catastrophe in motion, but she hadn't done so on purpose, and she'd risked her life, her livelihood, her other children's well-being to save Jessie. If that wasn't an act of love, Jessie didn't know what was.

That knowledge seemed to give Jessie permission to forgive her mother—and herself. Love wasn't perfect.

People made mistakes, poor choices. But if you were lucky, you had people in your life who loved you no matter what.

People like Cade.

She truly admired him for living his convictions. When Shiloh had needed more love and support than Cade could give her on his own, he'd reached out to Buck, the father who'd let him down—in his childhood and as recently as a few weeks ago. Did that send Cade into a panic? Did he hop in his truck and drive away? Of course not. He stayed and faced life's challenges head-on—even adding new and unexpected complications to his already complicated life. Jessie, Remy and, literally, trial by fire.

She picked up the phone on her lap and hit redial. "Why isn't he answering?" she asked Beau. That's what she'd named her new dog. He cocked his head and blinked in answer to her question.

She quickly punched in a second number. "Maybe Remy will pick up."

She did. On the third ring. "You are in such trouble."

"Me? What'd I do?"

"You ran away. Like a coward. In the night. I'm so ashamed."

Jessie scooted down so her butt was almost to the edge of the rattan bench and lifted her ankle to the railing to relieve the throbbing. Almost time for another aspirin. And a trip to a specialist to see about surgery.

"It was broad daylight. Ask Cade. I called to tell him goodbye. I had to think. I couldn't do that with everybody looking at me. You know how I am. Is Cade mad?"

"Furious."

Jessie groaned. "Is that why he isn't answering his phone? He hates me, right? I've been trying all morning."

"No."

"No, what? He doesn't hate me or that isn't the reason he isn't answering his phone." What if he never spoke to her again?

"He didn't answer because he forgot to turn his phone off in the airplane and it spent the entire flight roaming, which sucked his battery dry."

Jessie didn't have to ask what that meant. She had enough leftover twin-sense to know the convoluted explanation meant Cade was coming here. "How soon?" she whispered, her throat too tight with emotion to take a full breath.

"Now," Remy crowed triumphantly as a funky yellow-and-black taxi pulled to a stop at the curb. "Is that dramatic timing or what? I should have been the one to go to Hollywood, wouldn't you agree?"

Did Remy sound ridiculously self-satisfied? Yes. Did she deserve to? Yes.

Jessie jumped to her feet and hopped to the railing, because she simply couldn't bring herself to ask the Bullies for a pair of crutches. With all their kids, they were bound to have a few, but she wasn't yet ready to see the whole fam-damily, as her mother liked to say.

Beau gave a loud woof then planted himself on the

top step and began barking furiously at the man who was striding intently toward the house.

"You didn't tell me you had a dog," Cade called out over the racket.

"I have a dog," Jessie yelled back. "Does that change things?"

He stopped, then looked toward the driveway where Yota was parked. "Yeah. It means we're gonna have to drive back. I hope your car is up for it."

Jessie reached down and patted the dog's head to calm him. "It's okay, boy. This is Cade. You're going to like to him. I promise."

Cade approached cautiously. The taxi that had dropped him and Remy and Shiloh pulled away with a friendly toot. The dog flinched but didn't bark.

"Hey, fella, welcome to the family," Cade said, extending his hand. "I hope you don't eat raccoons. Sugar has been moping ever since your master left."

"I'm not his master. He sorta found me at a rest area. No tags."

Cade stroked the dog's head and earned a friendly lick. "I'm sure you have an interesting story to tell, old boy, but first things first." He looked at Jessie. "Why did you run?"

"I didn't run. I *can't* run," she said, resting her shoulder against the corner post. "My ankle's messed up bad. My career may be over."

"I'm sorry for your career's sake. But what does that have to do with us?"

"I never wanted to be the kind of person who needed

someone else to support me. If I can't work, I bring nothing to the table. My job is who I am."

He bounded up the steps in one smooth vault—the kind any free runner would have been proud of. "Jessie Bouchard, you drive me crazy. You're so much more than your job. How can you not see that? You're you. And I love you. I want you to be part of my life. Part of my daughter's life. If you need time to figure out how big a part that is, fine. You've got it. Just, please, never disappear like that again."

"You mean that?"

"Have you ever heard me say something I don't mean?"

She shook her head. "How bad was the damage from the fire?"

"The barn is a complete loss, but Buck is getting estimates as we speak. He said to tell you you can have your old room back, but he thinks it would look better if you moved in with me."

She looked over his shoulder to where Shiloh and Remy were standing with their suitcases. "Shiloh, are you sure about this? I'm not Remy."

Shiloh and Remy exchanged a what-the-heck sort of look.

"Yeah, I know," Shiloh said. "I get a cool mom and a cool aunt at the same time. What's not to love?"

Remy smiled broadly. "And aunts get to spoil their very cool nieces without dealing with any of the consequences. That is so me."

Jessie and Cade looked at each other and grinned.

"Can we come in?" Remy asked. "I emailed the Bullies before we left. They're probably on their way over here."

Jessie groaned, but Cade gave her a reassuring squeeze. "I should meet my future sisters-in-law, shouldn't I?"

Her jaw gaped. "You want to marry me?"

He took her hand and kissed her ring finger. "I've been told nothing says commitment like a big honking diamond. You give me the word and we'll make it official whenever you're ready."

She was ready now, but she didn't say so. No, she was done rushing through life in search of something she couldn't quite define. She knew what she wanted, who she wanted to be with and even when she wanted to make this happen.

"Have you and Shiloh ever been to Mardi Gras?"

His smile told her he was very possibly reading her mind—and liked what he saw. Maybe twin-sense was simply a matter of being so in tune with another person you were both thinking the same thought at the same time.

I love you, she willed him to hear.

"I love you," he said as he drew her to him for a kiss that told her everything she needed to know. She wrapped her arms around his neck, but before closing her eyes to lose herself in his kiss she glanced at Yota. On the bumper was the pristine new sticker. She'd peeled off the old, cynical "White Picket Fences

Make Good Kindling" before leaving the Black Hills. She'd found this new one under a pile of papers in her mother's desk. It summed up her feelings completely: "Love Happens."

* * * * *

COMING NEXT MONTH

Available May 10, 2011

#1704 A FATHER'S QUEST
Spotlight on Sentinel Pass
Debra Salonen

#1705 A TASTE OF TEXAS
Hometown U.S.A.
Liz Talley

#1706 SECRETS IN A SMALL TOWN
Mama Jo's Boys
Kimberly Van Meter

#1707 THE PRODIGAL SON
Going Back
Beth Andrews

#1708 AS GOOD AS HIS WORD
More Than Friends
Susan Gable

#1709 MITZI'S MARINE
In Uniform
Rogenna Brewer

You can find more information on upcoming
Harlequin® titles, free excerpts and more at
www.HarlequinInsideRomance.com.

HSRCNM0411

REQUEST YOUR FREE BOOKS!
2 FREE NOVELS PLUS 2 FREE GIFTS!

Harlequin®

Super Romance®

Exciting, emotional, unexpected!

YES! Please send me 2 FREE Harlequin® Superromance® novels and my 2 FREE gifts (gifts are worth about $10). After receiving them, if I don't wish to receive any more books, I can return the shipping statement marked "cancel." If I don't cancel, I will receive 6 brand-new novels every month and be billed just $4.69 per book in the U.S. or $5.24 per book in Canada. That's a saving of at least 15% off the cover price! It's quite a bargain! Shipping and handling is just 50¢ per book in the U.S. and 75¢ per book in Canada.* I understand that accepting the 2 free books and gifts places me under no obligation to buy anything. I can always return a shipment and cancel at any time. Even if I never buy another book, the two free books and gifts are mine to keep forever.

135/336 HDN FC6T

Name	(PLEASE PRINT)	
Address		Apt. #
City	State/Prov.	Zip/Postal Code

Signature (if under 18, a parent or guardian must sign)

Mail to the **Reader Service:**
IN U.S.A.: P.O. Box 1867, Buffalo, NY 14240-1867
IN CANADA: P.O. Box 609, Fort Erie, Ontario L2A 5X3

Not valid for current subscribers to Harlequin Superromance books.
**Are you a current subscriber to Harlequin Superromance books
and want to receive the larger-print edition?
Call 1-800-873-8635 or visit www.ReaderService.com.**

* Terms and prices subject to change without notice. Prices do not include applicable taxes. Sales tax applicable in N.Y. Canadian residents will be charged applicable taxes. Offer not valid in Quebec. This offer is limited to one order per household. All orders subject to credit approval. Credit or debit balances in a customer's account(s) may be offset by any other outstanding balance owed by or to the customer. Please allow 4 to 6 weeks for delivery. Offer available while quantities last.

Your Privacy—The Reader Service is committed to protecting your privacy. Our Privacy Policy is available online at www.ReaderService.com or upon request from the Reader Service.

We make a portion of our mailing list available to reputable third parties that offer products we believe may interest you. If you prefer that we not exchange your name with third parties, or if you wish to clarify or modify your communication preferences, please visit us at www.ReaderService.com/consumerschoice or write to us at Reader Service Preference Service, P.O. Box 9062, Buffalo, NY 14269. Include your complete name and address.

HSR.11

*With an evil force hell-bent on destruction,
two enemies must unite to find a truth that turns
all-too-personal when passions collide.*

*Enjoy a sneak peek in Jenna Kernan's next installment
in her original* TRACKER *series, GHOST STALKER,
available in May, only from Harlequin Nocturne.*

"**W**ho are you?" he snarled.

Jessie lifted her chin. "Your better."

His smile was cold. "Such arrogance could only come from a Niyanoka."

She nodded. "Why are you here?"

"I don't know." He glanced about her room. "I asked the birds to take me to a healer."

"And they have done so. Is that *all* you asked?"

"No. To lead them away from my friends." His eyes fluttered and she saw them roll over white.

Jessie straightened, preparing to flee, but he roused himself and mastered the momentary weakness. His eyes snapped open, locking on her.

Her heart hammered as she inched back.

"Lead who away?" she whispered, suddenly afraid of the answer.

"The ghosts. Nagi sent them to attack me so I would bring them to her."

The wolf must be deranged because Nagi did not send ghosts to attack living creatures. He captured the evil ones after their death if they refused to walk the Way of Souls, forcing them to face judgment.

"Her? The healer you seek is also female?"

"Michaela. She's Niyanoka, like you. The last Seer of Souls and Nagi wants her dead."

Jessie fell back to her seat on the carpet as the possibility of this ricocheted in her brain. Could it be true?

"Why should I believe you?" But she knew why. His black aura, the part that said he had been touched by death. Only a ghost could do that. But it made no sense.

Why would Nagi hunt one of her people and why would a Skinwalker want to protect her? She had been trained from birth to hate the Skinwalkers, to consider them a threat.

His intent blue eyes pinned her. Jessie felt her mouth go dry as she considered the impossible. Could the trickster be speaking the truth? Great Mystery, what evil was this?

She stared in astonishment. There was only one way to find her answers. But she had never even met a Skinwalker before and so did not even know if they dreamed.

But if he dreamed, she would have her chance to learn the truth.

Look for GHOST STALKER by Jenna Kernan,
available May only from Harlequin Nocturne,
wherever books and ebooks are sold.

Fan favorite author
TINA LEONARD
is back with
an exciting new miniseries.

Six bachelor brothers are given a challenge—
get married, start a big family and whoever does
so first will inherit the famed Rancho Diablo.
Too bad none of these cowboys is marriage material!

Callahan Cowboys:
Catch one if you can!

The Cowboy's Triplets (May 2011)
The Cowboy's Bonus Baby (July 2011)
The Bull Rider's Twins (Sept 2011)
Bonus Callahan Christmas Novella! (Nov 2011)
His Valentine Triplets (Jan 2012)
Cowboy Sam's Quadruplets (March 2012)
A Callahan Wedding (May 2012)

Love Inspired.
HISTORICAL
INSPIRATIONAL HISTORICAL ROMANCE

*Introducing a brand-new
heartwarming Amish miniseries,*

AMISH BRIDES
of Celery Fields

Beginning in May with

Hannah's Journey

by ANNA SCHMIDT

Levi Harmon, a wealthy circus owner, never expected to find
the embodiment of all he wanted in the soft-spoken, plainly
dressed woman. And for the Amish widow Hannah Goodloe,
to love an outsider was to be shunned. The simple pleasures
of family, faith and a place to belong seemed an impossible
dream. Unless Levi unlocked his past and opened his heart
to God's plan.

*Find out if love can conquer all
in* HANNAH'S JOURNEY,
available May wherever books are sold.

www.LoveInspiredBooks.com

LIH828(